UNDEAD
MUCH

UNDEAD
MUCH

Stacey Jay

razor
bill

An Imprint of Penguin Group (USA) Inc.

Undead Much

RAZORBILL

Published by the Penguin Group
Penguin Young Readers Group
345 Hudson Street, New York, New York 10014, U.S.A.
Penguin Group (USA) Inc., 375 Hudson Street, New York, New York 10014, U.S.A.
Penguin Group (Canada), 90 Eglinton Avenue East, Suite 700, Toronto, Ontario,
Canada M4P 2Y3 (a division of Pearson Penguin Canada Inc.)
Penguin Books Ltd, 80 Strand, London WC2R 0RL, England
Penguin Ireland, 25 St Stephen's Green, Dublin 2, Ireland (a division of Penguin
Books Ltd)
Penguin Group (Australia), 250 Camberwell Road, Camberwell, Victoria 3124,
Australia (a division of Pearson Australia Group Pty Ltd)
Penguin Books India Pvt Ltd, 11 Community Centre, Panchsheel Park,
New Delhi – 110 017, India
Penguin Group (NZ), 67 Apollo Drive, Rosedale, North Shore 0632, New Zealand
(a division of Pearson New Zealand Ltd.)

Penguin Books (South Africa) (Pty) Ltd, 24 Sturdee Avenue, Rosebank, Johannesburg
2196, South Africa

Penguin Books Ltd, Registered Offices: 80 Strand, London WC2R 0RL, England

10 9 8 7 6 5 4 3 2 1

Jay, Stacey.
  Undead much / Stacey Jay.
    p. cm.
  Sequel to: You are so undead to me.
  Summary: Sixteen-year-old Megan Berry learns the secret of why she is such a
powerful Settler, gets help from a new friend in battling a siege from a zombie army,
and tries to reach second base with her boyfriend, Ethan.
  ISBN 978-1-59514-273-3
  [1. Zombies—Fiction. 2. Supernatural—Fiction. 3. Dead—Fiction. 4. High schools—
Fiction. 5. Schools—Fiction. 6. Interpersonal relations—Fiction. 7. Arkansas—
Fiction.] I. Title.
  PZ7.J344Und 2010
  [Fic]—dc22
                                2009021093
Printed in the United States of America

To Riley Roo, quite possibly the coolest five-year-old ever

CHAPTER 1

*O*kay, this was it. The BIG moment.

After two months of training so hard, we barely had the energy to shower before we fell into bed—let alone ravage each other the way two teenagers in love should *totally* be ravaging each other—Ethan and I were alone on Sunday night, the last night of winter break.

"I feel like I haven't seen you in weeks," Ethan mumbled against my lips, leaning into me until my back touched the inside of the car door.

"I'm so glad training is over until spring break." A part of me actually wished Junior Enforcer training was over forever, but I didn't tell him that.

Ethan loved having the chance to learn from what were basically the secret-service officers of the zombie Settling world. He wanted to join their ranks when he turned twenty, and the experience he was gaining would prove invaluable when it was time to put in his application.

Besides, he didn't seem to care that the only reason the Enforcers were hanging around Carol, Arkansas, was because of his freakishly powerful girlfriend, so the least I could do was keep my mouth shut about how grueling I'd found the past few months. A lot of boyfriends would *not* be cool with a girl being so much better than them at something. And I was better, way better. I was probably the most powerful sixteen-year-old zombie Settler in the history of the U.S.

On the days when it helped me put to rest a kid who'd crawled out of his grave with major issues or to kick black-magically raised zombie butt, I really appreciated the gift. The rest of the time . . . I kind of wished I was normal. Or at least a normal Settler of the Dead. Maybe then my entire body wouldn't hurt at the end of the day after an hour of pom squad practice and three hours of training with Kitty and her team of Enforcer tough guys.

And maybe Ethan and I wouldn't have had to wait *months* for the chance to be alone together for more than half an hour.

"This scarf has to go," he said, tugging the fluffy white fabric from my neck and throwing it to the floorboards. "But I love this Frisbee hat. Did I tell you how much I love this hat?"

"A few thousand times. It's called a beret." I laughed, then sighed as he trailed little kisses down my neck. Neck kisses. Who knew they would be so . . . fabulous?

"Now," he murmured, "if you could just say something in French while wearing that hat and doing that . . . thing you do . . ." I pressed my lips to his neck, dragging my teeth over his skin just the tiniest bit as I pulled away. "Yeah, *that* thing." The way his voice trembled made me feel oddly powerful and nervous at the same time.

But it was a good nervous. Everything Ethan made me feel was good. Good, good, good, good. So good, I couldn't believe he was really my boyfriend, that I was the one he called every night to say "I love you" to before he turned out the light.

Still, the whole "talk French to me, baby" stuff was pure guy weirdness.

"I think you've got issues with the French thing."

"Oh yeah?"

"Yeah. You might need therapy."

"Kiss therapy." He wiggled his eyebrows, but even that level of goofiness couldn't detract from his yum factor. He'd cut his dirty blond hair so it didn't hang down in front of his face quite the way it had when we first met, but he was still Greek-god gorgeous. And now I could see his amazing green eyes even better than before.

I stared into those eyes, grinning like a fool as I put a stop to the eyebrow wiggling with my fingertips. "You are such a dork."

"That's why we're a perfect match."

"Are you calling *me* a dork?"

"Total dork. A really hot dork, but—"

"Well, *that* makes it all better." I wrapped my arms around his neck, giggling as he tugged me through the narrow opening between the front seats and into the back of his Mini Cooper.

It was freakishly small back there, even with the seats folded down, and neither of us is particularly short, but I couldn't care less. I hardly noticed that my legs were folded into a pretzel when Ethan pulled me on top of him.

Man, he felt good. So solid and warm and the kisses . . . God, the kisses.

These were what kisses were supposed to feel like. Like your lips were on fire—in the good way, not the "I just ate three jalapeño peppers on a dare" way—and the fire was spreading to every inch of your body. Even if we hadn't left the car running and the heat on, I wouldn't have noticed the cold. I couldn't notice anything but him, and his lips, and his hands. I loved his hands, those hands . . . that were slowly moving up the back of my sweater . . . and sort of sliding beneath my bra strap.

Oh. Crap. Was this it? Were we going there? Was I ready to go there? I mean, heck yes, nothing felt as good as kissing Ethan, so I was sure doing other things with Ethan was going to be pretty fab too. And I turned sixteen over two months ago, so I was probably overdue for some groping, but—

Gah! Groping? Couldn't I think of a better word, something at least remotely romantic or sexy or something?

"You feel amazing," he said, before his tongue slipped past my lips.

"Mmmm." I moaned my agreement. Not agreeing that *I* tasted amazing, of course, but that *he* did. He tasted like coffee and caramel from the Starbucks we'd snagged on the way out to his grandfather's farm, and like . . . Ethan. Yummy, perfect, wonderful, hot, nineteen-year-old-in-college Ethan who was no doubt tired of taking it slow with his nearly-three-and-a-half-years-younger girlfriend.

Yep. He was definitely tired of taking it slow.

He eased apart the hooks on my lavender demi-cup bra with a practiced little flip of his fingers, making my heart race for reasons that had nothing to do with hormones.

Geez! Couldn't he struggle with the thing for a few seconds? Just to offer a little comfort of the "don't worry, I'm not waaayyyy more experienced than you are" variety? No, he had to unhook my hooks from their little circle things with an ease that left no doubt he'd done this many, many times before. Or at least many more times than I had.

Which was none. Zero.

God, what should I do?

On one hand I was really feeling the full-body tingleness of being with Ethan. But on the other hand, I was freaking out. I mean, we hadn't been able to go on a real date in weeks, not since we'd exchanged Christmas presents at his mom's house and then gone to a midnight showing of *It's a Wonderful Life* at the community center.

And then I'd had to be home right after, so there'd only been time for a little kissing. Shouldn't there be some sort of learning curve, a way to *ease* into this? I'm really an easing kind of person. I don't jump into the deep end—I wade slowly in from the shallow part of the pool, giving myself time to adjust.

Where was the time to *adjust*?!

Ethan paused. "Megan, I—"

Suddenly there was a knocking at the window.

I screamed a piercing, girly scream that made Ethan wince, but I couldn't help it. Give me creepy flesh-hungry Reanimated Corpses and I can get my Buffy on with the best of them. But interrupt me whilst making out and I am far more the hysterical-screaming-and-clutching-at-my-clothes, desperately-trying-to-rehook-my-bra-through-my-sweater type of girl.

"Um, sorry. Didn't mean to freak you out in there." The voice outside was male, but it didn't sound like anyone I knew.

He was definitely a young guy, however, which meant we'd escaped being discovered by Ethan's seventy-year-old grandfather. Thank. God. I really didn't want to look Pop-Pop in the eye while my bra was still unhooked.

Not that a complete stranger was a much better option.

"But, um . . . I'm here," the dude outside said. "So are you coming out?"

"Who the heck are you?" Ethan asked.

Excellent question. Who was he and why was he way out here at the edge of town, lurking in some old man's back pasture at nine o'clock on a Sunday night? Ethan and I had been sure even the cows would be shacked up somewhere warm.

"Megan? That *is* Megan Berry in there, right?" the guy asked.

"You know this guy?" Ethan grabbed the flashlight he left rolling around in his trunk, brandishing it like a weapon as he turned toward the window.

"I don't think so." I sighed with relief as I finally managed to get my bra back in position. Call me crazy, but I felt a thousand times more prepared to deal once the girls were properly strapped in. Even a possible stalker didn't seem as scary when securely undergarmented.

I noticed Ethan was looking frustrated. Or angry. Or something. Geez, you'd think I'd *invited* the strange dude to come hang out with us while we sucked face.

Groped. Sucked face. Yuck. I really needed to work on my descriptions of kissy-kissy behavior.

"Stay here, I'm going to check out your friend." Ethan had popped open the door and was sliding out into the night before I could protest. That dude was *not* my friend.

Not that it would have mattered. This wasn't the first time I'd noticed Ethan's hint of a jealous streak. Though it usually thrilled me to see him get all scowly when one of the other Settler boys checked me out during Enforcer drills.

I mean, Ethan was the hottest boy living—as far as I was concerned—and knowing he felt the same way about me was unbelievable. I'm no dog, but neither am I model material. I'm average height, with average long frizzy brown hair, which must be tamed with a scalding hot Chi to achieve any level of smoothness, and pretty decent brown eyes with a hint of gold around the irises. I'm a little too skinny, especially after all the training and dancing the past few months, and my figure is nothing to write home about. I mean, I have enough chest to keep strapless clothes in place, but still need creative padding to form any "luscious lady lumps" under my sweater.

"Megan? Did you hear me? You should come out and see this." Ethan stuck his head through the rear window. He sounded more shocked than jealous, which should have let me know right away there was some Settler weirdness going down. Wasn't there always? I mean, could we *ever* spend a night together without dead people being in some way involved?

No, *of course* we couldn't.

Still, I was legitimately surprised to see a dead guy standing next to Ethan, stomping his sneakered feet in the remains of the snow that had fallen the night before, looking amazingly lifelike for a zombie. His shoulder-length hair—brown or black, I couldn't quite tell in the moonlight—was clean and soft looking and his expression excited and friendly. In fact, if I hadn't been able to smell the funky grave odor clinging to his jeans and oversize striped sweater, I wouldn't have thought he was deceased at all.

"Hey! Megan, good to meet you. I'd recognize you anywhere. That's *some* mojo you've got going. I caught your energy the second I liberated myself from that crypt." He smiled, revealing two dazzling rows of super straight teeth and reached out to grab my hand. The guy had been very cute when he was alive, in a sort of saggy-pants-stoner way. "I'm Cliff."

"Cliff?"

"Clifford Joseph Frankincense Harvester, reporting for duty."

"Duty?" I repeated, so shocked I could barely bring myself to squeeze his hand and pump it up and down a few times before detangling myself. Manners are good and all, but the smell of fresh grave just doesn't come out of clothes without some major effort.

I would have dodged the hand entirely, in fact, if I'd *ever* had a zombie chat me up the way Cliff was doing. Usually the naturally Unsettled were kind of out of it until a Settler gave the cue to start blabbing. Even then, the majority of people who were troubled enough by unfinished business from their living days to crawl out of their graves and seek intervention weren't in the mood for idle conversation.

They came, they groaned and shuffled, I asked them what was up, and they confessed their issues. Then I promised to take care of their bidness and sent them back to their eternal slumber. End of story. All nice and tidy and relatively easy—except for the grave-sealing process. Now that I was a second-stage Settler, I had to follow them back to their place of rest and seal them in with a special ceremony so no one could resurrect them with black magic.

After having been nearly killed by Reanimated Corpses—RCs, as Ethan liked to call them—back in September, I took grave sealing very seriously. Really, I took just about everything very seriously. Learning that your best friend had been planning to kill you for years does that to a girl. My former BFF, Jess, was now in a Settlers' Affairs prison in Little Rock awaiting trial and sentencing, but that didn't really help me feel any safer. If I'd been stupid enough to be best friends with a witch who wanted to watch black-magically raised zombies munch my flesh, my safety wasn't something I could take for granted.

"Yeah, I figured it was a nice night, and I've never walked through a fresh snow before," Cliff said with a shrug.

"So you came to find me because you have never taken a walk in the snow?" Never in my entire life—either in the five years of Settling the dead when I was a kid, or in the past four months of being back in the business now that my powers have returned—had I ever heard a request like this.

Usually people had *real* issues. They wanted to tell someone they had been fighting with before they died that they loved them; they had unfinished business that affected the living or made them feel guilty in death; and sometimes they even had to get the name of their killer off their chests and into the hands of the proper authorities.

I'd had more than my share of murdered teens in the past few months. Unfortunately, my extraordinarily strong Settler power drew them to me like flies to a steaming fresh pile of cow poo.

Speaking of cow poo, we were bound to run into some if Cliff really wanted to stroll. Looked like my new suede boots—and my romantic date with Ethan—were shot.

"Um, yeah. That's not something you want to miss out on. So I figured I might as well crawl out of the old grave and go for a stroll. You game?" Cliff asked, then turned to Ethan with a sheepish grin. "If you don't mind, of course. I'm assuming you're the boyfriend?"

"No, sure. I mean, yeah. But that's fine," Ethan stammered, obviously thrown by Cliff as well. "I'll wait in the car—you two go ahead and stroll."

"Okay." I smiled at Cliff as I grabbed Ethan's hand and pulled him back toward the car. "Just let me grab my coat."

"No problem. You living people get cold." He laughed, a

strangely infectious sound that made me want to laugh too. Good thing I didn't, however, since Ethan didn't look amused. "I haven't been dead that long. I remember freezing my balls off at a football game last November. Who decided November was a good time for football? I mean, playing it, sure, since you're bound to get hot. But watching it? Mostly lame. Unless it's on television, and you've got lots of snacks for during the commercials."

"This guy talks more than you do," Ethan mumbled as he opened the door and grabbed my bright red peacoat.

"Thanks a lot." I shrugged my coat on and reached past Ethan for my scarf.

I got it that he was annoyed, but no need to take it out on me. I couldn't help my job any more than he could. So I drew a larger number of Unsettled than the average girl, and I hadn't dared ask another Settler to cover for me because I wanted to save up my favors for nights the pom squad had to dance at basketball games. It wasn't my fault I was still in high school. And balancing stage-two responsibilities was a lot harder than stage three—the level Ethan had been since his nineteenth birthday. He only had to be on duty a couple nights a week, and the rest of the time he could shut off his power and not worry about drawing the Undead.

I, however, was not granted such luxuries . . . even though I knew I could figure out how to turn my power off if I tried. I *was* abnormally advanced, after all.

Unfortunately, I'd also landed myself in an abnormally large amount of trouble a few months back while trying to get ahead, so now I was trying to walk the straight and narrow. Seemed like my boyfriend, who worked Protocol and was basically a Settler *cop*, should have been a little more supportive of that!

"I was just kidding." He rubbed my back as I wrapped my scarf around my neck. "You know I love listening to you ramble."

He kissed me on the cheek and I melted. I couldn't stay mad at him. "Then come with us. I'm sure Cliff wouldn't mind. He seems friendly."

"Too friendly," Ethan whispered. "I'm not sure he's giving you the real four-one-one on why he left his grave. Maybe he's holding back until you two are alone."

"Or maybe he's just . . . different?"

"Oh, he's different all right, but not that different. He knows your name, Meg, and didn't you say the only Unsettled who have known who you are right off the bat were—"

"The ones who died. Badly." I cut him off before he could mention "murder."

In the past few months I'd had a couple of kids who were murdered by black magic practitioners. Unfortunately, they hadn't been able to describe the practitioner very well, probably due to the trauma of being *murdered* and all that. They were the ones who knew who I was before I made the proper introductions. And no one, not even the most experienced Elders over at Settlers' Affairs headquarters, could guess how the dead kids knew who I was. It was a mystery, like so many other things about me.

For instance, why I had this incredible power and whether or not I'd be able to control it sufficiently to lead a relatively average life. Or why I still felt like I was living on borrowed time even though the people raising killer zombies had been locked away. No matter how normal I acted in front of Ethan and my parents, I still wasn't my old self . . . and I was beginning to think I never would be.

With those cheery thoughts in mind, I turned back to Cliff. "Okay, let's get strolling." Might as well get him taken care of and back in his grave, and maybe Ethan and I would have a few minutes to talk before my ten-o'clock-on-school-nights curfew.

"Call me if you need me," Ethan shouted as Cliff and I set off across the pasture.

"You won't need him. I'm harmless, I promise," Cliff said in a chummy whisper. "Not like the others."

I huddled deeper into my coat as a weird shiver raced down my spine. "The others? What others?"

"The . . . others. The . . . um . . . " His smile faded and he looked as confused as I felt, but seconds later his grin returned. "You know what? I can't remember. Let's just forget it and enjoy the walk. Cool?"

"Cool," I said. But it wasn't.

Nothing about the way this night was ending was cool. But then, what else was new?

CHAPTER 2

"Wow, Megan, looks like winter break *really* didn't agree with you."

"Thanks, Monica. Nice to see you too." I grinned, determined not to let the Monicster get to me. It was only our first afternoon back at practice. I couldn't let her evilness wear me down until at least February.

"Really, you could pack luggage in those bags." Monica Parsons wiggled into the girls' locker room like it was filled with guys ready to ogle her tiny size-two body instead of a bunch of girls changing into workout clothes for after-school basketball, cheer, and pom squad practice. "How is it possible to look so rough after a three-week vacation?"

As if she didn't know. She'd been training right next to Ethan and me every day down at the Settlers' Affairs compound. Monica was as obsessed as Ethan was with becoming an Enforcer candidate, even thinking she would be the first Settler to be accepted right out of high school.

She was delusional, of course, but I'd resisted the urge to tell her so. We'd finally forged an uneasy truce after helping contain a bunch of black-magically raised zombies last fall, and I was doing my best to keep the peace. She *was* captain of the pom squad, after all, and we were both bound to keep our identity as Settlers of the Dead top secret from the human world.

Still, that didn't mean I had to put up with her crap.

"I don't know, Monica, how is it possible to look so ho-like in jeans and a sweatshirt?" I asked, my tone sweet as honey. Shocked gasps erupted from London and Alana, the Monicster's partners in crime. Well, the ones left over after her ex-BFF, Beth, had gotten locked up for seriously creepy voodoo . . .

"It's easy." Monica tossed her long, silky, nearly black hair over her shoulder, clearly taking my insult as a compliment. "What's baffling is how you manage to make a perfectly cute miniskirt look so fugly."

"It's the cable tights." Alana smacked her gum. "They're totally short bus."

"Short bus means retarded, idiot," Monica said, turning on Alana with a critical glare.

"Right, those tights are retarded. Right?"

"It's pretty wrong to make fun of retarded people, Alana." London twisted her long auburn hair into a knot on the top of her head. "It's not like they can help it."

"Exactly. What's up with you today?" Monica shook her head sadly, obviously disappointed with the insult quality of her third-in-command.

Assuming I'd been forgotten now that Monica had found someone else to pick on, I wiggled into my black spandex dance pants, hoping I could get changed before I attracted any more attention.

"And what's up with that bruise, Megan? Has Ethan been beating you?" Monica asked, honing in on the giant black mark on my thigh. "That's totally going to show if we wear the black uniforms on Saturday night."

"I'll cover it up with base," I said, ignoring her questions.

For some reason, I couldn't think of a reasonable lie. All I could think about was the way Cliff had freaked out when I'd fallen down last night during our walk. We hadn't made it ten feet from the car when I'd tripped on a frozen cow patty—aka a large lump of bovine excrement—and bitten it big-time. Just average klutzy Megan stuff, but Cliff had been really worried, acting like the world would end if something bad happened to Megan Berry. It had creeped me out. Especially considering he still hadn't copped to any unfinished business besides a burning desire to traipse around in a winter wonderland.

Despite his sweetness, I'd been glad to get Cliff back in his crypt, all tucked in for a nice, long rest after his first—and final—walk in the snow.

"Makeup will rub off on the spandex." Monica sighed. "We're just going to have to wear the white and gold. Write that down for me, Alana."

Alana jumped to do her evil mistress's bidding while the rest of us finished changing. Or *tried* to finish changing. It wasn't easy, what with the twelve cheerleaders standing in a knot by the sinks, whispering and staring.

What was up with everyone today? You'd think three weeks off would make people *less* cranky. Apparently not.

But then, the cheerleaders and the pom squad had been enemies ever since the inception of the much more awesome dance team— aka pom squad—ten years ago. I personally believed the animosity stemmed from the fact that the cheerleaders were jealous that all they got to do was yell and jump around on the sidelines, while the pom squad commanded center floor and the entire crowd's attention during halftime when we did our latest routine. I mean, our superiority was clear to anyone with half a brain—which even most of the cheerleaders possessed.

I whipped my sweater off and was reaching for my sports bra just as giggles erupted from the cheer huddle, freezing me in place. I managed not to flinch or hunch my shoulders, but it wasn't easy. Old habits died hard, and I'd been the weirdly flat girl for too long to be able to strip with complete confidence even now that I had something up top. Penny, another sophomore on the pom squad, and a couple of the basketball girls also froze mid-strip, making me suspect I wasn't the only one with body-image concerns.

Monica, however, had no such issues.

"Is there a reason you and your clones are staring at us, Dana?" She unhooked her bra and flung it into her locker, then took her time grabbing her black sports bra from the top shelf.

"We're not staring, we were just . . . observing." Dana, the barely five-foot captain of the cheer squad stepped slightly in front of her clones.

Normally I wouldn't judge, but Monica was right. The cheerleaders were eerily similar. Every last one of them sported shoulder-length blond hair—some natural, but most from the bottle. Even Lee Chin, the Asian girl, was a blonde, as were Kimberly and Kate, the African-American twins.

"Well, I'm not really down for a strip show right now, so why don't you take your observation elsewhere?" Monica tugged her sports bra on and began pulling her hair back into a ponytail. "Maybe you could try, I don't know, *practicing*?"

Alana laughed and a few other pom girls stifled giggles. The cheerleaders were notoriously lazy, thinking that a bunch of backflips could make up for the fact that they spent most of their practices touching up each other's toenails and that no one would notice if they misspelled "Cougars" during the fight song. They'd managed to win the state cheerleading competition the year before, but only because Dana's aunt's friend's daughter was one of the judges. Otherwise, not even an unholy deal with the devil could have made up for all their slacking.

"Oh, we've been practicing. We've been working on new routines all winter break, enough to keep the crowd fired up through the entire basketball season."

"Fired up?" London muttered, making everyone giggle this time. Even me, I admit it.

The cheerleaders were like time travelers from a different age, a gentler time when people still said things like "gee whiz" and "golly" and meant it. It would have been kind of cute, if they weren't our sworn enemies.

"Yep, fired up and inspired to cheer the Cougars on to another state championship." Dana smiled and fisted her hands on her hips, every muscle going tight as if she were already standing on top of a pyramid. It made me wonder if it hurt when she sat down, like, if her muscles got sore from having her butt perpetually clenched. "And Principal Watkins and the booster club are totally behind us. They've got something special planned for the opening of the new gym, and they think it's a great idea for the cheerleaders to take their turn on the court at halftime."

A hush fell over our side of the room and the last of the lingering basketball players hustled out in a hurry. They were unusually tall and more athletic than the average girl, but they still knew a catfight in the making when they saw one.

After all, this wasn't just *any* basketball game. It was the *first* game of the season and the *first* game ever to be played on the new gym floor. This game was going to be broadcast on Little Rock's local station, photographed by every paper in the area, and generally be the biggest deal Carol, Arkansas, had seen in a *long* time. We'd prepped a dance routine more than worthy of the event. The cheerleaders trying to take over halftime was tantamount to replacing a famous-name Broadway star with some no-name understudy with badly conditioned hair.

It just wasn't going to happen, not if we had anything to say about it.

"What?" Monica's ice-blue eyes narrowed. "I'm not sure I heard you correctly."

"It's already been decided." Dana flipped her blond ponytail and grinned, making her twin dimples pop. "We're going to be the ones performing at halftime this basketball season."

"No, you're the ones who've been smoking crack," Alana said, stepping up her insult game. "The pom squad *owns* halftime. Everyone knows that."

"Not Principal Watkins or the booster club," Dana said with a smug little grin. "They agree with the rest of us and would like to see something a little more wholesome on our court."

"What is that supposed to mean?" London asked.

"It means we're tired of watching a bunch of stripper wannabes roll around on the floor for five minutes every game," Kimberly said.

"It's trashy," her twin, Kate, seconded. "Boys from other schools think Carol girls are easy."

"It's no wonder." Dana's eyes raked over every one of us, silently judging our bare midriffs and tight spandex pants. "The Slut Squad gives us all a bad rep."

Oh no she didn't.

Moving with a single-minded purpose, the rest of the pom squad filed in behind Monica, lending our silent support to our captain. If they wanted to rumble, we'd rumble, by God. I'd never scratched faces or pulled hair before, but I was getting in the mood to.

Or maybe Monica and I could try out some of our new moves on the platinum brats. Our Enforcer training had included hours of training in self-defense and combat strategy as well as spell work. It seemed a shame for all that to go to waste now that the black-magically raised zombie situation around Carol was under control.

"So you're telling me Principal Watkins and the boosters did this without even notifying the captain of the pom squad?" Monica asked, her voice surprisingly cool and controlled. "I find that hard to believe."

"Believe what you want. We'll all see I'm telling the truth come Saturday when we take the court at halftime." Dana nodded her head in that twitchy way she did right after giving the "ready, okay" that signaled her minions should begin a new cheer. "Come on, girls. We'd better go—Aaron said he found a top-secret place for us to practice."

Aaron was the only dude cheerleader as well as the newest member of the squad. He was a junior, vice president of the Honor Society, cute in an all-American kind of way, and had naturally blond hair, so it wasn't like he could help fitting in with the clones. But he was obviously a passenger on the cheerleader cruise liner of evil if he was scoping out "top-secret" practice locations.

What was with that? Like we were going to steal one of their lame routines? Between us we had over fifty years of combined dance training. *We* were the experts—*they* were the pretenders to the throne.

"What are we going to do?" Alana asked, as soon as the cheerleaders from heck had vacated the locker room.

"You're going to hit the old gym and practice," Monica said. "I'm going to hit Principal Watkins's office and remind him how things work here at CHS."

"Don't you think you should put on a shirt first?" I asked, then immediately wished I'd kept my mouth shut. "I mean, if what she was saying about Watkins is true, then wouldn't it pay to tone it down?"

Monica glared while I did my best not to cringe. Geez, she still scared me, even though I had stuff on her that would keep her from a full-out attack. She'd been dabbling in black magic last fall, in an attempt to steal Ethan away from the sophomore nobody who had somehow captured his attention. (The nobody would be me.)

I'd agreed not to tell Settlers' Affairs about her journey to the dark side as long as she let me have a special tryout for the pom squad— since I'd missed the first one due to potentially deadly situations beyond my control. But now that I was on the squad, she couldn't kick me off. I could, however, spill my guts to the Elders at SA and get her kicked out of Enforcer training. Not that I would, but it was a nice ace to have at times when Monica seemed primed to revert to her old Megan's-life-destroying ways.

Times like this one, for example.

But instead of ripping me a new one, she smiled. "Megan, I think I know how to handle men—even men old enough to be my grandfather." She pulled the ponytail holder from her hair, shaking her head until her glossy locks spilled over her shoulders in a sexy tangle.

How did she do that? Make it look so effortless?

"Okay, fine. I was just trying to help."

"Well don't. I don't need . . ." She paused at the door and turned back to me with this little gleam in her eyes. I knew I was in trouble before she opened her mouth. "No, you know what? Helping is a good thing. We're all sisters here, and we should help each other out."

"Right! We must stand united against our common enemy," I said, knowing Monica would get my insider reference.

We'd been forced to unite our powers before. Monica's former BFF, Beth, and my BFF, Jess, had been special friends (um, okay girlfriends) and partners in a plan to kill me and Monica for causing Jess's mom's death when we were just kids. Which was a totally bogus charge. Jess's mom had been raising the dead, and all Monica and I had done was work a *reverto* spell to send them back to their maker. We'd had no idea the zombies would munch on her until there was nothing left but bones.

But Jess and Beth didn't care that we hadn't meant to hurt anyone. They'd nearly killed me and Monica with a bunch of skeleton zombies. They'd even planned to film the event so they could enjoy the magic of our deaths again and again—the freaks. Sure, they were suffering for their evil now—Beth was in a mental institution in upstate New York and Jess was in SA prison and had been hospitalized twice for seizures brought on by working black magic—but the entire experience had still been pretty horrific.

21

You'd think that surviving something like that would have bonded me and Monica, but no such luck.

"Exactly. We have to unite." Monica crossed the room to link her scrawny arm around my waist. She was definitely up to something. "So I think Megan should come with me to see Principal Watkins." She grabbed the bottom of my T-shirt and tugged it up around my ribs.

I snatched the material from her hands and tugged it back down. "What are you doing?"

"Teaching you a thing or two about managing men." She rolled her eyes at my scandalized look. "Your sports bra is black and covers everything you *don't* have—what's the big deal?"

"I don't want to go talk to the principal with my stomach hanging out."

"Come on, Megan. You have pants on, for God's sake," she said. "You're dating a college guy and you're too shy to show less skin than you do in a bathing suit? Are you sure things are okay with you and Ethan? I mean, I know he's never been exactly what you call the innocent type."

Ooooh, she knew just where to aim her evil poison darts.

"Everything is fine with me and Ethan. Better than fine. But it's freezing outside. I don't want either of us to catch a cold before the big game," I said.

Monica glared and grabbed her T-shirt. "Fine."

Ha! Score one for Megan!

But as I followed Monica out into the late-afternoon chill and raced up the hill to the main building, I still felt like I'd lost a battle. I couldn't really put my finger on what that battle was any more than I could figure out what had been making me feel so restless the past few weeks. Was it just that I'd finally had the time for all the horribleness of Jess's betrayal and my multiple near-death experiences to hit full force? Or was it something else?

I didn't know, but that odd, unsettled feeling made me kind of glad the cheerleaders had stirred up a hornet's nest. It was comforting to be able to concentrate on a normal problem instead of the seemingly groundless fear that my entire life was about to fall apart.

CHAPTER 3

"What the heck is this?" Dad hit the brakes hard enough to give Mom and me whiplash and glared at the banner under the Kroger sign late the next afternoon. "*This* is the fund-raiser?"

Oh God. I should have known this would happen. Why hadn't I told my parents I would ride my bike? Sure, it was cold outside, but at least I would have been spared the embarrassment of having everyone stare while my dad malfunctioned in the grocery store parking lot.

"It's not what it looks like, Dad. It's just a joke and I'm already late so I'll just—"

"Stay in the car, Megan," he barked, his military background coming through loud and clear. He'd been retired from the air force for a couple of years, but his super-loud "obey me now or I'll throw you in a military prison where you will rot for a thousand years" voice was still in prime working order. "No daughter of mine is working at a topless car wash."

"Dad's right, it's barely forty-eight degrees," Mom said, twisting to give me the concerned-mom look.

"Who gives a crap how cold it is? I don't care if it was a hundred degrees, Jennifer, Megan is keeping her clothes on in public." He shifted into reverse and glared at me as he prepared to turn around. "*And* in private!"

"Dad! Stop! We're not going to be topless," I said, knowing I was blushing. Geez, why did Monica have to put up the sign so early? "We're going to wash everything except the tops of the cars. Get it?"

Dad stepped on the brake again, but didn't shift back into drive. The anger drained from his face and I could see he was starting to feel kind of silly. He looked nearly as angry as Principal Watkins had when he'd walked into school this morning and seen our posters advertising the car wash in the hall. Once we'd explained our gimmick, he'd calmed down fairly quickly, however. No matter what the cheerleaders said, Watkins didn't seem to care about taming the "Slut Squad" or what went on during halftime one way or the other.

He just wanted peace and had therefore gutlessly handed the decision of who did what at halftime over to the booster club. In a truly mercenary show of capitalism, the boosters then decided that whichever team could raise the most money by the end of the week would own halftime for the year. Hence, the last-minute borderline-scandalous Tuesday night car wash.

"Oh. Well, I still don't like it." Dad sighed in a way that made it clear raising a teenager was wearing him out. "But if your mother thinks it's okay . . ."

"I don't know." Mom wrinkled her nose, which made her look really young even though she was all dressed up. The woman had good genes, including great skin and the ability to eat like a pig and not gain weight.

Still, she was a mom, no matter how young looking, as evidenced by her next words. "Actually, I think it's pretty tacky."

"Well, tacky sells." I grabbed my backpack and mittens and prepared to evacuate.

"You mean sex sells," Mom said.

"Whatever."

"'Whatever'? What happened to the girl-power/feminist thing you and Jess were always . . ."

The car got really quiet, like it did every time someone accidentally mentioned Jess, the girl who had been my best friend for nearly six years before she'd tried to kill me.

"Yeah, well, we've got to do whatever it takes to raise more money than the cheerleaders or we lose halftime rights for the entire basketball season. The team that makes the biggest contribution to the boosters by Friday night wins," I said in a breezy voice, refusing to let Mom know how much thinking about Jess still bugged me.

She'd been after me to go "talk to someone" since last September, but I didn't have the time for therapy. I had zombie stuff to learn and pom squad and school and would like to spend some time with my boyfriend at *some* point. Maybe after the car wash. He said he'd come by once he got off his Protocol shift. In addition to going to college part-time, Ethan was a Settler cop.

Is there anything hotter than a cute guy who is also armed and dangerous? I think not.

"Call us if you need a ride home," Dad said.

"And don't get wet! You'll get hypothermia." Mom called as I slammed out the door.

I thought I heard her mumbling something about the idiocy of a car wash in winter but didn't respond. She was right, but what else were we supposed to do? We only had four days to make enough cash to win this stupid competition before Saturday's game, and a car wash was the only thing we could get up and running fast.

We had other irons in the fire, but for now scrubbing dirt from cars and trucks wrecked by the mess they'd put on the streets after the snow was the best we could do. Not a fun way to spend a Tuesday night, but at least we wouldn't have to wash the tops of the cars, and it wasn't cold enough to make the water freeze.

And we already had one customer. The senior girls were hard at work scrubbing a Mustang while a couple of juniors held up signs near the road and the rest of the team stood around trying to look adorable and worthy of the ten dollars per vehicle we were charging—plus tip, of course.

"Was that your mom and dad? They're cute." Penny was one of the three other sophomores on the team, and a girl I thought I'd like to get to know better if I had the time. She was always very sweet, and her curly copper hair and nose freckles reminded me of Lindsay Lohan when she was still the cute little kid from the *Parent Trap* remake.

"Thanks. Yeah, they weren't thrilled with the gimmick," I said, rolling up my coat sleeves and scoping out a bucket to commandeer for my personal scrubbing use.

"Oh God, my mom wasn't either. I thought she was going to have a stroke. And then she saw Monica and . . ." Our eyes drifted to where Monica was halfheartedly scrubbing the sides of the red Mustang. She had on a sweater and jeans, but both were so tight she looked like she'd been poured into a catsuit. And she was wearing stiletto boots. Who wore high heels to wash cars? "Well, after that I was lucky to get out of the car."

I laughed and Penny did too, and for a second I thought I might enjoy this evening of slavery. Penny was cool and we have never had the chance to just hang out and talk at practice.

Then I smelled it—death wafting across the parking lot.

It wasn't grave dirt or the sickeningly sweet odor of rotting flesh, but there was no doubt that whatever this was had been summoned from its grave with black magic. After months spent studying the various ingredients one could use to reanimate a corpse, I had the pungent odor of wormwood and gardenia memorized.

Still, I didn't want to believe it. This couldn't be happening again! Carol was a nice, sleepy small town, not a hotbed of black magic and mayhem. Or at least it hadn't been until four months ago. Now, it seemed the rules had changed.

I heard the unmistakable groans of flesh-hungry zombies and was running toward the tree line at the edge of the parking lot a second later.

"Monica! I saw one of your friends." I grabbed a handful of Monica's sweater on my way by and tugged her along with me.

"What the heck, Megan? I swear to God I—"

"One of your *special* friends." My eyes went wide and I prayed she got the message in the next ten seconds, because we were swiftly running out of time. If we didn't haul ass, those black-magically raised zombies were going to make it out of the cover of the trees and we'd both be royally screwed.

We'd have no choice but to fight them in the open to keep our friends from getting turned into zombie chow. Then Settlers' Affairs would have no choice but to send both us and our families far, far away. Being discovered by someone from the mortal world was just about the worst thing that could happen to a Settler. If SA even *thought* you'd been spotted by an average person, you were likely to find yourself in some seriously deep poo.

My parents had already been relocated once, from California to

Sticksville, Arkansas, and I really didn't want to find out where we'd be headed if I got caught kicking zombie tail on the Kroger parking lot.

"Oh shit," Monica hissed under her breath. "You're f-ing kidding me."

"No. In the trees. Hurry!"

She threw down her sponge and raced after me, making pretty good time for a chick in stiletto boots. I was going to have to reevaluate my opinion that movie people were stupid for always dressing women crime fighters in heels.

"Monica, Megan, where are ya'll—"

"We'll be right back, don't worry!" I called over my shoulder to London. *And please don't follow us,* I silently prayed. If the other girls got close to the edge of the trees, they were going to see what Monica and I were up to. It was getting dark, but not that dark, and there were no leaves to hide us.

On the upside, that meant there was nothing to hide the RCs, either.

Seconds after we stumbled through the first of the soggy, snow-covered leaves, I spotted them—four of the Undead hustling it toward Monica and me with a speed that was unnerving. It wasn't the full-on racing speed of a normal Unsettled, but neither was it the slow, horror-movie shuffle of a black-magically raised zombie.

These guys were different. They moved nearly as fast as the living and their eyes—though lacking that spark that said, "Yo, I'm not dead"—weren't glowing red. RCs *always* had red eyes—it was one of the key things that let you know they were RCs. In addition to the supernatural strength and the trying-to-munch-on-your-nummy-human-flesh stuff and all that.

And not only were their eyes *not* red, but their faces and clothes—which, oddly, looked like pajamas, not your average burial wear—weren't dirty. There wasn't a speck of grave dirt on them, and from the looks of their skin, they hadn't been dead more than a few hours, tops. They weren't decomposing and had a soft pink flush to their cheeks.

But thankfully, no matter how odd these guys were, there were only four of them. I should be able to work the *reverto* spell and get rid of them in no time. It was only if there were a bunch of Undead that Monica and I would have to resort to trickier spells to get the job done.

"*Reverto!*" I held up both hands and willed my power out of my palms, already feeling the relief that comes with getting a Settler crisis under control.

Until I realized the zombies weren't turning and heading back to their maker. Heck . . . they weren't even slowing down.

"*Reverto!*" I repeated, throwing everything I had into the command. My hands buzzed with the force of my power until it felt like I'd grabbed hold of the wrong end of my flattening iron, but still the RCs didn't stop. If anything, they seemed to move a little faster.

"Crap!" With a groan I reached down and grabbed a handful of snow, grateful for the relief of the cold against my burning skin.

"Jesus, Megan. What's wrong with you tonight?" Monica shoved in front of me and raised her own hands. "*Desino! Absisto!*"

I didn't know whether to be relieved or freaked that Monica's freezing commands didn't work either. On the one hand—good to know I wasn't having some weird power outage. On the other hand—zombies, coming closer, clearly wanting taste of girl flesh, "nom nom nom . . ."

"We're going to have to put them down the hard way." I risked a quick glance over my shoulder, relieved to see we were still alone and none of the girls had risked cold, soggy feet by coming to see why we'd run off into the woods like a couple of lunatics. "Do you have—"

"Of course I have my knife." Monica whipped her tiny blade from somewhere near her waist.

How she hid the thing in those skintight clothes was anyone's guess, but I was glad she had the metal required for the *pax frater corpus* spell. I had enough power that I didn't need to pierce the flesh of a zombie with metal in order to immobilize it—I just had to whack it with my fist while I chanted—but the average Settler did.

"You get Shorty and Baldy, I'll get the tall guy, and we'll split the dude coming up from behind," Monica said, taking the lead as usual.

I would have argued that *I* should take the tall football player guy since he looked a heck of a lot more threatening than the two smaller, thinner zombies on the left, but there wasn't any time. We were about to be surrounded.

"*Pax frater corpus, potestatum spirituum.*" I chanted the first portion of the spell as I rushed forward, catching the shortest zombie with a sharp thrust of my palm to his face, then crouching down to sweep the legs out from under the bald guy. Two seconds later, I was on top of him, pounding him in the center of the chest. But for some reason, Baldy didn't seem to be getting the message to lie down and die.

I poured even more strength into my punches and power into my spell. "*Inmundorum ut eicerent eos et curarent omnem. languorem et omnem infirm—*" I was nearly to the end of the chant when freakishly strong hands fisted in my hair and pulled me off the struggling corpse beneath me, dragging me through the snow.

At first I thought it was the fourth zombie who had snuck up behind me, but then I spotted that dude still a dozen feet away. It was the short guy I'd already put down! He should have been zonked out in the snow awaiting an SA retrieval team, not up and fighting for his pound of Megan meat.

The *pax frater* was long and tedious, but it was designed to put zombies down for the count permanently and was the strongest spell I knew that didn't involve setting things on fire—which might have been an option if I didn't think flaming pillars of zombie flesh weaving through the trees would attract the wrong kind of attention.

What the heck was up with these guys? I'd never heard of anything like them, not in four months of irritatingly constant lecturing. The Enforcers were *so* going to get an earful about withholding vital info.

I dug my heels into the cold ground and did my best to pull free from Mr. Short-and-Perky. But before I could twist around and break the dude's hold, a hot, slobbery zombie mouth was at my throat.

Barely resisting the urge to scream—and no doubt bring the rest of the pom squad running—I slammed my closed fist into the guy's face. He groaned and his teeth slid away without breaking the skin, but he *still* didn't let go. And now Baldy was up and at 'em, crawling through the snow toward where I struggled in the frozen leaves.

"Monica! A little help," I cried out, my words turning into a grunt as I contracted my abs, jackknifing my soggy tennis shoes into the face of the guy behind me. Thank God for flexibility and dancer muscles. Shorty groaned and released his hold on my hair just seconds before Baldy crawled on top of me.

"No one gets to do that but my boyfriend," I grumbled into the zombie's face as I slid one leg between the pair of his and shifted my weight. With a grunt, I flipped us over. Now I was on top, but I wouldn't be for long.

Shorty was already lunging toward me, and the straggler dude was closing in from behind. I didn't have time to pound Baldy's face. I had to find a more easily defended position.

I dove to the right, rolling through the snow until I'd put a good six feet between me and the boys. Only then did I spring into a crouched position and take a quick survey of the situation . . . and immediately wished I hadn't.

The news wasn't good.

There were more of them. At least two more, staggering through the darkening shadows beneath the trees, and the four we were already fighting weren't showing any sign of slowing down. The big guy had Monica pinned against a tree while she did her best to keep his teeth from her face, and all three of my guys were closing in with totally weird speed. Very soon we were either going to be discovered or dead, neither of which was a desirable state of being.

There was only one thing I could think of that might get rid of the zombies and get the two of us out of here in one piece. I hadn't had to borrow power from another Settler since I was a kid, but back in the days when Ethan had been my tutor, not my boyfriend, he'd made sure I remembered how. If I could just get past the dudes in front of me, liberate Monica, and get the two of us linked up, there was a chance we'd have enough juice to get rid of these guys.

Of course, getting past these three was going to be easier said than done. They were freaking determined to get a mouthful of Megan, which made me pretty certain I was the one they'd come for. Black-magically raised zombies were raised to hunt a specific target. I was going to have to check for totems—dolls resembling me, items of clothing, etc.—on their graves once we got them safe and snug in the ground again.

Assuming we managed to get them back in the ground at all.

"Megan! Do something." Monica's legs churned wildly in the air, and her face was turning an unhealthy red. The linebacker was going to strangle her if I didn't do something. Fast.

Praying that the pom squad had plenty of clients to keep their attention trained on washing cars, not burning zombies, I turned to Baldy and invoked the flame command. "*Exuro!*"

The good news was that Baldy's pajamas went up in flames like they'd been soaked in vodka, drawing the attention of Shorty and friend long enough for me to cut to the left and skirt around them. The bad news was that Baldy started screaming bloody murder, very likely drawing the attention of the living people only fifty or sixty feet away.

"*Opprimo.*" I tossed the smothering command over my shoulder, trying not to freak out that the zombie I'd set on fire was acting so very un-zombie-ish. I'd heard zombies shriek before, but nothing that sounded so human.

And not only should he *not* have sounded so lifelike, the other two guys shouldn't have noticed the fire or Baldy's screams, let alone been so distracted by them that they let their prey escape. There was something horribly wrong, and I wasn't sure even linking mine and Monica's power would do any good.

"It's going to work; it has to work," I muttered beneath my breath as I grabbed a hefty fallen limb from the ground and raced toward the big zombie at top speed. If Baldy could be distressed by fire, maybe Butch here could be bothered by a log upside the head.

Wood collided with melon with a sickening thud, making the big guy release his hold on Monica's scrawny neck. She sucked in a gasp of air and kneed the dude between the legs as hard as she could, triggering another non-zombie-ish reaction.

"What is wrong with these guys?" We both stared in shock as Butch's knees hit the ground and he collapsed sideways in the snow, clutching his wounded *cojones*.

"I don't know, but I suggest we get rid of them first and ask questions later," I said, grabbing Monica's hand in mine. "Let down your shields, give me everything you've got."

It was a testimony to how freaked the Monicster was that she didn't argue or make a single smart comment. Her shields simply collapsed and her energy came rushing into me, faster and faster, until my entire body burned with the force of the combined power. But still I waited, knowing I'd only have one chance to cast before the boys were on us.

Closer. Closer. I forced myself to hold back until Shorty was close enough to touch and the newcomers were no more than six feet away before throwing up my free hand and giving the RCs everything I had. "*Reverto!*"

The air in front of me buckled, wavering like water in a pond. Time seemed to hold its breath, the entire world gone silent as the zombies reached for me and the bubble of power reached for them.

Luckily for me, the power got to them first.

The spell hit the RCs with an audible pop and my body hit a tree behind me a second later. I'd been bounced by my own spell, something I'd heard of but never experienced. But I sure was experiencing it now. My body hit with enough force to knock the wind from my lungs, and my head smashed into the wood, making little black spots explode in front of my eyes.

By the time I slid to my side in the snow, everything was spinning. Still, through the cartoon birds tweeting around my head, I thought I saw someone hiding in the trees, watching the weird RCs stumble back through the darkened woods. Someone with dark eyes who didn't like what they were seeing. Didn't like it at all.

CHAPTER 4

"Come on, you can't stay there. Someone's coming." Hands tugged at my coat, and when that didn't produce the desired reaction, moved to my hair and tugged even harder.

"Ouch. God, leave me alone . . . my head."

"You won't care about your head if Penny and Terra see those zombies."

"Why? What?" What was she talking about? Nothing seemed to make sense. All I could think about were the eyes . . . and the sweater. Where had I seen that sweater before?

Monica's face swam into focus only inches away from mine. "Why? Because I'm going to smash it in with a rock if we're discovered. So. Get. Up. Now."

My brain felt like it was slam-dancing inside my skull, but I grabbed the hand Monica put in mine and held on as she hauled me to my feet. Then I let her throw my arm around her shoulders and drag me back toward the parking lot while I did my best not to throw up.

"You could help a little," she grumbled.

"I'm trying not to throw up."

"You're heavy."

"So you want me to throw up?" I asked, turning to face her,

relishing the idea of baptizing the Monicster in my partially digested lasagna. I mean, hadn't a part of me wanted to barf on her since third grade?

"No, no," she hurried to assure me. "Just keep moving and keep quiet."

"Why do I have to keep quiet?"

Monica cursed, then added in an urgent whisper. "Just agree with whatever I say, okay?"

"What? I don't—"

"Oh my God, thank God you guys are here! Megan has finally lost it." Monica's voice was as loud and supremely irritated as it usually was when discussing yours truly, which didn't do my poor head any good.

"What happened?" Terra, another sophomore I should have known better than I did, asked. Penny wedged her shoulder under my other arm and helped me limp the last few feet to the edge of the parking lot where I collapsed onto the asphalt with a grunt.

Oh, earth, sweet unspinning earth. I wanted to lay my cheek down on the ground and go straight to sleep, but settled for bracing my elbows on my knees and propping my head in my hands. Monica was right. I had to pull myself together and play this off so that no one else went into the woods.

"These dogs chased this baby raccoon up into a tree. We ran them off, but then Megan decides she has to climb up and save the thing, and I was all like, 'Hello, it's a wild animal, just *leave* it there,' but she wouldn't listen." She sighed, a sound so genuinely put-upon I nearly believed her story myself. "Two seconds later, the branch she's on breaks and Jane Goodall here falls out of the tree."

"Who's Jane Goodall?" I asked, tentatively lifting my eyes to look at the three girls, grateful to see only one of each of them. I wasn't seeing double. That was a good sign.

"I think she might have a concussion. Or brain damage," Monica added.

"I don't have brain damage. I've never heard of the woman."

"Isn't she the one who lived with apes?" Penny asked.

"It wasn't apes, it was chimps," Terra said. "I watched the special on PBS."

"You watch PBS?" Monica asked, wrinkling her nose.

"Don't judge," Terra said in a surprising show of chutzpah 'for a sophomore talking to the queen bi-atch of CHS. "Chimps are interesting. Their DNA is only one percent different from a human's."

Wow. Terra was way smarter than I'd realized. And cooler. Maybe she and Penny would consent to be friends with me once I felt ready to do the whole friends thing again.

"Whatever." Monica waved a hand breezily in the air. "The point is, Wonder Girl here is lucky she didn't break her freaking neck. She probably needs to go to the hospital."

"We could take you to the emergency room," Penny said. "Terra has a hardship permit, so she can drive even though she's only—"

"No, I should take her. I saw what happened and her mom will definitely want to know about it." Monica whipped out her cell phone with a meaningful look.

She was right. My mom would want to know about what had gone down in the woods. Mom didn't actively Settle the dead anymore—she was relieved of that duty when her offspring, me, started summoning—but she was doing her best to keep up with my training so she could help if I needed it. I hadn't so far, but now help was sounding pretty darn good.

I sure as heck didn't want to run into any more of those weird zombies without getting some help first. They were dangerous and could have even been deadly. If Monica and I hadn't been together and able to share power, I didn't know how well either of us would have fared.

"You two get back to washing cars. We've only got two hours before the supermarket shuts down and we need to raise at least two hundred dollars to be on our way to reaching our goal. We're not going to kick cheer butt by standing around staring at the brain-damaged girl." Monica shooed Penny and Terra away as she punched a number into her phone.

I watched them go with a grim smile. The other girls probably assumed it was my parents she was calling, but I knew better. Monica was a strict follower of protocol. She'd call Settlers' Affairs before she called anyone else, and in a matter of minutes, we'd have undercover Protocol officers swarming all over the parking lot. Not such a big deal, you might think, since my own boyfriend is a member of the team and was probably still on duty.

But for some reason, Protocol and I didn't mix. When they showed up, I tended to get into trouble. Usually I got out of it just fine, but right now I didn't feel up to the inevitable two hundred and twenty questions. So I pulled out my own cell and called Mom and Dad, interrupting their fancy dinner and thrilling them even further by announcing I needed to go to the SA hospital due to zombie-related injuries.

I hated to worry my parents, but I really did need to go the hospital—a fact made even clearer when I tried to stand up on my own and the world spun, my stomach lurched, and I ended up back on my butt losing my lasagna in the Kroger parking lot.

• • •

"Do you want me to run you a bath, sweetie?" Mom asked as we staggered into the house nearly three hours later.

It had taken over two and a half hours for the doctor to order a CAT scan and then to tell me that I had a mild concussion and I should go home and get some rest. (You'd think they'd do more for a head injury, right? Apparently not.)

But the SA infirmary *had* been unusually swamped. A six-year-old girl had summoned her first zombie, and her dad, the Settler in the family, hadn't been home to help her learn the ropes. The Unsettled had gone Rogue and injured the mom and three kids before the girl's mom could figure out what to do.

Rogues don't crave flesh like black-magically raised zombies, but they can cause a lot of damage when they start to lose their cool. That's why it's so important for Settlers to attend to the needs of the Unsettled in a swift and efficient manner. Heck, that's why it was so important to have Settlers *period*. If there's no one around to listen, the dead vent their issues in a much more violent manner.

So there had been that family's drama to deal with; then one whole section of the clinic had been closed off because they'd had to bring in a prisoner from the containment center downtown—a girl suffering from seizures caused by working too much black magic. It had taken me all of ten seconds to figure out who *that* was. Jess was the only black-magic artist presently being held at the SA facility in Little Rock. So I got to listen to my former BFF try to swallow her own tongue while I was sitting in the waiting room. Really fun. Really.

That she was *still* dealing with the fallout of her big bad plan last fall was more disturbing than I thought it would be. No matter that she'd planned to kill me and was a complete, psycho nutcase, I still didn't want her to be brain damaged for life . . . or worse.

"Megan?" Mom's hand on my shoulder was just the whisper of a touch, but it still made me jump. "Are you okay?"

"Yeah. I'm fine." I couldn't worry about Jess right now. I had plenty of my own crap to deal with. "I think I'll take a shower. My hair is . . . " I froze in the hall outside the kitchen and threw my arms up to keep my parents from going any further.

"Megan, are you—"

"There's someone here," I said, cutting my mom off with a harsh whisper. "Or at least someone has been here. Look at my backpack. I didn't leave it like that."

On the floor a few feet away, my L.L. Bean backpack lay open, every compartment unzipped and all my books, practice clothes, and makeup strewn across the floor. Ugh, and Mom's romance novel! But hopefully she wouldn't notice I'd liberated *Savage Kisses* from under her bed in all the excitement of our house being broken into.

"Give me your phone," Mom said. "I'm calling SA."

"No need. We're already here." Elder Thomas stepped into the hall and actually had the nerve to smile when Mom and I screamed. Like it was funny that she'd nearly scared us half to death. The white-haired, grannyish-looking woman had once been my favorite Elder, but now I wondered how I'd failed to see the evil in those rheumy blue eyes.

Okay, not *evil*, but she certainly didn't care about me or my family. She cared about the prestige that having one of the most powerful young Settlers in years had brought to her town, and she was determined not to lose what my freakiness had gained. The woman watched me like a hawk, always ready to praise my accomplishments, but even more ready to jump all over me when I made a mistake. Like she was in a position to criticize. It was her stubbornness and SA's unwillingness to believe teenagers could be deep into black magic that had almost gotten me killed last fall. In my opinion, anyone with their head that far up their you-know-what should mind their own business. But that was an opinion Elder Thomas obviously didn't share.

Hence the breaking into my house and nosing through my things.

"You went through my backpack?"

"And your room. The officers are finishing up now. We should be able to leave you to your shower in a few minutes."

"You're searching my room?" I asked, not bothering to hide my outrage. I'd managed to take down at least six weird zombies while keeping myself and Monica alive. What had I done to deserve a bunch of people pawing through my things?

What if they'd found my stash of *Babysitter's Club* books and thought I was an idiot who couldn't read age-appropriate material? Or what if, even now, the Protocol officers were *reading my diary*? What if *Ethan* was reading my diary, and getting an eyeful about my groping torment? Grrr . . . this was so not fair!

"Yes, we are." The friendly façade vanished, and Elder Thomas nailed me with that cold "I'm assessing a mutated specimen" look she did so well. "And we'd like to ask you some questions. I assumed you'd be too exhausted and the matter could wait, but your mouth seems to be in perfect working order. So if you'd like—"

"No, I wouldn't like." Damn straight my mouth was in perfect working order. "I didn't do anything wrong, and I—"

"No one is saying you did." Mom jumped in before I could say something even stupider. I shouldn't talk back to Elder Thomas. She might be inept at times, but she was an inept person who could get me in a heck of a lot of trouble But I was just so sick of being treated like a freak who had to be investigated every time something strange happened in Carol. "I'm sure the Protocol officers just need your statement."

"Actually, I'm allowing the Enforcement team to handle this."

"Enforcement? But we—"

Elder Thomas cut Mom off. "I'm not at liberty to discuss the matter. I'm sorry, Jennifer."

"Hey you guys, glad you made it home," Kitty said as she materialized next to Elder Thomas. "Megan, I thought I heard you come in. Long night." She smiled and blinked tiredly behind her thick glasses.

Kitty was barely five feet tall and looked more like a refugee from *Revenge of the Nerds* than a member of the Settler secret service, but I knew better. The woman could kick major butt, had a knowledge of Settler spells and history that was downright freaky, and was the big boss lady over the team of Enforcement officers who were hanging out in Carol until I was trained and my power was firmly under control.

"You want to get some Doritos and hang out at the kitchen table while we get this over with? I don't know about you, but I'm dying for a snack." She was also really nice, and I knew I'd forgive her for letting Barker and Smythe turn my backpack inside out . . . eventually.

"I think I'll just snag a Sprite," I said, moving into the kitchen. "My stomach isn't up to Doritos, but I'll get you a bowl."

"I'll be in our room, Jennifer." Dad escaped into his and Mom's room, clearly annoyed to have our lives invaded again. Poor Dad, it couldn't be easy being a normal dude in a world full of zombie-fighting freaks.

"I'll get the chips, Megan. You and Kitty go ahead and get started. It's a school night and I'd like to see you in bed in the next hour." Mom urged me toward the table and began bustling about the kitchen, fetching far more bowls than a single serving of Doritos required. She seemed . . . nervous. I guessed it was the Enforcement presence.

Usually a team of Enforcement officers searching your house would be a very, very bad thing. They didn't get involved in local matters unless some seriously illegal stuff was going down. But Kitty, Barker, and Smythe weren't just any Enforcement officers. They were my teachers, trainers, and kind of my friends. We'd all exchanged Christmas/Hanukkah/Kwanzaa presents, for God's sake.

So I didn't feel any huge need to freak. They were probably just helping our local SA chapter out. The Carol Protocol division was pretty small and no doubt unprepared to investigate something like the zombies Monica and I had encountered in the woods.

"Monica told you about the weird RCs, right? That's what this is about?" I settled into my chair with my Sprite while Kitty pulled a tiny tape recorder from her pocket. Mom set the Doritos down between us and then returned to puttering around the kitchen, clearly intending to eavesdrop, which was fine. I had nothing to hide from her or anyone else.

"She did, and she was thorough. As usual." Kitty winked at me and I smiled. "But I'd like to confirm everything with you. On the record." She pressed the record button and got her official voice on. "Interview with Megan Berry. January thirteenth, approximately twenty-two hundred hours.

"Due to the late hour and the fact that Miss Berry suffered head trauma earlier in the evening, this interview is purely for the confirmation of the incident, as per regulation four point three, subsections a and b. Are you ready, Megan?"

"Um, yeah. I mean. Yes." I cleared my throat, catching a bit of Mom's anxiety.

It was hard not to be anxious when Kitty started sounding like the FBI-type person she really was. I made a vow right then to keep my voice friendly when conducting Enforcer interviews. Assuming, of course, that I ended up becoming an Enforcer like everyone and their sister's friend's dog wanted me to be.

"Okay." Kitty smiled again, obviously trying to put me at ease. "When did you first notice the Out-of-Grave Phenomenon?"

"About ten minutes after I got to the car wash. Probably around five? I smelled something funny, then heard groaning, so I grabbed Monica—um, Miss Parsons—and we headed into the woods."

"You smelled something? Could you be more specific?" she asked, and I did my best to describe the smell of the herbs I'd noticed. "Great. So you entered the woods unobserved by any human witnesses?"

"The other members of the pom squad and the guy getting his car washed saw us."

"But they didn't see the Out-of-Grave Phenomenon?"

"I don't think so. No one came to look for us until we'd joined power and—"

"We'll get to that in just a second. First, could you tell me how many Reanimated Corpses you observed and briefly outline any unusual traits they may have had?"

I took my time describing as much as I could remember about the strange RCs—their fast movements, the lack of red eyes, the pink cheeks and apparent absence of grave dirt or any real signs of decomposition.

"So you're saying they appeared to be alive?" she asked casually, as if that weren't a huge weird deal.

"Well . . . I guess. I mean, the two I got really close to were pretty pale, but their skin wasn't cold or stiff." I hadn't thought of it at the time, but Shorty and Baldy's hands *had* been warm. "But they were both really strong, like zombie strong, and they definitely wanted a piece of me."

"They tried to bite you?" Kitty's eyes narrowed just the slightest bit and a shadow passed over her face. If she were someone else, I would have said she doubted my honesty. But this was Kitty. She knew I wasn't a liar, especially about something like this. So why was she looking at me like that?

"Several times. I managed to stop them, but it wasn't easy. None of the commands were working, even the *pax frater*. I don't know what we would have done if combining our power for the *reverto* spell hadn't worked," I said, a hint of accusation creeping into my tone. "You never told us there were RCs that didn't respond to spells. That would have been a good thing to know, you know. Like, *before* we almost died."

Kitty sighed and took off her glasses to rub her eyes. "All Reanimated Corpses *will* respond to Settler commands if there's sufficient power behind the spell and a manageable number of Out-of-Grave Phenomenons. Never in the history of our people have we had a documented case of—"

"But, I swear, there were only seven, four at first, and they didn't—"

"*Never* have we had a documented case of Reanimated Corpses behaving as you've described." Kitty slid her glasses back into place and nailed me with her clear gray eyes. "I'm afraid I can't tell you any more at this time, but be assured your training in how to manage the Undead has been thorough."

"Then what were those things?"

She looked sorry for me for a second, but apparently not sorry enough to answer my question. "Megan, could you tell me one more thing?" she asked, suddenly very interested in typing something into her BlackBerry. "Where were you between four o'clock and five o'clock this afternoon?"

"I was—"

"She was right here. Eating lasagna with her family, " Mom interrupted in a supremely pissed voice. She's a vegetarian and normally way more hippy than militant, but once you make her angry she can be pretty scary. "And this interview is over."

CHAPTER 5

"Jennifer, please," Kitty said. "I'm not trying to—"

"Oh, I know exactly what you're trying to do. You're trying to trick an innocent sixteen-year-old with a head injury into being interrogated without the benefit of representation." Mom grabbed the chips from the table and set them down on the island behind her with loud thunk. Clearly, hospitality time was over. "If Megan is a suspect, you'll need the proper paperwork, and we're going to need a mediator."

Settlers don't have lawyers, but mediators are basically the same thing. They step in and made sure people suspected of wrongdoing are treated fairly until their guilt or innocence is determined. After SA had decided to try Beth and Jess in Settler court, a mediator had been responsible for getting Beth's sentence transmitted to a stay in a mental facility instead of Settler Affairs prison. Tests had shown she was dealing with a bunch of different disorders and was a good candidate for rehabilitation once her memory had been wiped by Enforcement.

If Mom thought *we* needed a mediator . . .

"Okay, let's just calm down," I said, certain the maternal unit was overreacting. Kitty was my friend. She'd never think *I* had anything to do with those weird zombies. "I didn't do anything wrong and I'm sure Kitty and—"

"Don't say another word," Mom said, pointing a firm finger at me before turning back to Kitty. "I'd like you and your team out of my house."

"Mom! Please, stop it."

"Be quiet, Megan, and . . . and go to your room!"

"My room is full of Enforcers!" I jumped to my feet so fast my chair clattered to the ground behind me. "And this is crazy! I didn't make those zombies, if that's what everyone's thinking. Use a lie-detector charm on me, I swear it will—"

"I doubt the charm would work, Megan. You're too powerful." The way Kitty said the words made it clear she didn't think my power was all it was cracked up to be. Great. Neither did I.

"Then find some other way to test me. I'm telling the truth."

"Megan, listen to me," Mom begged. "You need to be very careful what you say."

"But I—"

"Your mom's right. You shouldn't say anything else." Kitty flipped off her recorder with a soft sigh and pushed back her chair. "I'll have the paperwork filed by tomorrow morning. You'll get your copy by early Thursday at the latest. After that, it will be your responsibility to file a petition for representation. In the meantime, it would probably be best if Megan didn't discuss this with anyone other than family members who, as you know, can't be called upon to testify against her in a felony case."

"Felony?" It felt like all the air had been sucked from my lungs.

I'd bent the rules a few times, sure, but what made Kitty and her team think *I'd* committed a felony? A felony was like . . . using black magic to *murder* someone or something horrible! Even the time SA thought I'd accidentally summoned a bunch of RC clones, no one had said anything about mediators or felonies.

An accident! Maybe this was something I'd done by accident. I still didn't have total control over my power, so it was possible.

"What if I did something without knowing I did it?" I asked, hurrying on before Mom could tell me to shut up again. "Like the time they thought I made those clones?"

"Not this time." Kitty's tone allowed no room for argument.

"We're finished in her room." Barker, another of my Enforcer trainers, appeared in the entrance to the kitchen.

He was so tall his head nearly hit the top of the doorframe and so wide he had to stand at an angle to keep his shoulders from hitting the sides. The dude was big enough to be flat-out scary and usually had a scowl on his face that completed the "fear me" look, but now he just looked sad. And disappointed.

My Sprite gurgled sickly in my stomach as I realized I was the one who had put that look on his face. Or whatever he thought I'd done. The man could barely look at me, which made *me* sad. And angry.

What had I ever done to make him and Kitty so ready to believe I'd raised those weird zombies? There had never been a Settler convicted of using black magic, so why were they assuming I was going to be the first? I might not have been the most eager little pupil, but I'd done my best to make them proud. I'd trained my ass off and studied until my brain felt like it was going to leak out of my ears, yet still, here we were.

It had to be my stupid super-Settler power getting me in trouble again. That was the only explanation that made sense. I was a suspect because I was *capable* of doing things the average Settler couldn't, not because I'd actually *done* anything.

"Did you find anything?" Kitty asked.

"No. It was clean." Barker didn't sound as happy about that as he should have. He probably thought I had stashed the evidence of my evil somewhere else. The jerk.

"Thanks." Kitty stood up and turned to face my mom and Elder Thomas, who had come to stand beside her sometime during the interrogation. "Please understand that we all care very much about Megan and your family. But as it stands—"

"As it stands, Megan is innocent. She didn't raise those zombies."

"Maybe not. We'll have to wait for all the lab work to come back to be sure," Elder Thomas said. "But we both know she *could* have. Don't we, Jennifer?"

It was exactly the thought I'd had a second ago, but for some reason it made my mom suck in a shocked breath, then dart a quick look in my direction before turning back to Elder Thomas. Like it was news I was weird? We'd known this for a while now. "That's . . . I thought we . . . This is crazy, Megan is innocent."

"Megan may be innocent, but mistakes have been made—"

"Are you suggesting . . . I can't . . ." Mom turned her back on me and dropped her voice to a whisper. "You know what? I'm not having this conversation. No one in this house did anything wrong, and I refuse to call that decision a mistake."

"I think we both know that—"

"Get out." Mom pointed a trembling finger at the door. The

words were soft but infused with more rage than I'd ever heard in my mother's voice.

"We'll be in touch." Elder Thomas headed toward the door, followed by a rather embarrassed-looking Kitty and a still sad-clown-faced Barker. The front door slammed seconds later and our house was suddenly disturbingly quiet.

But for some reason, I was afraid to break that silence. Maybe it was the fact that my mom was starting to cry, silent tears that leaked down her worried face. Or maybe it was the fact that, during her and Elder Thomas's decidedly odd conversation, I'd seen the look in Mom's eyes. It hadn't been anger or confusion I'd read there—it had been fear.

She was afraid of something. Afraid that Elder Thomas was right about me going over to the dark side? Afraid of whatever this "mistake" was? Afraid that the Enforcers would nail me to the wall whether I was innocent or not? I couldn't guess, and she didn't stick around to explain herself.

"Go to bed, Megan. We'll talk about this in the morning."

"But Mom—"

"Just go to bed. Please." She fled into her and Dad's room and slammed the door, but I could hear it when she started to cry even harder. Then Dad mumbled something in his deep voice and the sobs were muffled. Probably by his chest. He was probably giving Mom a hug, and telling her everything was going to be okay.

Meanwhile, I was out in the kitchen with no one, feet tangled in my overturned chair. Alone, the villain in this night's drama even though I'd done absolutely nothing wrong. For a second, I thought about calling Ethan and begging him to come over and let me sob on *his* chest, but realized it would be useless. No doubt he was still busy with Protocol duty and would be for the rest of the night. And even when he was finally dismissed, he might have been given orders not to see me. Girlfriend or not, I was apparently now a suspect in a felony, and surely SA wouldn't want one of their cops fraternizing with the enemy.

In fact, I wouldn't be surprised if I learned we were on a relationship time-out until this mess was sorted out. There would be no Ethan hugs, no Ethan kisses, no Ethan common-sense talks that always made me feel so much better—not even a big, warm Ethan hand to hold.

The thought broke down the last of my upper-lip stiffness. By the time I got to my bathroom and turned the shower on, I was crying like someone had died.

How could I have gotten in so much trouble for something I hadn't done? Why was I the only suspect when I *knew* they had no evidence to prove I'd raised those RCs? Sure I was the only super-powered Settler in our part of the country, but there had to be someone else who could have done this, because someone else *did* do it. I couldn't believe Kitty, at least, hadn't started to consider other suspects.

And what the heck was up with Mom and her "mistake" and this felony I'd supposedly committed? Trying to kill someone with zombies was a felony charge, but I was the one they'd been trying to bite! But then, the zombies *would* have tried to bite me if I was the one who raised them and a Settler had worked a *reverto* spell on them—a *reverto* spell sends them back to their maker for a bite of the blood that summoned them from their grave. So maybe that was why Kitty thought I was guilty.

Still, there had to be something more or everyone wouldn't be so sure I was the only one who could have done it.

There were obviously things going on I didn't understand. And whatever those things were, I was going to have to figure them out— fast. Sure, Mom seemed determined to stick up for me, but then, she was also withholding some kind of info and in her own room crying instead of in here rubbing my back. That just wasn't normal Mom behavior. And if I couldn't count on her for something as small as a back rub, how could I trust that she was going to keep me from going to SA prison for a crime I didn't commit?

The answer was, I couldn't, which made me cry even harder.

•   •   •

Wednesday morning dawned bright and horrible. My head felt like it was going to explode and my parents were still acting totally weird. I did my best to make a bunch of noise in the kitchen making breakfast, but even the smell of coffee percolating didn't summon the beasts from their lair. Mom was usually a freak about me drinking coffee, insisting it would decrease my bone density and infuse my cells with toxins and blah blah blah, but apparently she was too exhausted to worry about my vulnerable adolescent skeleton.

I had a huge to-go cup of French roast in my hand when I opened her door and said goodbye. All she did was mumble, "Be careful" and something about seeing me later, and then roll over to hug Dad— who was also still abed even though he should have left for work at the airport a good thirty minutes ago. He was never late and Mom never slept in. It was strange. And scary.

My mood was foul before I even arrived at school and only grew fouler as the day wore on. I was so *not* in the mood for acting normal.

English and world history seemed utterly pointless. Why did I need to learn about popular trends in twentieth-century literature or the evolution of Islamic culture when I could end up in jail for the rest of my life?

And who cared about the brilliant fund-raising event Monica and London had organized for Friday night? Sweetheart ice skating was not a giddy-making idea when you might have lost your sweetheart. Ethan hadn't called or sent a text all morning, and he had to know what went down. If he was allowed to contact me, he would have done it by now.

By lunchtime I hated my life and all the people happily chattering in the cafeteria. I hated raindrops on roses and whiskers on kittens and all that crap. I also hated ravioli and green beans from a can and brownies that weren't heavy enough. A brownie should be thick and weighty, not light and fluffy like some sort of cake. Brownies are NOT cake!

"Put the brownie down and step away from your lunch tray." He was whispering, but I would have known that voice anywhere.

"You're here!" I jumped off the chair I'd claimed in an abandoned corner of the lunchroom and flung myself into Ethan's arms, squeezing until he groaned in pain. God, he smelled so good, like that spicy soap he used and shaving cream and boy. *My* boy, my boyfriend who hadn't been told not to see me after all!

"I'm here, but I'm not supposed to be, so let's sneak while the sneaking is good," he said, leaning down to grab my backpack when I finally released my death hold.

"You're not supposed to be?"

"Nope. Good thing I'm not a compulsive rule follower anymore." He smiled and grabbed my hand, but I could tell he wasn't feeling any more lighthearted than I was. "Come on, I'm parked at the bottom of the hill. If we hustle, we'll blend in with the rest of the people headed out to lunch."

Only seniors were supposed to go off campus for lunch, but I didn't hesitate when Ethan pulled me out into the bright January day. My coat was still in my locker, but I didn't care about freezing my butt off either. All I cared about was being with Ethan and *away* from school.

"You know what? I don't want to come back," I said, a spring coming into my step as we made it past the teacher on duty without attracting attention. "I'm going to skip the rest of my classes."

"Sounds good," he said, though usually Ethan would be the last one to encourage ditching school. It was just another reminder that I was in a heck of a lot of trouble. "That will give us more time."

"More time for what?"

"I figured we should do some investigating of our—hey, are you okay?" Ethan asked as he opened the passenger's door of his car.

"Not really. But I'm better now that you're here. I assume you heard the news."

"I did, and it's ridiculous. I can't believe they think you had any part in raising whatever those things were."

"Thanks. It's nice that someone still believes in me." There were tears stinging the corners of my eyes, but I sucked them back into wherever tears come from. Tear ducts, I guess? "Kitty and Barker and Elder Thomas think I did it."

"They're insane. Of course you didn't," he said, leaning down to give me the softest little kiss. He closed the door and ran around to the driver's side, while I smiled and tried even harder not to cry. I really did have the *best* boyfriend in the world. "But like I said." He slid into the driver's seat and started the car. "I figured we should do some investigating of our own to help prove what we already know."

"Won't that get you in trouble at work?" I asked, as Ethan pulled into the line of cars heading out of the parking lot.

"Protocol got kicked off the case last night around midnight by the Enforcement team. Apparently they don't want a bunch of small-town losers screwing up their investigation. So it's not a direct conflict of interest."

"But I thought you said you weren't supposed to—"

"The Elders haven't said anything outright, but Kitty called and strongly advised me to stay away from you until you're cleared of suspicion." He pulled forward, taking a left out of the parking lot. "She made it sound like a request, but I got the order vibe loud and clear. I have a feeling I won't be invited back to training if I get caught helping you."

"Then take me back to school." I grabbed my backpack and pointed to a good place to turn around. "I don't want you to ruin your chances to do something you love."

"I love *you*, Schmeg," he said, using the old nickname that used to drive me absolutely insane. Now it seemed kind of sweet and made me want to cry again. But then, what didn't? "It's just work. You're my girlfriend."

I finally lost the tear battle and started sobbing. Ethan loved me, he *really* loved me. It was wonderful. I was so lucky! So why was it making me have a major, snotty come-apart?

"Meg, you okay?" Ethan asked, looking a little green to be trapped in a car with a sobbing girl, even one he loved. I nodded, but the tears didn't seem to want to stop. "I think there are some napkins left over from Sonic in the glove compartment."

Sonic! The site of our first pretend date months ago! Remembering how I'd been crushing on Ethan that night, and how I'd been certain he'd never think of me as anything but an annoying little-sister type, helped me pull myself together.

The impossible had happened. The proof was sitting in the driver's seat, telling me he loved me. And proving my innocence wasn't impossible either—it just felt like it because I didn't know what was going on. Hopefully, by the time Ethan and I were done today, that would no longer be the case.

"I'm better." I dabbed at my nose and eyes and took a deep breath. "Where are we starting this investigating?"

"I drove by Kroger on my way. Looks like the Enforcement team finally pulled out of the woods behind the parking lot. I figure it's as good a place to start as any."

"Right, sounds good," I said, but it didn't, not really. I didn't want to go back into those woods. Still, what choice did I have? Leads were few, and Ethan was right, the best place to start was at the scene of the crime . . . whatever that crime was. "Did Protocol get any information on why these zombies were so different? I mean, I know using black magic is a felony charge, but there's got to be some reason the Enforcers think I'm the *only* one who could have done this. I'm guessing it has something to do with having more power than the average Settler, but that's about as far as I've gotten."

"That's what I figured too. It's the only thing that makes sense."

"Right. But maybe if we can find out what's so special about the RCs—"

"They could be Settler-Resistant Undead," Ethan said, his tone making it clear he'd rather not share this information with me if he could have helped it. "Our Protocol task force leader said he'd heard about SRU attacks in Europe in the fourteenth century that wiped out entire towns. Back then the Settlers' Affairs people blamed the deaths on the plague to keep humans from freaking out about zombies."

"Geez. That's . . . very bad." And Megan wins the Understatement of the Year award. "But why—"

"And no one ever found out where they came from, who had raised them, or why Settlers couldn't control them. They just kind of disappeared in modern times. Until now, maybe?"

"Which would explain why the Enforcers are freaking out, but wouldn't explain why they think I did this." Must keep thinking logically, must not start imagining zombies swarming over the entire town of Carol.

"So we need to find out more about these SRUs, something that will help us start a list of real suspects."

"I don't know much, but I did hear Smythe and Barker saying something about checking the hospitals in Little Rock. They shut up pretty fast when they realized I was standing close enough to hear, but still, it's something." He turned into Kroger and pulled around to the back of the store. "If we don't find anything in the woods, we can start snooping around hospitals and see if we spot anything unusual," he said, parking beside a Dumpster.

I couldn't think of any connection between the Undead and a hospital, but I hadn't slept very well last night. Still, the whole situation seemed so overwhelming.

As if sensing my angst, Ethan turned and grabbed my hand before

I could open my door. "We're going to figure this out, Megan. I promise. Everything is going to be fine."

After that I just had to kiss him for a minute or two. Even if he was just saying it to make me feel better, it was wonderful having a boyfriend who knew exactly what to say.

CHAPTER 6

*T*hree hours and a fruitless search through the woods for clues later, Ethan and I were sneaking down the stairs at the University Medical Center, bound for the morgue. That's right, the *morgue*, where they cut dead people open and poke at their insides and then stick them in cold storage.

It was freaking creepy, even for a zombie Settler who regularly kicked it with dead people. I swore I could smell the horrible mix of cold flesh and antiseptic and industrial cleaner wafting through the air, and we still had three more flights to go.

"You're sure this is a good idea?" I shivered even as I wiped my sweaty palms on my jeans. How was it possible to be both sweaty and freezing at the same time? "Don't you think they'll have security?"

"Security for what? The people down here aren't going anywhere."

"I don't know, security to, like, protect the bodies," I said, trying to discreetly breathe through my mouth. "To make sure murderers don't come down here and destroy evidence or something."

"You've been watching too much *Law & Order*."

"I never watch *Law & Order*. I don't have time for TV." Which wasn't entirely true, but when I did have time, I didn't watch crime shows.

I'm more of a really heinous reality-TV kind of person, though I would never admit that to Ethan. He likes to watch films. Not just movies, but *films*, and I knew he wouldn't be impressed with my addiction to *Engaged & Underage* and *Wife Swap*.

"And what about security cameras? Don't you think—"

"Megan, if you don't want to go, you don't have to, but we both agree that the morgue is the most logical place in the hospital to look for clues about weird zombies. It's the only place we're likely to find a concentration of corpses. Right?"

"Right. You're right." I sighed and gave up trying to dry my hands as we descended the final flight of stairs. Obviously my sweat glands were as super-powered as the rest of me. "I don't know why I'm being such a chicken."

"Because morgues are creepy and the smell is seriously disturbing?"

I managed a tiny laugh. "I thought I was imagining how bad the smell was."

"No way, it's awful." He smiled before turning to peek through the door in front of us.

I saw bright fluorescent lights and clean white walls and caught a whiff of coffee mixed with the dead chemical smell. I couldn't decide if that made it better or worse, but at least it reminded me that there were living people down here. People who would have to be dealt with if we wanted to get our information.

"Okay, what's our story again? We're college kids doing a report for our cultural anthropology class?"

"Yeah, let me grab a notebook and pen from your backpack so we'll look official." He closed the door and turned me around so he could get to the zipper of my bag.

"Get me one too," I said, though I wondered if I'd even be able to hold a pen with the amount of palm sweat I was presently producing. "And shouldn't we have a thesis or something in case they ask?"

"Like what?"

"I don't know, like, Investigating Rituals of Death in the Twenty-first Century?"

"Did I ever tell you how totally hot it is when you get all smarty-pants?" Ethan finished digging around in my backpack and handed me a notebook and pen.

I smiled. "Not as many times as you told me you love that stupid hat."

"That hat is not stupid. It's sexy." He leaned down to kiss me, which was great for a second. But then I started to get this weird feeling . . . like someone was watching. Everything was quiet and I hadn't heard a door open or close, but the certainty that we weren't alone quickly grew so strong I thought I'd go crazy if I didn't check for peeping creeps.

"Sorry." I pulled away and glanced up. Nothing. There was no one there. But still, the feeling we weren't alone didn't go away. Maybe I was suffering from paranoid delusions as well as profuse palm sweat.

"Is something wrong?"

"No . . . my lips were just cold," I said, not wanting him to think I was chickening out again.

"Oh, okay." Ethan looked a little hurt, but shrugged like it was no big deal. "I'm sorry. I should have made you take my coat. Here, take it now."

"No, it's fine. It's just my lips."

"Megan, take my coat."

"No, really, it's—"

"Take the stupid coat," he said, loud enough I was afraid someone would hear. Great, now he was mad at me. Geez. Sometimes it seemed like things between us were easier *before* we threw all the kissy stuff into the mix.

"Fine." I ditched my backpack, put on his brown corduroy jacket—which did feel good and smelled yummily of Ethan—and then grabbed the pack off the ground. "Ready?"

"Let's go." Ethan opened the door for me, but he still didn't look happy. I was going to have to make it up to him by proving how addictive I found his kisses . . . later, in all my spare time, when I wasn't trying to avoid going to jail.

We found the front-desk guy within a few minutes of easing into the blindingly white hall. The morgue was a lot smaller than I'd thought it would be, even though I knew Little Rock had a lot of hospitals and they each had their own cold storage. It wasn't like the university morgue had to be big enough to handle all the stiffs in town.

Though that sure would have made it easier. If there were one central holding area, we wouldn't have had to worry about investigating five or six different hospitals trying to figure out where the weird zombies had come from. That is, *if* they had even come from a hospital and we weren't on some kind of wild goose chase.

"Hey, we're students from Williams and were hoping we could ask a few questions." Ethan quickly filled the skinny guy at the desk in on our cover story and asked if there was someone around who might be willing to talk to us.

"Someone like who?" he asked, picking at a dry piece of skin on the side of his nose. The guy looked bored out of his mind, not a condition I would have thought applied in his kind of work. But then again, I got tired of my job sometimes, and I work with the dead. And my dead people walk and talk and are generally far more interesting than your average corpse.

"Like, maybe a morgue supervisor," I said. "Someone who knows everything that goes down around here."

"That would be Dr. Blackmon, but he's not here today."

"Oh . . . well is there anyone else who could help us? We only need a few minutes," Ethan said with his most charming grin. Too bad bored skinny guy—Caleb, according to his name tag—didn't seem to respond to charm.

But maybe he'd respond to a little excitement injected into his humdrum life.

"Anyone who's been here in the past few days would work. We just need someone who might be able to explain all the weird stuff that's been happening." I did my best to ignore the scowl on Ethan's face. Sure, this wasn't the plan, but sometimes a girl had to improvise.

"Weird stuff?" Caleb perked up. Not much, but at least he stopped harvesting dead skin from his nose. Ew much? Someone should have taught him peeling dead skin was an activity best done in private *before* he reached his twenties.

"Yeah, we heard there's been some issues with the bodies," I said vaguely.

I couldn't get too specific since I had no idea if the zombies I'd worked the spell on last night returned to this morgue or not—if they had come from a morgue at all. The *reverto* spell was intended to send a corpse back to the person who had raised it for a quick bite and from there back to its grave. So I wasn't sure where the RCs would go if they had been morgue residents and not in possession of graves just yet. If they hadn't headed back to their lockers here at UMC, missing bodies would certainly be weird.

But even if they had, surely someone would have noticed that one of them had singed pajamas and that all of their feet were filthy from tromping about in the forest and—

No shoes! The zombies last night hadn't been wearing shoes. Duh, I should have thought about that before, but I'd been so focused on the pajamas that their feet hadn't crossed my mind. I'd seen a couple Unsettled who were buried in their PJs in my time, but every Out-of-Grave Phenomenon I'd gotten a close look at had sported some kind of footwear. People didn't like to bury their loved ones without shoes, even if it's just a pair of bunny slippers.

I was going to have to share this new clue with Ethan ASAP.

"I haven't heard about anything out of the ordinary around here, but . . ." Caleb narrowed his eyes and leaned a bit closer. "But there's definitely something going on upstairs. There were policemen all over the hospital today."

"Really?" Ethan asked. I could tell he was excited, but trying not to show it.

"Yeah, there wasn't a pastry left in the cafeteria by lunch. Not even a stale bear claw. I thought that stuff about cops and donuts was just some stupid stereotype, but it's totally true. I had to have a nonfat yogurt for dessert. It was disgusting." He sniffed, and his eyes became distant and unfocused as he slipped into deep thought mode. "I think it might have been expired, but the date was rubbed off the label so I couldn't be sure."

God, this guy was fascinating. Snore. Time to get him back on track. "So what were they doing here, besides scarfing down sugar-coated carbs?" I asked. "Did you talk to any of them? Did they ask you any questions?"

"No, they weren't interested in talking to the basement dwellers." Caleb sighed and returned to his skin picking. "And no one at my table knew what they were up to. It's being kept very hush-hush, though, so it must be something big. The suits were in an uproar, scenting lawsuit in the wind."

"Wow, sounds serious." Ethan scribbled something on his notepad and then tore off the piece of paper. "Would you be willing to call us if you hear anything more?"

"Sure, but weren't you here to learn about the morgue?" Caleb looked suspiciously from me to Ethan.

"My mom is a reporter for the *Arkansas Sentinel Gazette*," Ethan said, the lie falling from his lips without a moment's hesitation. "I try to keep an ear out for stories I think she might be interested in, and this sounds like it has scandal potential. She'd want to interview you if she gets the scoop. As a secret informant, of course."

Caleb nodded and glanced down at the number, clearly intrigued by the idea of being a secret informant. "Cool. I'll give you a call if I hear anything else. And I'll ask Dr. Blackmon if he has time to answer a few questions. Maybe you could even interview him on the phone, save you a trip down to the crypt."

Well now, wasn't he helpful? We should have told him we were reporters from the beginning. "That would be great. Thanks so much—we really appreciate it," I said, beaming down at him.

Caleb returned my smile, his grin transforming his pale, scrawny face into something a lot more approachable—if he'd quit the skin-picking thing, of course.

Ethan and I thanked him and headed back upstairs. This time, however, we went ahead and used the elevator. No need to skulk. It didn't seem like anyone cared that we were here. Ethan had been right—I'd obviously been smelling danger where there was none. Speaking of danger . . .

"Hey, I have to get back to school. My parents didn't go to work this morning, so I'm not sure whether they'll be in the parking lot after pom practice or not. Sometimes Mom shows up unexpectedly."

"Yeah, about your mom . . ."

"Yeah?" I asked, a funny feeling in my stomach. "What about her?"

"Elder Thomas gave Kitty a file last night and it had your mom's name on it," he said. "You have any idea what that's about? Why she would be digging up stuff on your mom when you're the one they suspect of raising these zombies?"

"I don't know. Elder Thomas said something about a 'mistake' Mom made last night, but I haven't been able to get the four-one-one," I said, unable to believe I'd forgotten to share that with Ethan. Some investigator I was. "Do you think it might have something to do with when Mom and Dad got relocated to Arkansas?"

"Could be." He nodded, but I could tell he wasn't totally convinced. "I'll see what I can dig up over at SA headquarters."

"I could go with you." I suddenly didn't want to be separated from Ethan, and the suspicion that my mom was hiding something made me a lot less worried about not being there for her to pick me up.

"No, you're right, you should get back to class. I'll drop you behind the gym just in case your parents are parked out front," he said as we exited the elevator and headed toward the parking garage. "Then I'll probably come back here and do a little more poking around before heading to headquarters. Definitely sounds like something big went down."

"True, but we can't be sure it was Undead-related." I hated to be the voice of doom, but I was doing my best not to get too excited. This could still be nothing and we could be back where we started—square one and clueless.

"My gut is telling me to check it out."

"Oh, my gut also told me something," I said, excited to share my clue. "While we were talking to Caleb, I remembered something about the zombies last night. They weren't wearing shoes!"

"Really? Monica didn't mention that in her report."

"Yep, no shoes. And they were also all in their pajamas. I mean, I think the big guy Monica fought might have been wearing sweatpants and a sweatshirt, but the others were all wearing PJs."

Ethan froze just inside the door to the hospital and turned to face me. "Dudes? They were all men?"

"Yeah, all four of them."

"What about the others? You said you saw a few more coming through the woods before you and Monica linked up."

"I'm not one hundred percent sure, but I think they were guys. Why?"

"Check the left pocket of my coat," Ethan said. I reached in and pulled out a hair ribbon, white with hints of gold streaked through the fibers. "I found that in the woods today. I didn't figure it was any big clue, since things fall off corpses all the time, but if it belongs to someone living we might be able to—"

"These are CHS colors," I said, my anxiety building as I stared at the seemingly innocent ribbon.

"True, but it's also the kind of thing any chick could wear in her hair, right?"

I shook my head. Ethan was incredibly cute and fairly fashion forward, but he was still such a *guy* sometimes. "No, no 'chick' over the age of eight or nine would wear a ribbon like this, and I doubt someone that young would be hanging out in the woods behind the grocery store. Besides, I've seen this exact same ribbon every other game night for the past four months."

"No way." He shook his head. "Someone from your pom squad?"

"Not this time." My fist tightened around the ribbon. "It's a cheerleader ribbon."

"Cheerleaders have been raising weird zombies?" He sounded dubious, and for once I was with him. Usually Ethan was the skeptic and I the voice of creative thinking, but he was right. There was no way I could believe that the cheerleaders were raising the dead.

"Of course not, but this ribbon means one of them was in the woods last night. Probably spying on our car wash to see how much money we were raising for the booster club."

Ethan sighed. "They might have seen the RCs."

"Or even worse, they might have seen Monica and me fighting the RCs." I shoved the ribbon back in Ethan's pocket. I didn't want to look at it anymore, or think about how much more trouble I could be in. Even if I managed to prove my innocence, my family could still be relocated if a nosy cheerleader had seen something she shouldn't have. "I'll try to figure out who was in the woods and just how much she saw tomorrow at school."

"Get Monica to help you." Ethan took my hand as we headed out to the parking lot.

"Monica? Help *me*? What kind of crack have you been smoking?"

"It's her butt on the line as much as yours," he said. "If you were spotted, she was too. Besides, she seemed upset last night when the Enforcers headed off to search your house."

"Why, because she couldn't come along and personally watch me being taken into custody for a crime I didn't commit?" I said, opening the passenger's side door.

Ethan stopped me from getting inside with strong hands on my shoulders. "Listen, Monica isn't the same person she was a few months ago. She doesn't have it out for you. Honestly, I think you two would get along really well if you'd give her a chance."

"I've given her tons of chances. She's a total witch, Ethan."

"She's not a witch, she's just . . . difficult. I'll admit that, but she can also be a valuable person to have on your side. You two have let this jealousy and competition thing go too far."

"Jealousy and competition?" I asked, inwardly seething though doing my best to keep my voice soft. What the heck was he talking about? "You think I'm jealous of Monica?"

"I don't know, maybe? A little bit? She's definitely jealous of you," he said, trying to backtrack. But it was too late—the damage was already done.

I didn't say a word, just frowned up at his face, hurt that he felt so compelled to defend the Monicster. *I* was the one who was in deep trouble, while *she* got away without anything more stressful than a few questions. She spent most of the day today planning an ice skating fund-raiser, not worried that she might be thrown in prison.

Besides, even if Ethan was right, was now the right time to be lecturing me about bonding with my Settler bitches and hos? The answer was no, it definitely was not.

"Let's go. I need to get back to school."

"Listen, Meg, I'm sorry." He ran a hand through his hair and I could tell he was feeling almost as mixed-up as I was. "I shouldn't have said anything—I just thought you could use some more help, that's all. I don't want to fight," Ethan said, fingers moving to my cheek. "Especially about Monica."

I sighed and bit my lip.

"Forgive me?" he asked, green eyes so magnetic in their repentance there was no chance of resisting.

"Forgiven." I looked up at him and smiled. "And thanks, by the way."

"For what?"

I shrugged. "For picking me up today, for helping me, for just being there."

"You don't have to thank me. This is what boyfriends do," he said, before he closed the distance between us.

His lips were surprisingly warm despite how cold it was outside, and they heated up mine in no time. I wrapped my arms around his neck and he moved even closer, squishing me against the side of the car as our lip-lock quickly went from sweet to something more serious.

There was an urgency in the way his mouth met mine that had never been there before, an intensity that made my heart race and my head spin. It was easily both the best and the scariest kiss I'd ever had. Even as every cell in my body lit up with a hard-core case of the tingles, my mind couldn't stop thinking there was something horribly final about the whole thing. It felt like we were characters in a movie, shooting that scene just before the hero runs off to battle and gets killed or the heroine dies of some tragic disease.

Gah! I didn't want to die of some tragic disease! I didn't want all this drama, even if it inspired kisses like this.

I sucked in a breath and ripped my mouth away. We were both breathing hard, very hard, like we'd been at this a lot longer than a minute and a half. I was surprised to find my hands were shaking as I detangled them from where they'd been buried in Ethan's hair.

"Wow." His breath puffed against my lips, hot and smelling of mints and Ethan.

"Too wow." I tried to laugh, but it came out sounding more like a grunt. Way to go, Megan, very alluring.

"Is there such a thing as too wow?"

"I don't know. Maybe?" As smoothly as possible, I pulled away and slid into the passenger's seat.

Ethan sighed and tightened his grip on my door until his knuckles turned white. "What do you mean, maybe? Is there something I should know, Megan? Because it seems like . . . "

"Seems like what?" I asked, my voice small and nervous sounding.

He paused, then let out a deep breath. "Nothing." But I could tell it wasn't.

"I just don't want to be late getting back to school. That's all."

"Okay." He forced a smile I could tell he didn't feel. "Fine, let's hit it."

As he circled around to the driver's side, I tried to tell myself everything was fine, that Ethan and I were good and everything was going to work itself out. But for some reason, I was having a hard time buying my own pep talk, especially when that weird "watched" feeling returned with a vengeance.

I scanned the parking lot but saw nothing out of the ordinary. Still, I was glad when we pulled out onto the road and the creepy feeling vanished. Now if only I could banish the awkwardness between me and my boyfriend as easily.

CHAPTER 7

The world was coming to an end. There was no other explanation for why there was a bag of cheeseburgers—real cheeseburgers, not veggie burgers, and from *McDonald's* no less—on our kitchen table later that afternoon.

"I couldn't remember if you didn't like mustard or ketchup, so I ordered all of them without either," Mom said around a mouthful of burger. She always talks with her mouth full, and it drives me insane, but at the moment I found it oddly comforting. At least I knew she hadn't been body-snatched by an alien or something. "I figured you could add whatever you liked and leave the other off."

"Thanks." I eased into my chair while discreetly shooting Dad a "what the heck is going on?" look. I'd never seen Mom eat meat, not once in sixteen years of life. It would have been disturbing on a normal day, but after her crying fit last night and her staying in bed this morning, it made me . . . nervous. And suspicious. What the heck was going on with her that she felt compelled to throw away decades of meat-avoidance on a bag full of McDonald's hamburgers?

"There are french fries in the microwave," he said with a weary smile, not seeming to notice my pointed stare. "We were trying to keep them warm until you got home from school."

"We skipped lunch, so we were starving by four o'clock."

Dad reached out and tucked a strand of hair behind her ear with this goofy grin on his face. "I can't remember the last time we stayed in bed all day."

I finally overcame my cheeseburger shock enough to notice they were both still in their pajamas. What the heck was up with everyone? First the zombies and now my parents. Didn't anyone actually get up and get dressed anymore?

Mom had always said staying in her pajamas all day depresses her, but she didn't look depressed. She didn't look upset at all, which for some reason made me even more certain she was hiding something.

"Too long." Mom leaned over to give Dad a quick kiss, then moaned her appreciation as she shoved the last bite of burger in her mouth. "God, these are so good."

Okay. That was it. "Mom, you do know those are meat, right? Like, real meat, not something made from a soybean?"

"I know, I'm probably going to be sick as a dog later." She and Dad laughed together, like they were sharing some private joke that involved retching hamburger meat.

Charming. And completely annoying! I was in deep trouble and they'd spent the day chilling out in bed, rekindling their marriage or whatever, and pigging out on cheeseburgers. And now they were acting like everything was okay and this was just any old afternoon, not the first afternoon since I'd been accused of a *felony*! My parents were huge jerks, and that was not okay!

"You guys suck," I said, throwing the burger I'd just snagged back into the bag. "You do realize I'm in huge trouble right? That I could go to jail? Like, for forever? I mean, I hate to interrupt your grown-up bonding time or whatever the heck this is but—"

"Honey, calm down," Mom said in her reasonable tone of voice. "Everything is going to be fine."

"No, it's not going to be fine." I stood to pace around the kitchen. "People who *know* me think I raised those zombies even though no Settler has *ever* been convicted of using black magic. And no one will tell me why. There's got to be more to it than black magic, otherwise—"

"As soon as we get the official paperwork, we'll know exactly what you've been charged with, and we can go from there," Dad said. "Until then, we would only be guessing at—"

"Mom is a Settler and she's smart—I'm sure she can make a pretty good guess. They're going to say I raised those zombies to do something horrible. Like kill someone or something, right?"

"I don't know, Megan. I can't know for sure until we get the paperwork."

Paperwork. Right, like Mom had ever been one to wait for the paperwork. Why was she acting like this? "Well can you at least tell me what was up with Elder Thomas last night? What's the big 'mistake,' Mom?" I pinned her with an accusing look but was surprised when she stared guiltily at her hands.

"That has nothing to do with you. I promise," she said.

"It sure sounded like it did."

She answered me with a long, sad sigh. My real mom would have sassed me right back and told me not to be ridiculous, that of course she didn't know anything she wasn't telling me. But this mom just sat there, fidgeting and letting Dad do the talking.

Maybe she had been body-snatched after all.

"Believe me, Megan, Mom and I are on your side." Dad came around the table to pull me in for a hug. Even though I was still mad, I couldn't resist leaning into him and wrapping my arms around his waist. He just felt so solid and dadlike and safe. "As soon as the written charges arrive we're going to be completely focused on clearing your name."

"Okay." I sniffed and hugged Dad tighter while Mom started gathering up the empty paper wrappers littering the table.

"Mom and I just needed a little time for ourselves today," he said, patting me on the back like I'd wanted Mom to do last night. "I know it's hard to believe, but parents can feel overwhelmed sometimes too."

"It's not hard to believe." I pulled away and took a deep breath. "I'm not a baby anymore, Dad. I know you and Mom have a life." Well, sort of, anyway. "And I know it can't be easy having a freak for a daughter."

"You're not a freak." Mom threw the wrappers in the trash with a lot more force than required, then pulled me in for a hug so tight I could barely breathe. "You're a beautiful, talented girl and a damn fine person." Tears were leaking from her eyes again when she pulled back to cup my face in her hands. "From the time you were a little girl, I've always been so proud of you. Do you know that? You have such a good heart. I couldn't have wished for a sweeter, more loving daughter."

Geez, now I was getting all weepy. "Thanks, Mom."

"You're not one of the bad guys, Meg, and we're going to make sure everyone at SA and the Enforcers and anyone else who thinks they know you better than we do understands that."

"Okay." I nodded and pulled away to fetch the both of us a Kleenex. I knew I should feel better after the pep talk, but I couldn't shake the feeling that something was wrong. It was sort of like that line from *Hamlet* we studied during our Shakespeare unit last fall, "The lady doth protest too much."

Mom did protest too much. But why? Was she just scared, or did my parents know more than they were letting on? I was trying to think of a way to get Mom to spill whatever it was she thought I didn't need to know when the doorbell rang. "I'll get it," I said, and hustled toward the front door.

"Cliff?" I asked, shocked to see the Unsettled I'd put to rest three days ago standing on my front porch. Unsettled didn't come back for seconds! Crawling out of your grave was a one-time deal. I'd never had a repeat customer, never even heard of such a thing. That must mean Cliff had never gone back to his eternal rest—despite the fact that I'd sealed his grave—which meant he'd been Unsettled for *three days*, which meant I probably had a Rogue zombie on my hands.

I braced myself for a fight, but Cliff just smiled.

"Hey, what's up, Berry? Great to see you again." The friendliness of the grin made him look *almost* human. Heck, he *did* look human. If I hadn't met him before, I wouldn't know he was a zombie at all. He seemed . . . cleaner. His long dark brown hair was shining with health, his clothes were different—light-colored khaki jeans and a dark brown sweater—and obviously clean, the grave smell was gone and he—

"You're wearing glasses." My statement of the obvious was met with a laugh.

"Nothing's getting past you, B."

"But why?"

"I sort of need them to see," he said, winking at me in a way that was kind of flirty. Or maybe just a shade too friendly. Or maybe I was the one who was too friendly, since he obviously hadn't gotten the message that our business was finished. But at least his eyes weren't glowing red behind his glasses. He wasn't anywhere close to going Rogue, at least not yet.

"Megan, who is it?" Mom called from the other room.

"A friend from church," I yelled back, giving our code phrase for "an Unsettled at the door."

I gestured for Cliff to shush and grabbed my coat, hat, and scarf from the coat tree by the door. "Be back soon!"

"All right, but take your cell phone. And call us when you're done if you need a ride. I don't want you walking by yourself after dark."

"Okay." Grabbing Cliff by the arm, I urged him down the steps and across the snow-dusted lawn. It was still an hour or so before sunset. There was enough light that my parents would be able to see how oddly clean Cliff was if they thought to look out the window, and I really didn't want to deal with trying to explain Cliff to them or anyone else.

"So we're in a hurry?" Cliff asked.

"Yes, we are," I hissed, risking a look over my shoulder and breathing a sigh of relief as I realized we'd made it out of the line of sight without being observed. "What are you doing here?"

"Coming to see you." He grinned and tucked his hair behind his ears. "It was really nice talking to you the other night. Even before I was dead I didn't meet many girls who could carry on a conversation."

"Cliff, I—"

"I mean, about girl stuff, sure, but not about life stuff. But I did hang with a lot of potheads." He laughed as we continued down the sidewalk in the general direction of his cemetery. "Not to judge, but . . . yeah. I just really enjoyed hanging out with you."

"Well, thanks, but Cliff . . ." God, how was I supposed to tell him to get lost after that? "I don't know how to say this, um . . ."

"I wasn't supposed to come back, was I?"

I breathed a sigh of relief. The dude was weird, but at least he was perceptive. "Not really. Actually, not at all. I've never had someone come back."

He nodded. "You looked pretty surprised, and I haven't seen anyone else like me hanging around the cemetery. I couldn't go back to sleep, or death or whatever, so I thought I'd try to find some fellow dead to chill with, but . . . no luck. "

"I'm sorry," I said, patting him on the back. He sounded so sad. The poor guy must have been really lonely, not to mention scared. "So you've been at the cemetery all this time?"

"Mostly. I hit a homeless shelter for a shower and change of clothes and then sort of um . . . liberated some reading glasses from the drugstore." He grinned, and for the first time I noticed how warm his eyes were. They were this rich, greenish brown that seemed to glow when he smiled. "But it was theft for a good cause. I didn't want to go home and risk getting caught trying to sneak clothes or glasses out of my room. I figure my parents have been through enough."

Wow. He was really strong. I can't say I would have been able to keep from running home to Mom and Dad, no matter how upset it would make them to see me come back from the dead.

"That must be hard."

He shrugged. "It's what I've got to do. I can't go home, at least not until I see . . . until I know if . . ." His words trailed off as he came to stop in the middle of the sidewalk. I turned to see him wincing in pain.

"Are you okay?"

"Yeah . . . no . . . I mean, I always had these headaches, but they're worse now. And sometimes I can't remember . . ."

"Can't remember what?"

He groaned and squeezed his eyes shut even tighter. "I can't . . . I see them, I know they're coming," he said, his breath getting faster and his hands gripping his head. "You have to stop them . . . there are so many . . . red eyes, pieces of blue and gray . . ."

"Cliff!" I grabbed him as his legs collapsed, but I wasn't strong enough to hold him upright. He was fairly short for a guy—maybe only an inch or two taller than my five-four—but he was pure muscle. In fact, I was surprised at how solid he felt as I guided him to the ground. He was hiding a pretty decent body under those baggy jeans and sweater.

A pretty decent dead *body, Megan. Don't start setting this guy up with your friends. Figure out how to get him the rest he deserves.*

The inner voice was right. Cliff was nice and funny and a hidden hottie, but he was also dead. Besides, I didn't really *have* any friends.

"They won't listen . . . the heart . . . one heart . . ."

"What heart? What are you—"

"*Habeo are transit.*"

"What?" Was he speaking in tongues or was this the beginning of a seizure? Should I grab a stick and try to wedge it between his teeth?

"One heart, just one heart." He groaned and rolled onto his side, curling into a ball on the cold ground. "Crap, I lost it. It's gone."

"Just try to breathe." I smoothed his hair out of his face and tucked it back behind his ear, relieved he seemed to be recovering from his episode. "Take deep breaths in and deep breaths out."

"I don't think I breathe anymore. But thanks." He pulled off his glasses and rubbed his fingers above his eyes. "Dude, that was a bad one."

"It looked like it."

"And pointless." He shoved his glasses back on and slammed a fist down onto the concrete, making me jump. "It's so hard to tell what they mean anymore. It's making me nuts."

"What they mean?"

Cliff rolled onto his back. "The pictures. I get these pictures in my head when the headaches come. Most of the time they're things that are really going to happen."

"Like, future things?"

"I'm sort of psychic." He darted a nervous look up to where I sat beside him. "I know that sounds crazy, but—"

"Hey, I talk to dead people and fight zombies—who am I to judge?"

Cliff laughed. "You're also pretty cool."

"Thanks, that's what all the Undead say." I rolled my eyes, unable to keep from thinking about all the people who didn't think I was cool at all. I still couldn't believe the Enforcers thought I was a Very Bad Thing, let alone all the Elders over at SA. They'd known me since I was a baby and should realize what type of person I was.

"I sense all is not well in the world of Megan Berry. What's going

84

down with you?" he asked, putting on this new age guru accent.

For some reason I couldn't keep from answering him. "Some people think I did a really bad thing I didn't do."

"People who should know better?"

"Yeah. And there's no evidence that I did anything wrong, so . . . I can't understand it."

He stared at me for a few seconds, then reached out and took my hand. "It's not what you did or didn't do. It's who you are."

"Who I am?" I asked, startled by how nice it felt to hold Cliff's hand.

His skin was pretty cold, but his touch was as comforting as Dad's hand rubbing my back. He gave off good vibes, even as a dead person, so I could only imagine the kind of energy he must have had in life. Cliff had probably been one of those people who made everyone smile, just by being around. It was a shame the world had lost him.

"That's what I see," he said.

"I thought your visions didn't work any more?"

"I didn't say that. I said it was harder to see what they mean."

"And you see that I'm in trouble because of who I am?" I asked.

"Or maybe . . . *what* you are? There's something different about you, and it scares a lot of people. That's all I can tell for sure."

I sighed and tried to hide my disappointment. For a second there, I'd thought Cliff was going to tell me something I didn't know, but it was just the same old thing. "Yeah, I know. I'm like a supercharged Settler of the Dead. Rare and weird and scary."

He smiled and his thumb ran lightly over the top of my hand. "I don't think you're weird or scary. Maybe a little rare, but in a good way. I certainly feel better than I did half an hour ago. I was so drained, but talking to you . . . well, it's just good."

For a second energy jumped between us, an awareness that, had I not had a boyfriend and had Cliff not been dead, I would have called attraction. My entire body buzzed and my head spun dizzily. It was a cross between the low-blood-sugar feeling I get when I skip breakfast and the seconds right after I pull away from Ethan's kisses, which was more than disturbing enough to make me yank my hand away from Cliff's.

"Come on, we've got to get you back to your crypt," I said, jumping to my feet when the dizziness passed. "Maybe I didn't seal your grave right last time. I can't remember doing anything different, but it was late and—"

"No, it's cool. I'll show myself back," he said, standing beside me. "You did everything fine. I could feel your mojo big-time, but my body wouldn't do what you were telling it to do. I'm not ready to rest. I've got something I have to do."

"I'm supposed to help you with that, you know, help you complete your unfinished business. That's sort of my job."

"Not this time." He smiled. "I think this time it's my job to help you. I saw you in the woods the other day. The others almost killed you."

The brown eyes I'd thought I'd seen right after I'd hit my head. It had been Cliff. "You were spying on me?" I asked, backing away a few steps, thinking about the weird feeling I'd had at the hospital. "Have you been following me?"

"No. Well . . . maybe," he said. "But I'm not the only one. You've got a living tail too. Don't look now, but that beige car down the street isn't empty."

"Crap." I closed my eyes, not needing to look at the car to guess who was inside. Settlers' Affairs had someone watching me. Beige was, after all, their signature color. "Great, now we really have to go." I turned and headed down the sidewalk, knowing my SA watchers would start to get suspicious if it took much longer to put Cliff to rest.

"Fine. But please believe me," he said, hurrying after me. "I would never hurt you. I only want to help."

"Thanks, but really, I don't need help." Well, I did, but not from an Unsettled. "The best thing you could do for me is to go back to your grave and try to rest in peace. Believe me, I'm in enough trouble already, and if the Enforcers or anyone from Settlers' Affairs sees any more weird zombies hanging around—"

"Zombie. Wow, it's really weird hearing that word and knowing someone is talking about me." His voice was soft and that ghost of a smile still on his face, but I could tell I'd hurt his feelings.

"I'm sorry. I didn't mean to—"

"No, it's cool. I'm a zombie, guess I better get used to it," he said, a hint of anger in his eyes. "But that doesn't mean I'm worthless. There's something I need to do and I'm going to do it, and nothing anyone says is going to stop me. Not even you, Megan Berry."

He turned around and raced off the sidewalk and through my neighbor's yard, headed toward the cemetery. I yelled his name as he left, but all he did was wave.

For a second I thought about really going after him, but decided against it after peeking around to see that the beige car hadn't moved from its position a few blocks away. Didn't look like they planned on following me to make sure I Settled Cliff even though I hadn't marked him with a halo like I was supposed to.

"Stellar work, guys. At least spy thoroughly if you're going to spy." Typical SA. For an organization that had stayed a secret from humanity for hundreds of years, sometimes I was amazed at how half-assed their work was. But then, the older I get the more I realize a *lot* of adults don't give a crap about doing their jobs well—including important people like teachers and policeman and doctors who are supposed to be *educating the precious youth of America* and *saving people's lives.* So why should I be surprised that SA had its share of incompetents?

I didn't know. But I was.

This time, however, my tail's laziness would work to my advantage. I'd just cut through my neighbor's yard and chill out in their tree house for a few minutes before circling back to my house. If I waited even twenty minutes, the SA spies wouldn't know that I hadn't gone to seal Cliff's grave. My mom and dad had deliberately chosen our house for its prime location, only minutes' away from two of the town's four graveyards.

As for Cliff, I had no idea how to handle him, but at least he didn't seem dangerous. Besides, the sun would be setting soon, and I really didn't want to be out in the dark with a dead guy. Of course, I didn't want to be back at my house under surveillance either. I didn't know where I wanted to be, but I couldn't deny that the last half hour with Cliff had been one of the nicest I'd spent in awhile.

What that said about my social and home lives, I didn't want to examine.

CHAPTER 8

I suspected the world was ending when I caught Mom chowing meat, but when Monica stopped me on the way into school Thursday and insisted I let her help me clear my name, I knew the earth was in serious trouble. Monica Parsons being concerned for my welfare was totally a sign of an impending apocalypse.

"This is the stupidest thing I've ever heard. SA and the Enforcers have their heads so far up their asses it's ridiculous. We have to figure out a way to prove you're innocent."

"Did Ethan call you?" I asked, suspicious of my meddling boyfriend.

Sure, he'd apologized for pushing the Monica issue, but that didn't mean he wouldn't give her a call and plead for help on my behalf. He'd do just about anything to help me . . . which made me feel warm and fuzzy and guilty as all heck.

The weird moment with Cliff was still bugging me. I'd never felt anything but pity or concern—or occasionally irritation—for an Unsettled, never friendship, and certainly never *more* than friendship. No one had ever made me tingle except Ethan, and the fact that the second guy to incite anything moderately tingle-esque in me was dead, bothered me. Big-time.

"Why would your boyfriend call me?" Monica wrapped her scarf around her neck and huddled inside her puffy white coat. It was freezing out this morning, and I kind of wished we'd taken this chat inside the school rather than over by the benches near the parking lot. "Is there trouble in paradise?"

"Everything's great. Better than great," I snapped. "He just said something yesterday about asking you for help. He thought you'd be interested to know we might have had a non-Settler watching us with those zombies that day in the woods."

"What? You're kidding me."

"Unfortunately, no." I quickly filled her in, then pulled the ribbon out of my pocket. "He found this. I'm betting it was from a cheer spy trying to scope out our fund-raiser."

"Those little biatches." Monica snatched the ribbon from my hand. "If we get relocated because of one of those freaks, I'm going to shove a spirit stick right up—"

"There's a chance they didn't see anything and we'll both be fine," I said, cutting her off before she could totally flip. "But I think we should try to figure it out for sure one way or the other. I was planning to crash the cheer table during lunch to see what I can find out."

"You have first lunch, right?" she asked. I nodded. "I have second, so I'll do the same thing. They're going to be at Pizza Pie tonight for the joint fund-raiser, so at least we'll have something to talk about."

"Right," I said, silently cursing myself. I'd totally forgotten about the joint fund-raiser at the new pizza place near the highway. They'd promised us 5 percent of sales and to let the customers choose which team they wanted to support when they paid their bill. Our job was to hang out and solicit supporters and bring in business. Unfortunately, I'd also booked myself for a late-night investigation session with Ethan. "What time does that start again?"

Monica narrowed her eyes. "You forgot, didn't you?"

"No, I didn't, I just—"

She sighed and turned to trudge up the hill as the first bell rang. "Don't worry, it's cool. I can't say I'd be stressing about fund-raising if I were in your place." Wow, Monica was being so nice. It was quite possible she had been body-snatched along with my mother. "But seriously, you've got to figure a way out of this mess. I heard my dad talking to one of the Elders last night. Whatever forensic tests they've been waiting for came back, and it doesn't look good for you."

"What kind of forensic tests?" I asked.

"I don't know, I couldn't tell from hearing just Dad's side of the conversation, but I did get this much, they're totally planning to lock you up and throw away the key." She paused and cocked her head to the side. "I'm actually sort of surprised to see you. I thought the Enforcers would have taken you into custody last night."

"What?" God, this couldn't be happening! Everyone had lost their minds! Was there no sanity left in the world? I hadn't done anything! What in the world could these "tests" have shown them, besides that I was completely innocent?

"I mean, I could be wrong, but—"

"No, you're probably not wrong." I sighed, swallowing the burnt rubber taste that had risen in my mouth. I couldn't let Monica's news make me lose it. I had to stay sane and focused so I could prove to all the crazy people how crazy they really were. "But maybe they figure the spies are keeping an eye on me for now." I nodded to my right, in the direction of the beige sedan that had followed me to school.

"Wow, you've got spies." She made a sound halfway between a snort and a laugh. "Aren't you a bad girl?"

"This isn't funny, Monica."

"Of course it isn't. You're screwed unless we figure something out. It's a done deal. I mean, you'll get a trial and everything, I guess, but it sounds like a formality. Everyone's sure you're guilty."

"I know," I said, trying not to let my terror and confusion show. Did we really need to go over this? I *knew* I was in trouble, what I didn't know was how to get out of it.

"I don't know what they have on you, but if it's enough to totally discount the fact that no Settler has ever been convicted of—"

"Nothing!" I yelled, then lowered my voice when a couple of guys in front of us turned to stare. "Nothing, I swear. They won't even tell me what I'm being accused of. I mean, I know it has to do with raising those zombies, but I don't know why I'm the only suspect. They're supposed to be sending the formal charge to my house today, and hopefully that will give me something to go on, but—"

"Well then, whoever really raised them must be a Settler, and probably a super-powerful one like you."

"Right." Duh, Monica. I figured that one out a while ago.

"And whatever forensic evidence they've got must prove that."

Okay, not so duh. She was probably on to something. Settlers' Affairs' tests must have implicated me in some way. But how? I knew I hadn't done anything. At least . . . not on purpose, which made me wonder again if there was any way I could have made something happen without even knowing it. Of course, if that were the case, I was in as much trouble as if I *had* raised those zombies on purpose.

If SA thought I was raising SRUs with my super-Settler mojo, I'd be stuck in a magical containment unit and never set free.

"I didn't do it. Not even by accident," I said, panic making me babble before thinking.

"Of course you didn't. Don't be a freak. You can't *accidentally* raise zombies. Besides, those things the other day stank of wormwood. Someone raised them on purpose, and we're going to figure out who it was," she said, opening the door for me and letting me pass before following me to my locker. "We'll just have to figure out what kind of evidence the Enforcers have and how it might make you look guilty even if—"

"Hold on a second, I—"

"I'll do some research tonight and let you know if I find anything interesting."

"Monica, why are you doing this?" I asked, unable to help myself. I was suspicious of everyone lately. "Why are you helping me?"

She froze, looking as surprised as I felt, as if she'd just realized helping was exactly what she was doing. She recovered quickly, however, and her surprised look turned into a glare. "Why wouldn't I? You didn't do this. You're such a goody two-shoes it's vomit-inducing. SA and the Enforcers are crazy, and I don't want to see someone innocent go to jail."

"Even me?"

Monica cocked her head to the side, like she was studying some strange bug she'd discovered under a rock. "I don't hate you. You know that, right? I mean, I actually thought we were becoming friends."

"Friends," I repeated, shocked to the tips of my new Uggs.

"Friends who constantly rip on each other?"

"That's just kidding around, Meg. Toughen up. I make fun of all the sophomores on the squad." She shrugged. "But I don't want to see anything bad happen to any of them, and I don't want to see anything bad happen to you. Especially since the Enforcers are only here for you in the first place. They'll be gone the second you set foot in jail."

Ah. Now it made sense. "And you won't have a leg up on your competition if you don't keep training with them. Nice to know your motivations are selfish, as always."

Monica rolled her eyes, but there was a smile on her face. "Whatever, Berry. I'll text you after lunch to let you know what I find out at the cheer table." Then she turned to flounce away down the hall.

"Ditto." I grabbed my English notebook and slammed my locker shut with a smile. I didn't want to admit it, but I was glad Monica thought we were becoming friends. I could use a few friends, even ones who constantly insulted my lack of fashion sense and thought I was a vomit-inducing goody two-shoes.

Hey, beggars can't be choosers.

• • •

I was in luck at lunch. Only four of the twelve cheer clones had first lunch, so I wasn't nearly as intimidated as I had thought I'd be. Still, it was awkward figuring out exactly how to insinuate myself with people I'd never dared—or desired—to hang with before. Luckily, I tripped over my own feet and spilled spaghetti all over their table before I had a chance to get too angsty about my method of approach.

"Oh my God, ew!" Kimberly shoved her chair back just in

time to avoid a red-sauce splatter, while her twin, Kate, dodged a rogue meatball. Lee Chin just stared at me, her almond eyes clearly unimpressed.

"I'm so sorry!" I blushed as I plunked down my now-spaghettiless tray and grabbed a bunch of napkins from the dispenser at the center of the table. "I just tripped and I—"

"You did that on purpose." Kate glared at me and snatched the napkins from my hand. "Are you pom losers so desperate to make us look bad that—"

"It was an accident, Kay. Relax." Aaron, the lone boy on the squad and the only person still smiling, grabbed some napkins and mopped up the noodles on his side of the table. "Hey, I'm Aaron. Megan, right?"

I returned his smile, though I was already a little uncomfortable with the flirt factor of his grin. What was with me and boy-type attention lately? First Cliff and now Aaron. Of the two, most would say Aaron was the more tempting—what with the whole all-American hottie thing and being *alive* and all that—but he didn't tempt me for a second. In fact, he kind of gave me a mild case of the "ews." Now Cliff, on the other hand . . .

Nope. *Not* going to think about that. Focus, Megan!

"Yeah. I've seen you at the Honor Society meetings," I said as I casually slid into the only seat not splattered with sauce, which happened to be right next to Aaron.

"I'm vice president. Pierce usually insists on me being there," he said. It was a smart-ass remark, but it was impossible to get my feelings hurt with the way he was looking at me. Aaron was obviously interested. Leaning-close-and-staring-into-my-eyes interested. How weird and uncomfortable was that?

But at least it gave me an excuse to hang around the table, something that would have been difficult without him, given the glares of the three other cheerleaders at the table. The "you're not wanted here" vibes were pretty intense. I was going to have to think fast if I was going to figure out a way to casually find out where these four had been Tuesday night just before dusk.

"So, how has the fund-raising been going? I heard you all had a great turnout Tuesday night," I said, my heart racing. I was such a bad liar! I didn't even know if they'd done anything Tuesday night, let alone how the turnout was.

"It's none of your—"

"It was pretty good." Aaron interrupted Kimberly before she could tell me to mind my own business. "But nothing like that topless car wash." He laughed and leaned even closer, until I could smell the peanut butter on his breath. It wasn't a bad smell per se, but hello? Had the dude never heard of personal space? "You don't know how many guys were disappointed to find topless meant you weren't washing the tops of the cars."

"Yeah, well, my dad wasn't disappointed. I thought he was going to bust something until I told him what was really going on."

"So you were there?" Aaron asked, obviously not getting my "back away from me" vibes. He scooted his chair even closer. "I came by but didn't see you."

"Yeah, Aaron left us high and dry at our Parents' Night Out to go give his hard-earned money to the competition." Kimberly shook her head in disappointment while her twin sniffed her disapproval.

"He's a boy. He can't resist the pull of the Slut Squad." Lee Chin smirked.

"I was there, but I had to leave early for a . . . family thing," I said. "What about you guys, how long did you work Tuesday night?"

"From five thirty to almost midnight. Some of those parents really took that night-out stuff seriously. I couldn't believe it. We still had two five-year-olds at eleven thirty," Kate said, warming up as the whining about kids ensued.

"It was crazy. I had no idea kids were so much work," her twin agreed.

"I'm never having children." Lee Chin shuddered. "They're so . . . childish. And they smell funny."

I did my best not to laugh, but almost lost it when I caught Aaron rolling his eyes. He thought the girls at his table were crazy too. Maybe he wasn't so bad. Maybe he had no depth perception or something, or there was some other reasonable explanation for his weird closeness.

"And the whole squad was there the entire time, except Aaron?" I asked.

"Why do you want to know?" Lee Chin glared in my direction. "Were you sent here to spy on us or something?"

"No! No way, I mean, what would be the point, right?" I shrugged and took a bite of my cake. *Just act casual and they'll calm down, and nothing's more casual than cake eating.* "Whoever has the most money Friday wins, so it doesn't really matter—"

"It matters if you're trying to psych us out. And if that's the case, you'd better back off." Kimberly added her glare to Lee Chin's.

"Ladies, chill out. Megan here is cool." Aaron wrapped his arm around the back of my chair and squeezed my face with his free hand. "Look at these chubby little cheeks. Is this the face of a spy?"

"Thanks." I laughed and acted like I was comfortable with the touchy-feely stuff, but was relieved when Aaron let go.

Until he started running his finger along my lips, of course.

"You had a crumb," he said, holding the finger with said crumb on it up between us.

"Oh, thanks. Well . . . guess I should go get some more spaghetti before they close the line." Aaron was starting to skeeve me out, and it seemed I'd gotten as far as I was going to get with the cheerleaders anyway. "See you guys tonight." I grabbed my backpack and made a beeline for the entrance to the hot line, pretending I didn't hear Kimberly call that I'd forgotten my lunch tray and better come back and put it away because she wasn't in charge of cleaning up my messes.

After all the crap the cheerleaders had pulled lately, leaving them at a spaghetti-splattered table seemed the very least I could do.

CHAPTER 9

"I'll pick you up around nine," Ethan said as we pulled up in front of Pizza Pie just before the dinner rush. "I think I found someone at the hospital who's willing to give us the four-one-one on why the cops were there. She gets off her shift at nine thirty. Sound good?"

"Sounds perfect, I'll see you then."

"Bye, love you."

Sigh. Hearing those words coming from his lips still made my heart flip over and do a cannonball into my stomach. In the good way.

"Love you too," I said, smiling as I opened the car door. I really had the best boyfriend ever. He had skipped all his college classes, gotten someone to cover his Protocol shift, and devoted himself completely to keeping me out of jail.

God. Jail. It seemed more likely with every passing second.

I waved goodbye and trotted across the parking lot toward the entrance, trying not to think about the deep poo I was in. Though, after the past two days, it wasn't easy.

"You look like heck. Did you eat anything today?" Monica looked me up and down with a critical eye as I joined her and the other girls at the rear of the pizza joint. Geez, it almost made me wish I'd headed to the opposite corner to hang with the cheerleaders. "You didn't, did you?"

"Yeah, I did," I said, though I honestly couldn't remember consuming anything other than a few bites of oatmeal and one nibble of cake. They were out of spaghetti by the time I reached the lunch counter, and I'd been too freaked to think any further about food, which was saying something. I was usually a stress eater. Give me Doritos and sour cream and onion dip in a time of crisis and I can usually find a way to live another day.

"Fine, but you're getting too skinny. It's not attractive."

"Like you're one to talk." I glared pointedly at Monica's size-two body, which was way skinnier than my size-four or six—depending on the brand.

"Honestly, you have no butt anymore. Not that I care, but it's not a good look for you."

"Thanks, Monica," I said, unable to think of a smart response. She was really starting to hurt my feelings with the constant criticism.

"Are you like . . . " Monica trailed off with a shake of her head, then grabbed my arm before turning back to London. "Get everyone assigned to schmooze a section of the restaurant. I'm going to feed Megan and I'll be right back."

"Wait. I'm not hungry. I—"

"I don't care, you're eating something. We all ate when we got here and you obviously need some food." She pulled me through a hole in an accordion partition separating the main restaurant from the party room and back toward a table littered with the remains of a pizza feast. "Now eat. At least two pieces, preferably three."

"Listen, I appreciate the fact that you think I look like crap," I said, crossing my arms and refusing to take a step toward the table. I felt sick to my stomach and there was no way I was letting Monica bully me into eating greasy pizza that would no doubt make me yack. "But you're not going to fatten me up in one sitting. So let's just go help the others set—"

"You looked like you were going to cry back there," Monica said, her voice soft. "And you really are getting too thin."

"Yeah, I got that the first five times," I said, getting angry. "Could you just lay off? It's pretty mean to keep—"

"I'm not trying to be mean. You're usually gorgeous, you know that."

My mouth fell open in pure shock. Monica telling me I was gorgeous? And seeming to mean it? Where was the punch line?

"Even worn out you look ten times better than most people," she continued, "but you're clearly not a hundred percent. You need to rest and take care of yourself."

"Right, in all my spare time."

"Taking care of yourself isn't something you do in your spare time." With a determined stride, she headed for the pizza table and started loading a plate with cheese slices. "It's something you make a priority, especially in our line of work. You can't afford to be run-down—it could get you or someone else killed if this black-magic crap keeps happening."

"I'm doing the best I can." I blinked back the tears stinging the backs of my eyes. "Sorry if that's not good enough."

Monica shook her head and turned back to me with a sigh. "I'm not saying you're not good enough. I'm trying to tell you I don't want you to get hurt."

"Because it would screw up your future?" I sniffed.

"No, because I'm worried and I care about you, idiot," she said, not a trace of sarcasm in her tone. "Now eat something."

Monica was being nice to me, not because she wanted something or was afraid I'd screw up her plans, but because I was such a wreck she felt sorry for me. Monica, who was easily the least empathetic person I'd ever met. How low must I have sunk to have earned her pity?

Very, very low indeed.

Swallowing the lump in my throat, I reached for the pizza. "Okay. I'll—"

Suddenly there was a loud crash from the door leading into the kitchen and someone screamed. Then someone else cursed, then a few more people screamed, then the door flew open and a wild-eyed girl with brown corkscrew curls dashed into the room.

"Could I get some help here, y'all?" she asked, as breathless as if she'd run a fifty-meter dash. "I've got two OOGPs in here, and they're freaking weird."

The girl's name was Bobbie Jane. I'd seen her two or three times during the fall Enforcer training, though I hadn't realized she worked at Pizza Pie until now. Her mom and dad worked full-time, and she usually had to watch her little sisters, so she didn't make it to every training session, but Settlers' Affairs didn't stress about her being there. She wasn't a very powerful Settler to begin with and wouldn't be going into Enforcement, but she wasn't a total slouch either. She should have been able to handle a couple of zombies without too much trouble. The two OOGPs—Out-of-Grave Phenomena—must be bad news if she needed help.

Monica and I ran for the kitchen. Even before we burst through the door, I had a horrible feeling I knew what we'd find.

"Shit," I said, even though I'd been trying my best not to curse as part of my lengthy list of New Year's resolutions.

My bad feeling was dead-on. Across the room were two zombies exactly like the ones Monica and I had fought in the woods—they looked amazingly lifelike and didn't reek of grave dirt, and *both* wore pajamas—crawling over the cold stove and dishwashers in their haste to get to the three of us.

"Yeah," Bobbie Jane said, agreeing with my assessment of the situation. "And it gets worse. I wasn't observed, but *they* were. There were five people in here. They all booked it out the back, but—"

"They'll be looking for help," Monica finished. "Which means we've got five, maybe ten minutes to *reverto* their—"

"But the *reverto* spell isn't working." Bobbie Jane shouted to be heard over the moaning and groaning of the zombies headed our way. "I haven't tried the *pax frater*, but—"

"It won't work either. These freaks are different." Monica grabbed my hand and dropped her shields, not wasting further time explaining, which was a good thing. Zombie One was already over the dishwasher—sending the dishes on top clattering to the floor—and had nearly cleared the industrial stove. Zombie Two wasn't far behind.

Taking a deep breath, I focused my attention on pulling Monica's power inside myself and prepared to cast. This would be cake compared to the last time. There were only two of them. Maybe if I took just a little bit of Monica's energy and waited until the RCs were close, then I wouldn't be so messed up afterwards.

Then I could follow them back to wherever they came from, trap the person who was responsible for raising them, and clear my name. If I just waited until they were a little closer . . . a little closer . . .

"Do it, Megan!" Monica yelled over the hungry keening filling the room.

"Just a second."

"Now!" Monica shouted just as Bobbie Jane screamed and hit the floor beside us.

We'd been ambushed from behind!

There wasn't time to lift my palm and cast before someone ripped Monica's hand from mine and a thick, solid body knocked me off my feet. I landed on the hard tile floor with a groan but did my best to flip over. I couldn't see who was on top of me, but I was betting it wasn't a friend.

"Gunh!" The boy groaned and lunged for my neck just as I shifted onto my back.

He—no, scratch that, *she*. It was a girl. The bald head had thrown me for a second, but it was definitely a girl's body under her red flannel pajamas, and decidedly feminine lips curled above her teeth as I knocked her foaming mouth away.

"Please help me!" Bobbie Jane was crying now, I caught sight of her tearstained cheeks and blood pouring down her arm out of the corner of my eye.

She was fighting the RC who'd taken her to the ground, but she'd been bitten—badly. Bobbie Jane wasn't one of those wimpy chicks who cried if they broke a nail. She wasn't the strongest Settler, but she was tough. I'd seen her get the wind knocked out of her sparring with Barker and she hadn't so much as whimpered. If she was crying, she was seriously hurt. Monica and I had to get hooked up again and get rid of these things before she lost any more blood.

I punched the chick on top of me straight in the nose and rolled swiftly to the side, knocking her off long enough for me to struggle to my feet. Monica was less than five feet away, slamming one Undead's head into the stove while delivering a roundhouse kick to the head of another lurching in behind her.

"Monica, over here, we—"

Her eyes darted to mine. "Behind you," she shouted.

Spinning on my heel, I delivered a sharp uppercut to the face of the girl I'd just knocked off of me a second ago. She cried out but rallied in time to block the kick I'd aimed at her solar plexus. Dammit, she was fast! No black-magically raised corpse should be able to move that fast!

"Megan! Megan, please!" I risked a quick glance over at Bobbie Jane, who was now struggling against two zombies—one who had her forearm locked between his teeth and another trying to get a mouthful of her leg. Bobbie Jane kicked and bucked and fought like a champ, but she was outnumbered and in an undefendable position. We had to get her out of here, had to—

"Ah!" I cried out as Red Flannel Girl slugged me in the face, then made a lunge for my neck that I just barely managed to dodge.

What was with the hitting? The Undead didn't possess the smarts to distract someone with a punch before making a bid for the blood and flesh they craved. They were soulless, mindless shells raised to pursue the will of another. They shuffled and groaned—they didn't dart and weave.

Apparently this chick hadn't gotten the memo, because ten seconds after slugging me, she kneed me between the legs—which *hurts*, even if you're a girl, I'll have you know—then swept my feet out from under me with the expertise of a trained fighter.

"Unnh!" I hit the ground a second time, wincing in pain as my tailbone felt like it exploded. If I hadn't broken a bone, I'd come darn close, which ticked me off sufficiently that the next punch I landed to Red Flannel Girl's face sent her careening backwards in one of those slow-motion arcs you see in the movies.

It was actually pretty sweet. Too bad I didn't have time to relish my small victory.

Sensing movement behind me, I spun my arms in a circle, twisting as far to my right as I could, shattering the kneecap of the dude reaching for my neck. He screamed like a five-year-old and collapsed, distracted enough by his pain that his grasping hands missed me as I jumped to my feet and leapt over him. I headed straight for where Monica was still holding her own near the stove, knowing time was running out.

Bobbie Jane screamed again, a bloodcurdling sound that made my skin break out in goose pimples. I didn't even care anymore that she was probably going to bring a bunch of average human people running, and all three of us would be exposed. All I could think about was getting to Monica and evading the zombies long enough for us to get linked up and accomplish the *reverto* spell.

But where could we go? The kitchen wasn't that big, and unless we knocked the zombies unconscious, there was no way we could get far enough away from them to buy the time we needed.

Then I saw the pots and pans hanging above the stove, strapped

106

to some sort of industrial grid bolted to the ceiling. It looked pretty strong, but was it strong enough to hold me and the Monicster? I wasn't sure, but we were getting ready to find out.

"Monica, up!" I shouted as I ran, pointing above her head.

She glanced toward the ceiling, then turned back to her zombies, clocking them both in the face before interlacing her hands, forming a foothold. Say what you want about Monica, but the girl thinks fast and is a kick-ass person to have on your side in a fight. I stepped into her hands and she gave me just the boost I needed to reach up and grab the edge of the grid.

I swung wildly back and forth for a second, pots and pans crashing to the floor as I climbed on top, but finally managed to leverage myself up and over the edge. Scrambling around as fast as I could, I reached a hand over the side just in time to grab Monica—who had climbed on top of the stove—and pull her up beside me. Once she was safe from the zombie hands snatching at us from below, I summoned her power.

"*Reverto!*" This time, the aftershock from the command sent me shooting across the metal grid on my stomach, bruising my hip bones and ribs and proving Monica right—I needed to gain some weight. If I'd had a little more meat on my bones, it wouldn't have hurt nearly as much.

As it was, I was still wincing in pain as the zombies streamed out the back door into the marshland behind Pizza Pie. Trying to ignore the throbbing of my ribs, I crawled to the edge of the grid. I was dizzy, but I had to get down. If people came in and saw me, I'd have a tough job explaining what the heck I was doing.

Of course, getting down would have been a lot easier if Monica had stuck around to help. Instead, she'd bolted the second the zombies headed for the door. I assumed she was checking on Bobbie Jane, but when she spoke it definitely wasn't a fellow Settler she was talking to.

"Your mom's Dr. Sampson, right? Okay, I need you to go get your mom and bring her back here, then I need *you* to call nine-one-one and tell them we have someone very badly hurt and we need an ambulance, and I need *you* to get Mr. Moretti. Do you understand?" Monica asked, her voice soft and kind of high-pitched, like she was talking to—

Kids. There were three kids standing in the door, I realized as I hit the floor, sending pans clattering to the ground. Two girls and a little boy were staring at the two of us with wide, frightened eyes, but nodding their understanding of their various duties.

"Good, now hurry." Monica waited until they scattered before rushing over to Bobbie Jane. The other Settler lay very still, a puddle of red smearing her Pizza Pie uniform and the white tile around her. She'd lost a scary amount of blood. We needed to stop it or the ambulance was going to be too late.

Heart pounding in my ears, I turned and surveyed the room, grateful to see some clean-looking dish towels near the sink in the corner. I hurried to grab one as fast as my dizzy head and wobbly legs would allow and then rushed back to Bobbie Jane. "Here, we have to press this to the wound and stop the blood. Apply direct pressure on—"

"It won't do any good," Monica said, ignoring the towel I held out.

"Yes, it will. I remember the first-aid classes we took last October.

If you apply direct pressure—"

"No, Megan. It's not that," she said, turning to look up at me with tear-filled eyes. "It won't do any good because . . . she's already dead."

CHAPTER 10

I couldn't remember ever feeling so cold. Sure it was probably thirty-something degrees outside and I'd been huddled on the ground for fifteen minutes, but I knew that wasn't the reason I couldn't stop shivering.

Bobbie Jane was dead. Not that I'd known her all that well, but what did that matter? Bobbie Jane, with her bouncy curls, heart-shaped face, and eyes that had seen far more than those of the average sixteen-year-old, was gone. Now those eyes would never open again, and it was all my fault. If I hadn't waited so long to cast, if I hadn't been more worried about clearing my name than about keeping people safe, maybe she would still be alive.

I was positive I couldn't feel any worse when the shouts came from the marsh.

"We've got another one! About a hundred yards back." Somber-faced policemen rushed into the swampy water, carrying guns and cameras, followed by the EMTs.

"Oh God, no. Please, no." Tabitha's mom was whispering, but I could hear the anguish in her voice all the way across the parking lot.

Once the initial chaos of learning Pizza Pie had been attacked by drugged-up cult members—the official story being spun by the Settler undercover on the Carol PD—had cleared, we'd realized one of the cheerleaders was missing. Tabitha, a sophomore, had gone to the bathroom a few minutes before all heck broke loose and never come back. Now they were pulling her from the swamp on a stretcher.

"No! Is she okay?" Her mom screamed, a sound that turned into a horrible wail as she rushed to her daughter's side. It was Tabitha. The blond hair and signature gold ribbon were clearly visible above her pale face.

"She's conscious, but she's lost a lot of blood. We need to get her to University for a transfusion." The EMT hustled toward the ambulance, followed by Tabitha's sobbing mother.

"I wish that was Bobbie Jane. I wish she was going for a transfusion," Monica said, her tone as flat and emotionless as it had been since we were pulled out of the kitchen and rushed to the ambulance for treatment.

Monica had a couple of bite marks, and I had the beginnings of a killer black eye, but nothing serious enough that we needed to go to the hospital. We'd insisted on waiting for our parents to come pick us up. No doubt we were both in need of parental comfort, but there was also the little matter of the Enforcers, who were on their way to investigate the death.

Dead. Bobbie Jane was dead. No matter how many times I repeated it, it just didn't seem to make sense. This couldn't have happened. People weren't murdered in Carol, especially not by zombies. Settlers didn't let things like this happen.

"Megan?" I turned to see Mom leaping out of the car before Dad had even fully pulled to a stop. Unfortunately, Kitty and Barker were in a car right behind them.

111

"We're just going to tell them the truth, right?" Monica asked in that monotone, which was starting to freak me out.

"Yeah. Probably the best thing," I said, awkwardly patting her knee. I had a feeling she was in shock, but couldn't remember what I should do about it. My brain didn't seem to be working, which made me suspect she wasn't the only one who was a little out of it.

"Honey, are you okay?" Mom crouched down beside me, cupping my face in her hands and running her fingers through my hair, as if she had to touch me to make sure I was alive.

"Yeah, I . . . no. No, I'm not." I swallowed hard but couldn't fight the tears pooling in my eyes. "Bobbie Jane is dead."

"I know. I heard," she said, looking as sad as I felt.

"It was more of those freak RCs," Monica said. "We tried to get rid of them, but they got to Bobbie Jane first. We couldn't . . . We tried, but we—"

Then she finally lost it, breaking down in full-fledged sobs that had my mom wrapping an arm around her and pulling her close. Monica's mom and dad had been an hour away at some political fund-raiser when she called and hadn't made it back to Carol yet, but I guessed any mom would do in a crisis. Monica clung to my mom's sweater and cried like the world was ending. If I'd ever had any doubt that there was a good person inside the often cruel girl sitting next to me, it was banished as I watched her grieve.

"We're sorry, but we need to talk to the girls." Kitty's voice was respectful, but firm. I looked up to see her and Barker standing a few feet behind my mom looking as pale and shaken as I felt. It seemed even the big, bad Enforcers weren't going to be able to take this one in stride.

"Can't this wait?" Mom asked, making no attempt to hide her anger. "Obviously they're both very upset, and—"

"It's okay." Monica sniffed and swiped at her eyes. "Let's get it over with. I want to go home." She rose and stomped off into the darkness at the edge of the parking lot. Barker followed without a word. Guess that left me with Kitty.

"Megan, you know you don't have to do this. You haven't been assigned a mediator yet, and until you have, you—"

"No." I stood up and brushed the gravel off my jeans. "I want to do whatever I can to help them find the person responsible for this."

"Just be careful," Mom said with a sigh. It was pretty obvious she didn't want me to talk to Kitty, but she knew how stubborn I could be when I set my mind on something. And my mind was definitely set. I had to help catch the real Very Bad Thing, even if it meant putting my own safety and future at risk.

If anyone else died in my town, I was going to feel responsible. Heck, I already felt responsible, so I couldn't even summon up any righteous indignation when Kitty started grilling me before we'd even reached a secluded corner of the parking lot.

"Where were you this afternoon, between the hours of three thirty and five o'clock?"

"I was at pom squad practice," I said. "Ethan picked me up at four thirty and we ran by my house so I could change clothes and then I came straight here."

Her eyes narrowed and her thin lips pressed together. She wasn't pleased to hear that Ethan had ignored her advice to leave me alone. "And where is Ethan now?"

"He's on his way," I said, though I couldn't actually be sure that was true. I'd tried to call him, but had been sent straight to voice mail. It wouldn't be any big surprise if he was underground scoping out another morgue and wasn't getting any signal.

Kitty nodded, and I could almost see her making a mental note to warn Ethan again of the risks of consorting with a suspected felon. "Did you notice anything out of the ordinary when you first arrived at the restaurant tonight?"

"No."

"Nothing at all? You don't want to think about it?"

"I don't know," I said, shocked by the harshness of her tone. "Nothing that I remember."

"Well, maybe you should try a little harder," she snapped. "A girl is dead, Megan, and—"

"I know a girl is dead," I yelled, before lowering my voice. There were still normal people here, not to mention normal *cops*, and I couldn't afford to attract attention. "But I swear to you, I have nothing to do with this."

"I'd love to believe you." She shook her head wearily, and for a second I could see how scared she was. "I really would, but—"

"Then believe me! Please, Kitty. Whoever raised those corpses is still out there, and it doesn't look like they're going to stop any time soon. While you're busy investigating an innocent suspect, more people could die. We have to—"

"*We* don't have to do anything. This is an Enforcement matter," Kitty said, all vulnerability vanishing from her face. When she spoke again, it was with the calm, efficient voice of an Enforcer who suspected me of evil. "All I need from you is a blood sample."

"What? I thought they had my blood on file down at—"

"They do. I'm just hoping a fresh sample might show something different from what the forensic experts have found so far. It might be your last chance to hang on to your freedom, at least for a few more days."

"Okay, fine. Sample away," I said, glad we were out of Mom's sight. I had a feeling she wouldn't approve. "But I'm innocent, I swear I am. I have not been raising bizarro RCs. I've been actively *fighting* them, in case no one has noticed." I held my torn and bleeding knuckles up between us as I tried to pull myself together. "I did everything I could to *stop* those things. I was only trying to do my job."

And to save your own ass. You should tell her that, tell her how waiting until the last minute to cast probably got Bobbie Jane killed.

I sucked in a deep breath, forcing myself not to cry. I wasn't going to lose it. Not here, not now. I could go home and crawl into bed and blame myself later.

Kitty didn't respond, just reached into her coat pocket and pulled out a syringe and a few individually wrapped packets of sterilizing swabs. "Can you push up the sleeve of your coat?"

"Sure." Tears fell silently down my face as Kitty cleaned an area near the crook of my arm, but I wasn't crying because of the needle sliding beneath the skin. I could hardly feel that pain, and what I did feel I knew I deserved. At least I could still feel something, not like Bobbie Jane, who would never feel anything again.

"You can go home," Kitty said as she capped the needle and tucked it back in her coat. "We can't legally take you into custody yet, but I'd get my bag packed if I were you. It probably won't take more than twenty-four hours to get the last of the proof SA needs to—"

"Thanks, I'll keep that in mind." I didn't bother to ask what "proof" she was talking about before I turned and walked away. I knew she wouldn't tell me. Even if she still had doubts about my guilt, she worked for Settlers' Affairs, and *they* wouldn't mind if I ended up zombie chow. I bet they thought it would spare them a lot of trouble.

Of course, they'd learn better when the zombies didn't stop once I was dead. When whoever was raising them kept . . .

"But what if they didn't?" I whispered, a horrible idea forming in my mind.

I hated to be paranoid, but both sets of zombies had seemed to be after yours truly. The first time I couldn't be sure, but now it had happened twice. I'd been targeted by black magic. Whoever was raising these RCs wanted *me* dead.

Or maybe just out of the way. It made sense to bring some super zombies to fight the super Settler. And if someone wanted me out of the way so they could wreak cataclysmic havoc with a bunch of SRUs, then they wouldn't care whether I was dead or rotting in a Settler prison—their goal would be accomplished. I'd be out of commission and they'd be able to . . .

Do something really, really bad. Like wipe out a town, or a state. Or maybe even the country, but I didn't want to think about that.

God, that had to be it, it was just like the night of homecoming when Jess had been trying to keep me and Monica from the dance. This wasn't just about me. Some black magician must be planning something very bad and wanted to be sure no one could stop them. I had to tell Ethan as soon as he got here, and Monica too if she was still determined to help me.

I turned in the direction I'd last seen her, but couldn't find her anywhere. I looked for a few more minutes before deciding I would just have to get in touch with her later. Now that the adrenaline rush was wearing off, I couldn't believe how tired I was. I felt like I could sleep for about a thousand years.

"Are you free to go?" Dad asked when I got to the car. Mom was sitting inside, glaring at Kitty and Elder Thomas (who'd just shown up a few minutes ago) through the window.

"Yeah, I want to go home." I'd call Ethan on the way and let him know I'd left Pizza Pie.

Dad nodded and patted me on the back before opening up the back door, but he didn't say anything. He'd been in the military and deployed to lots of places where violence and death were disturbingly common. So I guess he knew better than anyone that when lives have been lost, there just isn't anything you can say to make it better.

• • •

We'd been home for over three hours and Ethan still hadn't called, so I went ahead and swapped the jeans I'd put on for some pajamas. I'd already taken my shower and forced myself to eat some of the cheddar-cheese-and-potato soup my mom had whipped up. The last thing I wanted to do was eat, but Monica was right. I couldn't afford to let myself get run-down, especially not with whoever was raising zombies still on the loose.

Still, my stomach didn't feel right after dinner. Despite the exhaustion level, there was no way I was getting to sleep right away, so I figured I might as well do a quick e-mail check. I hadn't been on ten seconds when Ethan popped up on IM.

EthanzID: Megan! I've been waiting for half an hour. I was afraid to call. Can you chat? Is there anyone else in the room with you?

Megsalot: Hey, no, there's no one else here. I can talk, but why were you afraid to call?

EthanzID: My cell phone was tapped. I removed the bug, but I couldn't be sure your cell or home phones weren't tapped too.

Megsalot: What?!! Isn't that illegal? Even for Enforcement?

EthanzID: As far as I know, but I'm beginning to think our Enforcers aren't playing by the rules. Smythe was at the Presbyterian hospital tonight.

Megsalot: Oh no, did he see you?!

EthanzID: No, but I saw him. By the time he was finished, the nurse he was talking to was unconscious.

Megsalot: OMG! Did he . . . Is she going to be okay?

EthanzID: She'll be fine, but he had some sort of cattle prod thing and shocked her with it.

Megsalot: To clear her memory?

EthanzID: Exactly. I got your message and was on the way out of the hospital morgue when a bunch of police cars pulled up. I followed them to the intensive care unit, but they weren't letting anyone on the floor, so I tried to find another way in. I ran into Smythe and the nurse in the stairwell. Guess he'd had the same idea.

Megsalot: Do you think Smythe has something to do with the weird zombies? Do you think he could be the one—

EthanzID: I don't know, but I don't think so. He called Kitty right after he finished with the nurse and said something about having a situation contained. So if he's the one responsible, then all the Enforcers are in on it.

Hmm . . . could the Enforcers be up to something shady? I couldn't deny I'd had my doubts about them in the past. No matter how nice they were, there was still something a little scary about Enforcement. On the surface they seemed to be under orders from our local SA council, but in reality I had a feeling they were pursuing their own agenda and our local Elders had a lot less power than they thought they did.

Megsalot: You know, I hate to think they're shady, but I didn't want to believe the truth about Jess at first either. Sometimes it's hard to know who your friends are.

EthanzID: Yeah . . . I heard Jess was back at the SA clinic tonight. More seizures . . .

Megsalot: Can we not talk about Jess? I know I brought her up, but . . .

EthanzID: No, that's fine. But as far as the Enforcers are concerned, I don't know what they'd have to gain from getting rid of you.

Megsalot: Which reminds me—I think that whoever is raising these zombies wants me out of the way.

EthanzID: I figured as much. Why do you think I've been so worried? I mean, I don't want anyone else to get hurt, but I really don't want this freak to get to you.

Okay, now I felt dumb. I guess Ethan thought the fact that I was the target was so clear it didn't even need to be discussed. We were going to have to have a talk about stating the obvious. For a smart girl with a 3.8 average, sometimes I can be pretty dense.

Or maybe I was just too tired to think straight. It seemed like this week had been going on forever.

EthanzID: You still there?

Megsalot: Yeah, I'm here. Just thinking . . .

EthanzID: I heard about Bobbie Jane. I'm so sorry. I wish I could have been there.

Megsalot: I wish you could have been there too. I really messed things up, Ethan. I can't believe I let her die.

EthanzID: You can't blame yourself. You're an amazing Settler, but you can only do so much. These zombies are unlike anything anyone in the U.S. has ever faced before. I can't find anything in my books talking about SRUs after the eighteenth century.

Megsalot: Monica is looking for answers too. Maybe she'll find something.

EthanzID: And I'm going to head back to the hospital tomorrow morning and see if I can get on the ICU floor. There's something going on there, I'm sure of it, and I'm betting it's connected to the attack tonight. The timing and Smythe being there are too much of a coincidence.

Megsalot: I'm sure they'd think it was a weird coincidence that YOU just happened to be at the hospital too. If something fishy is going on, you have to make sure no one finds out you were there.

EthanzID: You're right. Delete this chat as soon as we sign off.

Megsalot: Speaking of deleting messages, did you find out anything about why the Enforcers were checking into my mom?

EthanzID: No, nothing concrete yet. I'll let you know as soon as I know something for certain.

Something about Ethan's text made the suspicious-of-everyone alarm go off in my head, but I ignored it. If he'd found something, he'd tell me. I was just being paranoid. Though who could really blame me, what with the phone tapping and being followed by SA officers and the like? I really had to find some way to clear my name before I became one of those weird twitchy people who live in a van and refuse to drink tap water because they're convinced the government is putting tranquilizers in it to keep the population calm while they implant tracking chips behind our ears.

Or something like that . . .

Megsalot: Okay. Sounds good. I miss you.

EthanzID: I miss you too. I wish I was there . . . I'm worried about you.

Megsalot: I'm worried about you too. Please be careful.

Ethan promised to send me an e-mail the next day giving me a new phone number where I could reach him. Then we both signed off. I deleted our chat and crawled into bed.

I would have sworn I'd never be able to get to sleep, but I obviously drifted pretty darn close. By the time I heard the tapping at the window, I had to fight to cast off the cobwebs sticking to my brain. Good thing really, or I definitely would have screamed and brought Mom and Dad running. Even familiar dead faces are terrifying when they're floating in the darkness outside your window.

CHAPTER 11

"A girl died." Cliff looked as traumatized as I felt, but still showed no signs of going Rogue. Whatever breed of Undead he was, he didn't seem like he'd be turning all red and glowy-eyed on me anytime soon. He was an anomaly, much like other people I knew . . .

"I can't believe she's really dead. I mean . . . this wasn't supposed to happen," he continued. I didn't even question how he knew. He'd obviously been lurking again. I knew I should tell him to cut it out, but I didn't have the heart to yell at him.

"I know," I whispered through the crack in the window. "I'm sorry, I—"

"It wasn't your fault," he said with such conviction I almost believed him. "It was them, the others."

The others. That was like the third time Cliff had mentioned the weird zombies. "What do you know about the others, Cliff? Who's raising them?"

"Raising them? Don't they just get up?"

"No, they're not like you," I said, briefly outlining the difference between normal Unsettled and ones raised with black magic. "Reanimated Corpses aren't themselves anymore, not the way you are. That usually makes them easier to control, but that's not the case with these guys. Do you have any idea why? Why they're so resistant to Settler magic?"

He shrugged. "I don't even know why *I'm* resistant to Settler magic."

Hmm . . . I hadn't really thought about that, but I should have. Cliff wasn't one of the bad guys, but his timing was pretty suspicious. The chances he and the other zombies-not-behaving-normally were connected was better than good. But how? I couldn't help but feel that Cliff knew more than he was letting on.

"If you don't know anything, then why do you keep mentioning the others? How did you even know they exist?" I asked. "I mean, you mentioned them the first time we met, before there was even an attack, which makes me—"

"Now hold on," Cliff said, raising his hands as if to prove he had nothing to hide. "I told you I had visions when I was alive. I still have them—they just don't work as well. But I remembered the others. They were one of the first things I saw when I woke up."

"You saw them?"

He nodded. "Them, and you . . . and . . . the other dark-haired girl and . . . I just knew I had to find you and try to help. No matter how strong you are, you're not going to be able to handle them or the other ones that are coming on your own."

"The other ones," I repeated, pinning him with my most piercing stare. "There are *more*? More of these unstoppable freaks?"

"Don't ask, I can't remember. I just know there are going to be more zombies, a lot more. And not friendly, fabulous guys like me."

I sighed. Great news—Cliff was just full of it. "And I guess you don't know why you happen to be around every time I'm attacked, either."

"No, *that* I know." His gaze grew sort of unfocused. "I . . . feel them . . . when they wake up, but I'm always too late. Tonight I ran as fast as I could, but they were already pulling the second girl from the woods by the time I got there."

Cliff's voice echoed the failure I felt so completely that I couldn't bring myself to ask him any more questions. Besides, his visions didn't seem to be much more useful than a television report detailing a crime that had already happened.

"So, can I come in?" he asked. "Better yet, can you come out? Peeking through this crack in your window is cool and all but—"

"No, I can't. It's almost midnight." A burst of cold air rushed in. I shivered and crossed my arms, glad I was wearing my fleece pajamas. It had gotten colder since we'd left Pizza Pie, and the smoky scent of impending snow hung in the air. It was a sad smell, and it made me realize how very little I wanted to socialize. "Listen, it's been a long night and—"

"I know, I'm sorry. But I had to see you," he said, popping the screen out of my window with an expertise that spoke of many nights sneaking out. "I've got something to show you and I need some more Settling."

"Cliff, please, you can't keep coming here. I'm not supposed to keep Settling the same person over and over. It's against the rules."

"Oh God no. We wouldn't want to break the rules," he gasped, then grinned his infectious grin. It was a little more strained than usual, but I could tell he was trying to cheer us both up. "Come on, get your coat and shoes. If we hurry, we can catch the last bus into Little Rock."

"I'm not going to Little Rock. I've got a ten o'clock curfew on weeknights," I said, deciding pleading parental interference was the best way to handle Cliff.

He certainly didn't seem to care for the "but you're supposed to stay dead" argument. Couldn't say I blamed him, but it was complicating my life. With everything going on right now, the last thing I needed was a new zombie BFF.

"Your parents don't have to know. Come on, don't tell me you've never snuck out before. This window is perfect."

"Oh, I've snuck, but every time I have I've almost *died*. It's taught me respect for authority."

"Right." He laughed like I'd made some great joke.

"I'm not kidding. The first time I snuck out I was ten and ended up with this scar." I tugged at the neck of my black fleece top, revealing the silvery white zombie bite mark scar on my shoulder blade. "And amnesia and Settler power failure that lasted for *years*. Then, the second time, I—"

"Fascinating stuff, but let's talk while we walk." Cliff reached through the window and grabbed my hand. I didn't pull away. It was weird, but Cliff's touch was very comforting. It made me feel . . . safe. "I didn't realize how late it was getting. We only have about ten minutes to get to the bus stop."

"I'm in my pajamas!"

"Your pajamas look like clothes! Come on, let's hit the Rock."

"Why do you need to go to Little Rock, anyway?" I'd never had an Unsettled request travel privileges, but then, I'd never had an Unsettled who refused to stay in his grave, either.

"No, the question is, why do *we* need to go into Little Rock, and I'll tell you on the way. Just put on some shoes and let's go. Please,

Megan. It's important, or I swear I would leave you alone."

I sighed, feeling my resistance begin to fade. "How am I going to get back? If the last bus to Little Rock leaves in ten min—"

"The buses back to Carol run until two. I'm sure we'll be done by then. I know exactly where we're going."

"And where is—"

"I'll tell you—"

"When we get there, yeah, yeah, yeah." Geez, I was *so* going to regret this, I could feel it already. But that didn't stop me from dropping to my knees and digging under my bed for my Uggs. "Okay, let's hit it." I tugged on my shoes and grabbed the Williams sweatshirt I'd stolen from Ethan from the mostly clean pile on the floor. No time to waste sneaking down the hall to grab my coat.

Cliff helped me leap the few feet from the ledge down to the frozen grass below. He dropped my hands to close the window and scoop a large camouflage backpack from the ground, but then threaded his cold fingers through mine before turning to cut through the backyard, avoiding detection by the SA spies still parked in front of my house.

For a second I felt guilty. Here I was, in my boyfriend's sweatshirt, holding hands with another man—or boy, or zombie, or whatever. But then I decided to ignore the little voice saying I should pull away from Cliff. Holding his hand still made me feel safe and weirdly energized despite that hint of dizziness that always seemed to accompany his touch, and I needed that comfort right now. Somewhere out there in the darkness was a person raising nearly unstoppable killing machines with my name on them.

Cliff might be stalking me, but at least he was a friend, and that was all the persuasion I needed to keep my hand right where it was.

• • •

An hour later, I stood at the top of a long, rolling hill in a posh Little Rock neighborhood, certain, for the second time that night, that I was going to die.

"I can't do this! It's too dark. What if there are holes in the pavement that I can't see and my skate gets stuck?" I asked, my palms sweating inside the hand guards Cliff had brought for me to wear—along with knee guards and a pair of Rollerblades in precisely my size.

He said he was good at guessing things like that, which would make him a great friend to have when it came time for birthdays, but I couldn't let myself think about him that way. He wouldn't be around for my birthday next October. He was dead, and he had to go back to his grave and stay there.

Unfortunately, that was getting harder to imagine the more time I spent with him. Cliff was fun, sweet, and way more perceptive than your average boy. In fact, he would have been well on his way to being my new partner in crime if he weren't a zombie.

And if it weren't for that weird spark that flared between us every once in a while, that dizzy, giddy, almost high feeling—not that I'd ever smoked up, but I could imagine this was how being high felt— that resulted from being in his presence. Ninety percent of the time I felt only chummy vibes coming from Cliff, but the other 10 percent . . .

"Megan, you're going to be fine." He smiled and squeezed his fingers around mine, sending a little shiver across my skin that I tried to ignore. "You know how to skate and you're wearing safety equipment. Besides, this hill isn't nearly as intense as it looks."

"I thought you said you'd never skated it before?"

"I haven't, but look at it. It's not that bad."

"Cliff, I've already got a black eye. I really don't want—"

"Yeah," he said, his expression angry even though his fingers were gentle as he smoothed down the side of my face. "I don't like seeing you hurt."

"It's my job." I shrugged, trying to ignore how breathless he was making me feel.

Now his touch wasn't safe at all—it was tempting in a way it shouldn't be to a girl totally in love with someone else. I should have pulled away that very second, but I didn't. I just stood there and watched Cliff's mouth get closer to mine while I slowly forgot how to breathe.

"I don't care. I'm not going to let you get hurt again. I promise." His lips brushed softly against my cheekbone, right under where my skin was swollen and bruised.

My eyes slid closed, the world spun, and for a second the temptation to turn my head and find Cliff's lips with mine was so strong I wasn't sure I'd be able to resist. Wearing Ethan's sweatshirt, loving Ethan like I did, it didn't matter. I wanted to kiss Cliff, wanted that connection with him so badly something in my chest ached when I forced myself to roll away.

God, this was crazy! And against Settler rules, and boy/girl rules, and just about all the other rules I could think of. I had to put a stop to this before it was too late.

When I spoke again, my voice sounded angrier than I intended, but better angry than any of those other feelings. "Cliff, why are we here? You said you had something to show me, something that couldn't wait."

"I do."

"Then why are we wasting time Rollerblading?"

"This isn't a waste of time," he said, sounding irritated himself. "Life is short, Megan, shorter than I ever realized. You have to make time to play."

"There are zombies *killing* people. A girl is *dead*! I don't have time to—"

"Yes, you do. You deserve to have a little fun, even when things are bad. Heck, especially when things are bad." He rolled closer, pinning me with those soulful eyes that made me certain he knew all of my secrets. "Promise me you'll make time to enjoy your life, no matter what happens. I don't want you to wake up in a crypt someday wishing you'd spent less time smoking up and more time living."

"But I don't smoke pot."

He grinned. "You know what I mean."

"Yeah." I returned his smile, but it wasn't my happy grin. I was going to miss Cliff. He was the first new friend I'd made since Jessica tried to kill me. Well, and the Monicster, if you could call her a friend.

For the first time in my life I actually understood the lure of black magic. I'd never lost anyone I cared about so much before. It didn't matter that Cliff had already been "lost" before I'd even met him, I still didn't want him to go. If I'd known a spell to keep him from having to crawl back in that crypt, I would have been sorely tempted to cast it. Even knowing what I did about the consequences to my own soul and that a spell like that might change Cliff in some frightening way. Even knowing that Jess still wasn't out of the woods for all the dark power she'd channeled last fall, I was still . . . tempted.

I shivered at the darkly seductive warmth curling through my veins.

I was a good person, I'd been raised to fear black magic, and I personally knew a girl who was having seizures and heart attacks as a direct result of summoning the wrong kind of mojo, but still, it called to me. I guessed maybe that was why Kitty and Elder Thomas needed proof I was innocent. No one was immune.

"Okay, enough heavy stuff," Cliff said. "Let's take this hill."

"Agreed, but then we have to get down to business. I'm not trying to be a fun-killer, but we've only got forty-five minutes to get back to the bus stop before the last bus leaves."

"We'll be there in plenty of time."

"I'm serious, Cliff, I can't miss that bus or—"

"Megs, have a little faith." He shook his head in mock disappointment. "I didn't choose this spot simply for its beauty or astoundingly long, rolling slope alone."

"You didn't?"

"Our true destination also happens to a mere half-mile away, right at the bottom of this hill, and a block from a bus stop."

I raised my eyebrows. "Wow, I'm impressed."

"Good planning for a zombie, eh?"

"Good planning for a boy." Even Ethan, the smartest guy I knew, seemed to have trouble doing more than one thing at a time.

"I've always been a good planner."

"Maybe you're just in touch with your girly side."

"Or maybe you've just been hanging out with the wrong guys." He was halfway down the hill before I could think of how to respond, which was probably just as well. Flirtation must be avoided at all costs.

Still, Cliff was right—a little fun would probably be okay.

The thought made me smile as I pushed off, my pulse racing as I picked up speed and the cold air whipped through my hair. By the time I'd gone fifty feet, my nose was frozen and my teeth chattering, but I didn't regret being here for a moment. There was just something magical about zooming down a deserted street in the dark, feeling the night come to life around you, knowing that—at least for a few minutes—all you had to think about was wind and speed and letting gravity take charge.

I wasn't usually the sort to enjoy giving up control, but for the moment it was perfect. So perfect, I was sad to see the hill come to an end so fast.

CHAPTER 12

"You want us to break into my doctor's office? Are you crazy?" I asked, looking nervously around as we walked. The parking lot was deserted, but just thinking about breaking and entering was enough to give me hives. I might push the limits when it came to Settler law, but when it came to the human variety I was a model citizen.

"We're not going to steal anything." Cliff paused near a darkened window and pressed his face to the glass. "Well, not anything that doesn't belong to you anyway. I say your parents' medical records *are* your business. After all, *they* have access to *your* records."

"They're my parents!"

Cliff turned to me, blinking in confusion. "So?" He pushed at the bottom of the pane, nearly giving me a heart attack. It was all I could do to not whip my cell out and call the police myself.

Monica was right—I was a hopeless goody two-shoes.

"Don't touch that! There might be an alarm." I grabbed the sleeve of Cliff's sweatshirt and tugged him back into the shadows.

"If there's an alarm, you can run and I'll go in and get the records."

"But what if there's a security camera? The police could see. You could be—"

"I'm dead. What are the police going to do?" he asked. "Megan, this is no big deal. This building is old, and I doubt the practice is making enough money to go super high-tech with the security."

"I don't care." I crossed my arms and glared. "I don't break or enter, especially not to steal my parents' medical records. It's illegal and pointless. My parents are both perfectly healthy."

Cliff cocked his head. "I never said your parents were sick."

"Then why are we—"

"Listen, Megs, you love your mom and dad and they love you, but that doesn't mean you can trust them. Parents lie too."

My lips parted in silent shock. I wasn't sure whether to be angry or hurt by what he was implying. I mean, my mom had been acting strange lately, and I suspected she wasn't telling me something. But that was *withholding*, not lying. There was a big difference. "My parents wouldn't lie to me. We're like . . . friends. They don't treat me like a kid."

His eyebrows lifted. "And the ten o'clock curfew is because . . . "

"That's different. Sure I have a curfew and stuff like that. But in other ways they treat me like an adult, like I'm smart enough to understand things and be part of the decisions that are made for our family."

Cliff's face was a study in pity as he brushed a strand of hair away from my face. "Megan, those zombies you've been fighting lately aren't the only things that are different. You're different."

"I *know* that."

"Well, haven't you ever wondered why?"

I stepped away, hating the way my skin lit up when his fingers lingered just behind my ear. What was wrong with me? Why did Cliff make me feel this way? I had a perfectly wonderful boyfriend, one who was *alive* and didn't accuse my parents of being liars. I should turn around, march across the parking lot to the bus stop, and never look back.

But I didn't.

Hadn't a part of me been suspicious of Mom and Dad for days now? It wasn't just Ethan's announcement that the Enforcers had been looking into Mom's file. Mom and Dad just hadn't been acting like Mom and Dad. There was a good chance that only stress was to blame, but what if it wasn't? What if Cliff was right and they weren't just keeping private grown-up stuff private? What if they'd been lying to me?

"It's just the way I am," I said, but my weakening resolve was clear in my voice. I huddled deeper into Ethan's sweatshirt, suddenly feeling the cold.

"Are you sure?" Cliff asked. "Are you sure there's not an explanation, one your parents have kept from you? Maybe because they thought it would be best for you?"

Well . . . when he put it that way . . . no, I wasn't sure. But neither was I sure I trusted Cliff, at least not more than my own mom and dad. "If you know something, why don't you just tell me? Why drag me down here to steal things?"

"You won't believe me without proof," he said. "Besides, I'm not exactly sure what we're going to find. I just know we need to get our hands on those records. Specifically your dad's . . . I think."

"You *think*?"

Cliff sighed and leaned against the side of the building. "I told you, my visions don't work as well as they used to. Even when I was alive, they didn't tell me everything. They just sent me in the right direction. Now, it's even more vague, like a dream I can't quite remember."

"A dream you can't quite remember." The eye-roll I sent his way was well deserved. "Then why should I—"

"We're running out of time." He cast a frustrated glance at his watch and then turned pleading eyes back to mine. "Please, Megan, let's just get the records. If there's nothing there, then I'll admit I was wrong. I'm fine with being wrong. I just . . . I don't want . . ."

"You don't want what?"

"I don't want you to die." The desperation in his tone told me Cliff hadn't been totally straight with me. Not about why he kept seeking me out, and not about his visions.

"You've seen it, haven't you? You've seen me die." My voice wasn't much more than a whisper, like I could keep the words from being true if I didn't say them too loudly. "Those weird RCs kill me, don't they?"

"No, I didn't see that," he hurried to assure me. "But I've seen things that make me worry. A lot. There's a fire, girls screaming. I see you running and then . . . and then there are these hands . . . on your throat . . ." He didn't finish his sentence. He didn't need to. "It makes me worry constantly. About you and about the people who will get hurt if you're not around anymore."

Our eyes held as we came to a silent understanding. We both knew I couldn't afford to ignore his warning.

"So how do we do this?" I crossed my arms again, making it clear I still wasn't thrilled with this plan. "I'm assuming you have experience with breaking and entering?"

Cliff smiled. "Come on, I think I saw something on the other side of the building." He grabbed my hand and pulled me around to the front, pausing under a row of narrow windows about six feet off the ground. "I'm betting those are in a bathroom. What do you think?"

"No . . ." I closed my eyes, struggling to remember the layout of the Pleasant Mountain Family Clinic. "There aren't any windows in the bathrooms. It's been a while since I've been here, but I think these are in one of the doctors' private offices."

"Even better. They might have the files in there. Here, let me lift you up."

"Wait a second, I—"

"Just push on the bottom of the window and see if it opens. Those look really old, and I'm betting they don't lock from the inside."

I sighed, but didn't bother putting up a fight. I'd already agreed to do this—might as well get it over with. I stepped into the basket Cliff made with his hands, and for the second time that night let someone else boost me up into the air. The bottom of the window budged almost immediately.

"It's loose. I think I can get in," I said, not knowing whether to be excited or terrified. There was no way I'd be able to lift Cliff up high enough for him to slide in through the window. I was going to have to do it myself.

The knowledge made my heart beat faster, made my blood pump so loudly in my ears that I didn't heard the footsteps until it was too late.

"Freeze! Little Rock Police," a deep male voice ordered. Seconds later, the hands holding me disappeared. I was left dangling in midair, clinging to the window ledge as Cliff ran like a bat out of heck into the shadows surrounding the parking lot. He was gone before the men behind me could finish yelling for him to stop.

Great. My first act of juvenile delinquency and I'd not only been caught, I'd also been abandoned by my accomplice. Now I was going to get a ticket or thrown in the hoosegow or something even worse.

I dropped to the ground and turned around, hands in the air.

"We're going to need your home phone number," the second policeman said as he tucked his gun away in its holster. "We're calling your parents."

Yep, this was definitely something worse.

Too bad I hadn't retrieved my parents' files. It would have been good to have some dirt on them *before* they got the call from the police. Then maybe I would have had something to bargain with to keep from being grounded for the rest of my natural life.

• • •

"What the hell were you doing?" Mom asked through gritted teeth, the real interrogation starting before we'd even pulled out of the police station parking lot. Since I had a clean record, the cops had given me a stern warning not to trespass and sent me on my way. It had just been bad luck they'd spotted me and Cliff while they were out patrolling, and, strangely enough, I think they felt a little sorry for me for getting caught. I *had* nearly broken down three times while explaining that I'd *never* done something like this before and would *never* do something like this again.

In the end, I'd gotten mercy from the law, but I knew better than to expect the same from my mother.

"I had an Unsettled?" I winced when it came out as a question. I sounded like I was lying even when I wasn't. This wasn't going to go well, not well at all.

"So you decided to sneak out of the house in the middle of the night?"

"I didn't think you'd let me go."

"Damn straight we wouldn't have. At least not alone. You could have been seriously hurt. What if there'd been another attack? What if you were—"

"I know. It was stupid. I'm sorry," I said, sinking lower in the passenger's seat. It was past two in the morning, but I wasn't tired. Being in police custody had banished any shred of sleepiness. At this point, I was fairly sure I'd never close my eyes again. "He wanted to go into Little Rock to Rollerblade down this hill, and—"

"Don't try it, Megan," Mom snapped. "I want the truth, not some story about this boy falling and cutting himself and you needing supplies from the doctor's office." She jerked the car onto the highway with a squeal of the tires. Mom isn't the best driver under normal circumstances, but when she's angry . . . Well, we'd be lucky if we didn't wind up in a ditch. "The police weren't buying it and neither am I. Especially since I *know* it didn't matter if that boy lost a leg on that hill as long as you got it back in his grave along with him."

"Would you believe I had to use the bathroom?" I asked, stalling for time.

How could I tell Mom I was sneaking in to steal her and Dad's medical records? Not only would the lack of trust freak her out, but I'd have to explain how I'd gotten the idea in the first place, and I really wasn't up to telling anyone about Cliff.

"You're lying." Mom's voice was chilly enough to make me shiver, even with the heat blasting in the car. "I'm not as stupid as you seem to think I am, and I don't—"

"I don't think you're stupid. It's just that . . . there are . . . things . . ." Crap, I sucked at this. I should just tell her the truth. Maybe she'd let me know what was in those records and it wouldn't be any big deal.

"Megan, you know you can tell me anything, right?" she asked, her voice softer than it had been before. "If you're in some kind of trouble, if you've . . . done something . . . even if it's something awful. I will always love you. And I'll—"

"God, Mom," I said, that mix of anger and hurt rearing its ugly head once more. "You sound like Kitty. Do you think I'm guilty too?"

"No, of course I don't . . . I just . . ." She trailed off and I did my best to stop sniffling. I really didn't want to cry again tonight. "I just don't want you to hide anything from me."

I couldn't have asked for a better opening. If I chickened out now, I'd never get a better chance. "And I don't want you to hide anything from me. Even if you think it's for my own good."

Mom spun to face me. The car swerved off the road onto the rumble strip, making the entire vehicle shake until she regained control. It wasn't the reaction of an innocent woman, and I felt the first real crack snake its way through the bedrock of my faith. I'd always taken my mom's honesty for granted, but now I wasn't so sure.

Neither of us said a word as the exit for Carol came up and Mom turned left onto Main Street. Finally she broke the silence. "Have you been going through my things?"

Oh God, Cliff was right. She *did* have something to hide. "No, but I guess I should have been."

"Don't smart-ass me. There are things you don't understand."

"Duh! And whose fault is that?"

"You're still a kid, for God's sake. You're too young to know some truths."

"I'm not too young to go to Settler prison for the rest of my life," I yelled, no longer trying to keep a lid on my freak-out. Screw my withholding explanation—she'd been flat-out *lying* to me. The woman who had drilled the importance of honesty into my skull since I was practically a fetus had *lied*. And she was *still* lying. "I know Enforcement has been looking into your past."

"So what? I'm your mother, I—"

"And I'm not deaf, either. I heard you and Elder Thomas talking. What the heck was all that about? What mistake was she talking about?"

"That's none of your—"

"Tell me, Mom. Tell me what you're hiding."

"Some mistakes are better left in the past, Megan. Leave it alone."

"If you don't tell me, I'll find out on my own, and when I do, I'm not going to—"

"Don't you dare threaten me," Mom snapped, turning to glare at me while the car veered toward the median. "I am still your mother and I have never—" We hit a pothole on the side of the road with a loud thunk that made the car rattle.

"Shit, watch the freaking road!"

"Don't curse!"

"We're going to have a wreck!"

"I've been driving for decades, Megan, I don't need—"

"Yeah, driving like crap. You're an awful driver, just ask Dad." I didn't know why I was taking the argument in that direction. I guess a part of me didn't want to stay on topic, didn't want to know the obviously awful secret she was keeping.

Still, my lips kept flapping, almost against my will. "Does Dad know? Does he know you lied to—"

"Leave Dad out of this," Mom said, though she did turn her eyes back to the road and directed the car between the lines. "Your Dad and I agreed I should handle it. He's not a Settler, and he doesn't understand how sensitive this situation is."

"Neither do I, and I *am* a Settler. Thanks to you I always will be, whether I like it or not."

"God, Megan, don't start that again. I am *so* sick of hearing you whine about not being normal. What the hell is 'normal' anyway, and who wants to be—"

"I do!"

"Obviously. And you know what, I wish you *were* normal," she said, her volume rising to match my own. "Then all you'd have to think about is clothes and makeup and boys and that fucking pom squad you're so obsessed with, and you could be even more shallow and selfish than you already are."

My mom had said "fuck." To *me*. It was shocking enough to bring fresh tears to my eyes, even without the "shallow" and "selfish" comments.

"I am not shallow or selfish," I whispered, fighting to swallow the cantaloupe-size lump in my throat. "I work hard, harder than you ever did when you were my age!"

"Really? And how do you—"

"I hardly ever get to see my boyfriend, I have no friends since my best friend tried to kill me over *Settler* crap, and I've risked my life at least four times in the past year to—"

"And how many of those situations were your own fault?" she asked, stopping at the red light two streets before our own.

"It's *my* fault weird zombies keep attacking me?"

"I don't know. Is it? You tell me, Megan." I could tell she regretted the words as soon as she'd said them, but it didn't matter.

"I'm walking home."

"No, you're not." Mom grabbed my arm hard enough to make me wince.

"Whatever happened to 'You're such a great girl, I'm so proud of you'? Was that all bullshit?"

"I'm sorry, I shouldn't have . . . I didn't mean . . . I've never doubted—"

"Yes, you have. You just *did*, and so do Kitty and Barker and Elder Thomas. You all doubt me, even though I've done *nothing* wrong." I was sobbing now, big, heaving, donkey sobs. Never had I dreamed my life would become *this* unfair.

I mean, I still felt guilty over hesitating a few seconds too long before invoking the *reverto* command tonight, but I had done my best. I wasn't perfect, but I'd done everything I could to get rid of those RCs and every other OOGP that had ever stuck its decomposing nose into my life. That my mom could doubt that, even for a second, made me feel like my entire world was falling apart.

"Megan—"

"So don't ask me what I was doing tonight," I said, "or what I'm doing any night until I prove I'm innocent. If you think I'm such a bad person and refuse to be honest with me, then you don't deserve to know."

I wrenched my arm away, flipped the automatic unlock button, and threw myself out of the car. I was sprinting across the newly bulldozed lot next to the Sonic before Mom could roll down her window.

"Megan Amanda Berry, get back in the car!"

But I didn't slow down for a second. All I wanted to do was run. Run and run and run until I was far away from my mom, her doubt, and all our dirty family secrets.

Whatever those were.

I was still in the dark, but I wouldn't be for long. I'd find a way to get those medical records and dig up every little last thing my mom and everyone else didn't want me to know. And then I'd prove them wrong. All of them.

I'd make them sorry they'd ever doubted me, that they'd ever thought I was a murderer or a witch. I'd use all that stupid power I'd never even wanted and I'd show them what I could really do, how I could make them hurt, suffer, wish they'd never been—

"No." I froze at the edge of the lot, where the road turned residential and tidy streets spun off toward organized little subdivisions, feeling like a dark, wretched thing intruding into the innocent land of suburbia.

The longing for revenge was understandable, but I'd *never* use my power to hurt people, not even people who had hurt me. I couldn't believe the thought had entered my mind, no matter how upset I was. It made me afraid in a way I hadn't been since all the weird zombie stuff started.

What if there was really something different about me? Something more than just being extraordinarily strong? What if, deep down, I wasn't one of the good guys like the rest of the Settlers?

"Megan, please. I'm sorry. Get back in the car." My mom pulled up beside me, but I didn't turn to look. I couldn't. Not right now, not when I suspected she might see a shadow of that bad person she feared I was still lurking in my eyes.

"I'm going to Monica's," I said, surprising even myself. I'd clearly hit rock bottom if the Monicster's was the safest place I could think of.

For a few minutes, the only sound was the purring of the engine and the scratch of something rustling around in the industrial Dumpster a few feet away. Normally that would have sent me racing back to the car, but even the threat of coming face-to-face with a bunch of swamp rats couldn't persuade me to go a step closer to my mom. I didn't know who she was anymore. With the rats, at least I'd know what to expect.

Finally, Mom sighed, a weary sound that let me know I'd won before she even spoke. "Won't you need clothes, your makeup, other stuff for school?"

"I'll just borrow some of hers and run in and grab my backpack on the way," I said, my jaw tightening. She was giving up. That easily. My old mom would never have let me get away with telling her to butt out of my life or going over to a friend's house unannounced in the middle of the night.

Despite the fact that I *really* didn't want to go home, I suddenly wished she'd jump out of the car and tell me she wasn't taking no for an answer. But she didn't, which I supposed meant I'd won.

So why did I feel like I'd lost everything that mattered?

"All right." Mom paused, and for a second I thought she was going to change her mind. But when I looked over at her, all I saw was a scared woman with the beginnings of a worry line between her eyebrows who didn't know what to do. With me, or with herself. "Can I at least give you a ride?"

I swallowed, hard. "It's only five blocks."

"Megan, I—"

"See you later, Mom." I ran again, as fast as I could, telling myself the cold wind was the reason for the wetness on my cheeks.

CHAPTER 13

"Get up, Berry." A bony finger jabbed me between the ribs hard enough to make me twitch and seek shelter beneath the covers. "If I have to listen to you snore for another minute I'm going to lose it."

With no small degree of effort I cracked open my eyes. According to the clock by Monica's bed it was six o'clock. I'd only been asleep for about three hours. "Wake me in an hour."

"No, you're getting up now. Get. Up." The last two words were accented by more finger jabs. Clearly, the sweet, vulnerable Monica from the night before had vanished and the real Monicster had returned to continue her reign of terror. Still, she *had* let me into her room and offered me clothes to sleep in at nearly three in the morning. I couldn't afford to be too critical. "Now, freak, or I'm going to cut you with something sharp."

"Why not something dull? It would hurt more," I muttered as I forced myself into a seated position. The room spun dizzily for a moment, either a side effect of too much stress and not enough sleep, or of the shocking orange and pink paisley wallpaper.

No matter how tired I was, I was betting on the wallpaper.

"Here, get dressed." Clothing smacked me in the face. "Those jeans should fit. They're too big on me."

Ah, an insult first thing in the morning. "I thought you said I was too skinny?"

"You are, for your body type. Not everyone can have delicate bone structure," she said, then turned toward the source of the lovely smell filling the room. "You drink coffee, right?"

"You have a coffeemaker in your room?" I asked, my envy clear though my voice was muffled by the black sweater I was pulling over my head.

"Coffeemaker and espresso machine." She poured a large cup from the pot sitting on top of the little refrigerator/microwave combo in the corner. There was also a sink, a few feet of counter space, and two cabinets above the mini kitchen. The Monicster's room was even more tricked out than Ethan's dorm. "But there's no way I'm making you a latte, so don't get any ideas. Cream or sugar?"

"Both." I leaped from the bed and struggled into Monica's jeans—which were still a little too tight, so there was hope my butt hadn't fallen off completely.

"Here, drink. I need your brain functioning in the next ten minutes," she said, handing me the coffee and tapping her booted foot.

For the first time, I noticed she was already dressed, complete with makeup and flatironed hair. What time had she gotten up? And why did the fact that Monica was a morning person make me suspect her of greater evil than ever before?

"What's happening in ten minutes?" I gulped coffee, not caring that it burned the back of my throat. What was a little pain when there was such sweet, coffee-y goodness to be had?

"Ethan's coming to get you to take you to school. He called last night looking for you. Good work forgetting your cell."

"I didn't forget it—I had reason to believe it was tapped."

"What?" Monica's brow wrinkled.

"The Enforcers are getting sketchy with their methods. Ethan's phone was tapped too."

"Wow. He *was* calling from a new number," she said, then shrugged as if phone tapping were an everyday affair. "Still, it's probably a good idea to bring your phone with you next time you sneak out of the house in the middle of the night. Better overheard than dead. And it will keep your parents from calling your boyfriend on the Settler dorm phone at one in the morning when they can't reach you on your cell."

Oh, crap. Why hadn't Mom said she'd tried to call Ethan? Now I had to figure out what I was going to tell him, and quick. I took another deep pull on my coffee, praying the caffeine would dash straight to my weary synapses.

"He made me promise to call if I heard anything." Monica straightened the orange bedspread with quick, efficient motions. Who would have thought Monicster had such a taste for pink and orange? I would have pegged her as a black-like-her-soul kind of decorator. "I waited to call him back until this morning since I thought you needed sleep. Otherwise, I'm sure Prince Charming would have been over here in the middle of the night, and my dad would have lost his shit if he'd seen another guy in here."

"*Another* guy?" My eyebrows lifted above the rim of my cup.

"And I really didn't want to deal with that fallout." Monica ignored my question, and I resisted the urge to make a joke about the string of men she invited back to her lair, figuring I couldn't afford to alienate one of the few people on my side. Besides, my curiosity about what she was pulling from under her bed was sufficiently intriguing to banish all thoughts of boy-themed interrogation.

"What's that?"

"It's a dry-erase board." Her pointed "duh" look inspired another big gulp of coffee. Obviously she was serious about the whole brain-functioning thing. "I thought a visual aid would help organize the information."

"Okay." I perched on the edge of the bed, squinting at the chart Monica had drawn. "What exactly is this?"

"It's everything I could find on Settler-specific forensic evidence down in the archives at the SA library in Little Rock. I was there until almost midnight last night, and believe me, my parents weren't too happy," she said, circling various sets of letters on the board. "If they hadn't been so trashed on cheap wine from that fund-raiser thing, I never would have gotten out of the house. You so owe me one."

"Or two or three," I agreed, though I still had no idea what I was looking at.

"Yeah, well, if you're grateful now, you're totally going to offer me your firstborn in a few minutes." She turned back to me with a satisfied smile.

"I didn't think you liked kids."

"I don't, but you do," she said, her pity for me and my breeder's heart apparent. "I bet you and Ethan already talk about how many puppies you're going to squeeze out by the time you're thirty."

"Ew. That's a really gross way to put it."

"Not as gross as researching the differences between Settler sperm and normal guy sperm. Do you know that Settler men have little hooks on the end of their sperms' tails?" she asked, her lip curled in disgust, even though I could tell she was totally intrigued by weird Settler spooge. "It looks the same as sperm mutated by a fungus, so human doctors have never gotten suspicious but—"

"And the reason we're talking about this is?" I asked, earning myself another "duh" look from Monica and an eye roll for good measure.

"Forensic evidence. You know, hair, DNA, spit, sperm, *blood* . . . "

"Blood." Even if she hadn't emphasized the word, it made sense. Blood was the only one of those things used to raise zombies. "You found out something about our blood?"

"Your blood in particular. I did a little reading about the other stuff, but I figured the forensic evidence the Enforcers had on you *had* to be blood."

"Blood they found on the graves of the weird zombies or at the morgue or wherever."

"Right. So I did a little digging, trying to find out how Settler blood is different from normal blood, and how super-Settler blood might be different from either."

"Makes sense," I said, starting to get excited. Monica was definitely on to something. There had to be a difference between my blood and normal Settler blood, and that was why SA was so positive I was the person raising these weird zombies. "So what did you find?"

"Nothing." She smiled, and for a second I wondered if the evil Monica had made a reappearance. "There isn't anything weird about Settler blood. Nothing you could see under a microscope or learn from a lab test, anyway. Whatever makes our blood special seems to be more magical than scientific."

"But then why did Kitty want a blood sample last night?"

"What? You didn't tell me that." Monica glared down at me from where she stood at the end of the bed. "How am I supposed to help you if—"

"I couldn't find you. I was going to tell you today. She said she wanted a fresh sample and that it might keep me out of jail for another twenty-four hours."

"Hmm." She narrowed her eyes. "And it might. Or longer."

"How?"

"See all these letters?" Monica pointed to her chart. "They stand for different blood types found in people with paranormal powers. People who can move things with their mind, psychics, witches, fire starters, things like that."

Psychics?

Cliff was psychic. I wondered if that meant he had weird blood, and if that might somehow be responsible for keeping him out of the ground for so long? It was almost enough to make me spill the beans to Monica, but I held my tongue. I didn't know why, but I wasn't ready to tell anyone about Cliff, at least not until I figured out whether it was somehow my fault that he couldn't rest.

"Anyway, none of these blood types are found in normal people or Settlers, and they can't be detected with human medicine, only with special tests, and only on fresh blood. And are you ready for the real kicker? Bad little Settlers and witches and people like that have a major jones for this stuff. Supernatural blood types mean big magical bang for your buck. So whoever is raising these super zombies has to be using some of it, whether they got it from you or someone else."

Someone else. Someone like . . . Cliff? Oh God, I didn't even want to think about that. Cliff would never betray me, I was sure of it.

As sure as I could be of *anything* these days. Besides, I wasn't psychic, so why would Cliff's blood and my blood be at all similar? In fact, if my blood matched whatever the Enforcers had found, I didn't see how any of this information was going to help. "I'm sorry, Monica. I really appreciate all your work, but I don't see how any of this makes a difference."

"Don't you see? You *must* have one of these blood types."

"But my mom's just a Settler, she's not—"

Monica sighed and let her chart drop to the bed. "So maybe your dad or somebody has one of these types of people in his family and you're getting mojo from both sides. Maybe that's why you're so much more powerful than the rest of us."

My dad was the least mojo-y person I knew, but I was willing to entertain the possibility, not that it really mattered. "Let's say you're right. But even if Kitty does her test and it shows something the first test didn't—like that I'm part fire starter or whatever—how will that prove it isn't my blood that was used to raise the weird zombies?"

"It would prove that it's different!"

"Not really. If the test can only be performed on a fresh sample, then the stuff used to raise the zombies wouldn't show the hidden blood type even if it was there. It won't do any good."

"But . . . I . . ." Monica sat down heavily in the orange computer chair behind her. "You're right. I hate to say it, but you're right."

"I'm sorry," I said, knowing how much those words had cost the Monicster. "I wish I wasn't."

"Yeah, me too." She sighed and ran a hand through her perfectly flatironed hair. "Bet you wish you hadn't given Kitty that sample last night now, huh?"

"What do you mean?" I asked, earning my third "duh" look of the morning.

"If the test comes back positive for one of these supernatural blood types, you just handed her all the evidence she needs to prove you had the power to raise these freaks of zombie nature. And considering those blood types are only found in, like, point-two percent of the population . . ."

"She tricked me." God! "Crap."

"*Now* who feels stupid?"

I sighed. "I've felt plenty stupid since all this started," I said, fighting the despair that threatened to shut off the tiny lightbulb our conversation had lit up in my mind. "But I think I might be rallying."

"Oh yeah?"

"Yeah. If these blood types are only detected in fresh blood, then that means they did some other kind of test to see if my blood matched the blood used to raise the zombies. Probably a normal, human test."

"Probably."

"They couldn't have done a DNA test in such a short amount of time, so—"

"How do you know?"

"Haven't you ever watched those 'who's my baby's daddy' Springer episodes?"

"Um, no. Somehow I managed to miss those."

"Well, DNA tests take weeks, even when they put a rush on them," I said, refusing to have my enthusiasm dampened by Monica's sneer of Springer disapproval. "So that means they must have used a human blood type to decide I was their girl. I'm AB negative, which is super rare, and—" I smacked myself on the forehead with my palm, nearly causing coffee to splash out of my cup. "I'm so stupid. I can't believe I didn't think of that before! When I was ten and l lost all that blood in the attack, my mom was the only Settler who could donate for my transfusion. They didn't have any of my blood type in the bank in Little Rock."

"That's why the Enforcers were checking out your mom. She's the only other Settler around here with your blood type."

"Right. This also means we're both going to be cleared. All we have to do is insist on a DNA test," I said, torn between giving in to relief and the anxiety pressing in just as heavily from the other side of my brain.

What if that DNA test didn't clear us for some reason? What if there was something I was overlooking?

"And in the meantime, we'll try to find out if there are any other super Settlers around with AB negative blood and get ready to kick their ass. I knew SA was overlooking something blindingly obvious, as usual." Monica clapped her hands together as if that were the end of the matter. "Now, you should brush your hair. Ethan will be here any second. Makeup would be a good idea too. I normally wouldn't let you infect my brushes with your facial bacteria, but you need some cosmetic help. You heal fast, but there's still a little black-eye action going on."

"Ethan's seen me without makeup before and he doesn't care." The thought made me feel mushy and sad all at the same time.

My boyfriend thought I was beautiful even when I was pale and bag-ridden, and I hadn't even thought to call him last night. Not to mention the whole Cliff thing. In the cold light of day, I couldn't believe I'd had a single more-than-friends thought about a dead guy, but I had. Which probably meant I was the lousiest girlfriend in the entire world. Ethan deserved so much better.

"I'll just grab some lipstick and mascara from my backpack on the way to—"

"Um, no. You need more help than that. Go. Apply." Monica snatched my coffee from my hands and steered me toward the bathroom. "I recommend base and extra bag and black-eye concealer."

"Really, it's no big deal, I—"

"Have you forgotten what today is?" My blank look must have assured her I had. "The sweetheart skate is tonight and you, my friend, have not sold a single ticket. That means you've got to hustle today, and no boy is going to buy a couples skate with a girl who looks like she dug her way out of a grave."

"But . . . after all that's happened, are we still—"

"The competition is still on. Dana called me last night to assure me the cheerleaders were still 'in it to win it.' She said Tabitha was going to be fine, and that they were going to dedicate their first halftime performance to her recovery or something like that. So go, hurry, or you won't have time to—"

"Okay, okay." I hurried into the bathroom and set to fixing my face, even though the last thing I cared about right now was beating the cheerleaders at fund-raising. A girl was dead, I was in the midst of World War III with my mom, and someone was trying to kill me. Even if our DNA breakthrough was going to clear my name, there was still a lot of bad crap going down. The fact that Monica was still interested in pom squad stuff was just . . . weird.

But then again, that was probably why she'd live a long and well-balanced life, easily juggling her paranormal and everyday activities and I'd be a complete basket case by the time I was twenty. After all, wasn't that why I tried so hard to be normal? Because I could feel the Settler stuff slowly taking over, consuming me until there was nothing left of the girl I'd wanted to be before my power came back last fall?

I shivered and did my best to apply a thin line of eyeliner without looking myself in the eye. My face was freaking me out as much as my thoughts. I just looked so . . . hollow—empty in a way I'd never seen before.

The phone rang outside and I heard Monica talking softly. She stuck her head in the bathroom a second later. "Come on, time's up. Ethan's outside."

"Just one second, I'm almost—"

"Nope, we've got to go. Both of us, and we're not going straight to school." Her grim tone indicated this side trip wasn't going to be to the donut shop or Sonic for a sunrise smoothie. "The Elders have called an emergency meeting and our attendance is mandatory."

"But Kitty and Barker took our statements last night."

"Apparently there was a loose end or three we forgot to mention," she said, the dread clear on her face as she grabbed her backpack from the floor. "And one of those loose ends told her mom quite a story last night."

"Oh God, the kids." Settlers were *never* supposed to let themselves or the OOGPs they dealt with be observed. It was the number one rule, the one we all learned from the first second we started drawing zombies when we were kids. Heck, it was why a lot of little Settlers were homeschooled. If you couldn't get your power to summon Unsettled under control, you didn't leave the house. SA was *that* serious about making sure our world and our job remained top secret.

"Elder Thomas's nephew is in the same practice with Dr. Sampson and got an earful over the phone this morning. Apparently the doctor is thinking about taking her daughter to a psychiatrist and was looking for some good names."

"Crap." I followed Monica out the door and down the steps, shivering as the cold air cut through my borrowed sweater. It was freezing. Of course it would be freezing on the one day I forgot my coat. That was just my luck lately. "I didn't even think. But surely they didn't see much—we would have noticed if they'd been there the whole time. Wouldn't we?"

"I don't know. Guess we're about to find out." Monica gave Ethan a limp wave as he emerged from the driver's side of his Mini Cooper, then she climbed into the backseat.

I, however, didn't play it nearly as cool. Before I knew what I was doing, I'd hurled myself at him. I buried my face in his chest and sucked his familiar smell deep into my lungs, wishing I never had to move. As soon as I touched Ethan, any doubt that this was the only boy for me vanished. He was home in a way even Mom and Dad weren't, especially right now, and I couldn't believe I'd let myself even *think* about anyone else.

"Hey, it's going to be okay," he whispered, his breath warming my hair. "You and Monica aren't in trouble. I think they just want to talk to you, let you know what they're doing about the kids."

"It's not that, it's just . . . everything." I squeezed him tighter. "But I think Monica and I figured out something important." I briefly filled him in on my and Monica's powwow, but wasn't surprised to see he didn't look totally relieved.

"That's great, but there's still somebody out there—"

"Raising crazy zombies and trying to kill me. Yeah."

"Hey, don't worry. We're going to figure this out."

"Right. And once the DNA test comes back, and SA realizes they've been after the wrong person, it's bound to get easier."

"Exactly. Positive thinking." He kissed the top of my head, and my heart did a tragic modern ballet in my chest. Why did it feel like this was the last time I'd ever be with Ethan like this? That after today, everything was going to change? "Listen, I was going to head to the hospital to check out the ICU, but I can—"

"No, you should go." I reluctantly pulled my cheek from Ethan's sweater. "The less time the Enforcers have to cover up whatever happened, the better. Until I'm cleared for sure, we can't stop trying to figure out what's going on."

"That's what I thought." He cocked his head to the side, contemplating me with that same looking-through-you kind of look Cliff had given me last night. "Is there something else?"

"Um . . . no," I said, squashing the urge to confess where I'd been last night, even though he hadn't asked.

He would eventually, however, and I'd have to be ready with a feasible lie, or the truth, or some sort of hybrid that would keep my conscience quiet while concealing the fact that I kept summoning the same Unsettled dude over and over again. If I hadn't had the sneaking suspicion my growing feelings for Cliff were in some way responsible for keeping him from his eternal rest, I would have just told Ethan the truth. After all, Cliff's appearance might still have something to do with the weird RCs, and Ethan, as one of the only people trying to help me, should know that.

Then why didn't I spill my guts? It wasn't like I owed Cliff anything, and nothing had really happened. Nothing that I felt forced to tell Ethan in order to cleanse my sinful soul or anything like that. And wouldn't it feel good to tell *someone*?

"About last night, I—"

"Tell me in the car. We've got to run. I stopped by your house and grabbed your backpack and coat so that will save a little time. I also stuck a new pay-as-you-go cell in the pocket of your coat. That way I can call you on a secure line." God, he really was the best boyfriend ever. "But we have to hustle to make it to headquarters by six thirty."

"Okay, we'll just talk later then," I said, secretly relieved. My intentions were good, but my resolve was weak. "I don't want to share everything with the Monicster."

"Though she's been pretty helpful so far, hasn't she?" he asked, looking very satisfied with himself.

I smiled and fought the urge to squeeze him again. He's unbearably cute, especially when he gets that cocky little smirk on his face. It makes him look younger for some reason, like the boy I'd first met when I was five and he was eight. Truth be told, I think I'd started crushing on him right then, in a kindergarten, "I want to share my cookies with you" sort of way.

"I'd still share my cookies with you." On impulse I stood on tiptoe, capturing his lips for a real kiss, not some early-morning peck. Immediately, my body felt shot through with electricity and my weary synapses fired to life. Kisses. *So* much better than coffee.

By the time we pulled apart we were both breathing faster. "Weren't they animal crackers? That you'd already eaten the heads off of?"

"I think they were."

He smiled, a mushy smile that took what was left of my breath away. "I'd still eat them, even all wet and spitty at the ends. I love your cookies and I—"

"God, get a room or give me a barf bag," Monica shouted from inside.

Ethan and I smiled, but neither of us was embarrassed. There were just some things people like Monica would never understand, and mushy, cookie-sharing love like ours was one of them. I'd been an idiot to stress out about me and Ethan. Nothing—not my second-base anxiety and certainly not some dead guy—was going to get between us.

Yeah, but being dead or in prison for the rest of your life would probably—

"Let's go." I refused to acknowledge the inner voice of doom. Things were looking up. Monica and I had pretty much locked down a way to prove my innocence, Ethan had a lead, and by this afternoon we'd be that much closer to shutting the real zombie-raiser down and clearing my name. I was going to stay positive, no matter what.

CHAPTER 14

*B*eige was the color of despair. After twenty minutes sitting in a beige chair, staring at a beige table full of Settler Elders—most of them also dressed in beige—I was certain the awful color even had a smell. It was a sad, musty smell, like that of the ancient swimming pool locker room down at the Y, shot through with the sharper, metallic scent of fear.

Or maybe it was the Elders' fear I could smell, and it had nothing to do with beige. Because they were all afraid. I could see it in the tight set of their jaws, in the hands that twisted into fists on top of the table. Just looking at them was enough to terrify me, even if they hadn't just finished telling me and Monica the scariest story I'd ever heard.

"I assume you understand the seriousness of this matter?" Elder Crane asked, his nasal tone grating on my already raw nerves. But then, it was easy to get twitchy when you had just learned one or two screwups on your part could lead to the end of life on earth as we knew it.

Yep. The. End. Like, the BIG end. We'd just been informed that if the Settler world became common knowledge among the human population, Rogue zombies could eventually take over the world. That was what had caused the Settler-Resistant Undead in Europe all

161

those hundreds of years ago and why Settlers had stopped working with human governments and gone underground. Whenever too many humans found out about zombies and the people who attended to them, Settlers started to lose their power over the dead. Before the development of hypnotism and, later, mind-wiping spells fueled by modern technology, there was no way to control the spread of information. Which meant there was no way to stop a zombie plague from destroying a village or, at times, whole cities.

In today's information age, if a YouTube video got into the wrong hands, we could have a global epidemic on our hands in no time. It wouldn't matter if not everyone who saw the thing believed in zombies or Settlers. Even a few hundred believers would be enough to put a serious dent in our magic.

We were like the opposite of Tinkerbell. We needed people *not* to believe in order to maintain our power and keep Rogue zombies from infesting the world like packs of rabid, rotting dogs.

Yet Monica and I had allowed at least three people to see us in action, little people with big mouths who had told the tale of what they'd seen to every grown-up who would listen before SA had finally gotten wind of what had happened and sent out Enforcers to contain the situation. Now they were just praying they'd gotten to everyone and cleared the memory of last night from their minds before the Settlers of the greater Little Rock area began to lose their power and Arkansas was sucked into the grips of a zombie plague.

And it was all our fault.

So much for staying positive.

"Yes, I understand," Monica said. "And I swear I'll do my best to make sure this never happens again."

"Absolutely. I mean, I've always taken the rule seriously, but now . . . yeah," I added, wincing at my stunning lack of coherency. Not that it mattered. None of the ten Elders sitting around the meeting table spared me a glance.

They'd steered clear of any discussion about my possible involvement in the zombie raisings, but their unspoken belief in my guilt hung in the air. It made me wonder why they'd even bothered telling me what they'd told Monica. I guess they thought the news would convince me to change my evil ways and quit raising super zombies with black magic and risking the exposure of the Settler world. After all, not even super-big bad guys want to live in a world populated by violent Rogues.

Rogues weren't the same as black-magically raised corpses, but they were still very bad news. Any Unsettled who was out of their grave long enough could go Rogue. After an hour or two, if they didn't make contact with a Settler, the typical Unsettled lost their power of speech and reason and began venting their frustration with whatever was still bothering them from their human lives by wrecking everything in their path.

Rogues could kill people, destroy the peace, and basically make the world a terrifying, unlivable place if there were no Settlers around to take care of them. Considering nothing could kill RCs, the only way to get rid of them would be some sort of explosive, and as soon as the police or army or whoever took care of one batch, there would be another to take its place. After all, people would keep dying, and those dead people would keep having issues and rising from their graves. Without Settlers, Rogue numbers would get out of control and the world would be plunged into the midst of a zombie epidemic.

I, for one, thought this would be something good for Settlers to know from the get-go. With so much at risk, why did SA feel the consequences of exposure were something to be concealed until there was no choice but to drag people like Monica and me into their secret beige meeting room and scare us half to death *after* we'd screwed up? It made about as much sense as extremely conservative parents not telling their daughters about the consequences of sex until *after* they were already pregnant. Shutting the barn door after the horse was loose, much?

But then, I was beginning to think SA wasn't nearly as smart as they believed themselves to be. Our remaining undiscovered for so long seemed due more to humanity's tendency not to see things they didn't want to see, rather than cleverness on the part of Settlers' Affairs.

"I want to be certain you both understand the facts as they have been presented." Elder Crane stared at us, his watery blue eyes drilling a hole in the air above our heads. He didn't do eye contact, but Elder Thomas did.

Her eyes met mine and I wished I could sink through the floor. If I never saw another accusing glare in my life, I would die a happy girl. I couldn't *wait* for the chance to talk to Kitty about the DNA test and be on my way to being Miss Goody Two-Shoes again. "If our world and our work were to become matters of common knowledge, our power to Settle the dead would fade and eventually disappear completely."

"We would be helpless to prevent the chaos we've described," another Elder added. I thought it was Elder Nevins, but couldn't be sure. I'd only seen the man a couple times. He was from the Little Rock council and usually didn't bother meddling in our small-town affairs.

"We understand, sir," Monica said. "And I think I speak for both of us when I say—"

"I'd be careful of whom I aligned myself with, Miss Parsons." Nevins didn't bother to hide his contempt for me the way the others had. I expected Monica to take the hint, but she didn't.

"I'm always careful, Mr. Bevins." Bevins, not Nevins. I'd been close. "Neither Megan nor I have done anything wrong."

She was either crazy or way more loyal than I'd ever dreamed. Either way, I had to fight the urge to lean over and hug her. The Monicster was standing up for me, and it meant a lot. A whole lot. Ethan hadn't been allowed into the meeting and had headed down to the hospital to continue his investigation, so I would have been completely on my own in hostile territory without her.

"That remains to be—"

"We've simply been responding to hostile Out-of-Grave Phenomenons in the way we've been trained to respond," Monica said, interrupting Elder Crane as though she smart-mouthed Settlers' Affairs council members on a daily basis. "Considering Megan hasn't even passed her third-stage exam yet, I feel our work has been more than adequate and—"

"That's enough, Monica," Elder Thomas said.

"And I think the move to condemn Megan before she's even been tried," Monica pressed on, raising her voice to be heard over the grumbles of the council, "before she and her family have even been made aware of the evidence gathered in the case against her is—"

"The evidence was delivered to Miss Berry's mother yesterday afternoon," Elder Thomas snapped, which succeeded in shutting Monica down rather effectively.

Oh God, not again. My mom had lied to me *again*. My eyes slid closed and my chest did that horrible squeezing thing it did whenever my world turned upside down. At this rate, you'd think it would eventually do a complete three-sixty and be right-side up again.

So far—no such luck.

"But Elder Thomas," I said, ashamed to be confessing my own family couldn't be bothered to be honest with me. "I had no idea. I'd really like to see the evidence for myself, since it is my—"

"It's in your guardian's hands." Elder Thomas stood and the rest of the council began to gather briefcases and purses from the floor. We were all working people here and had to be at school or the office in the next half hour. Life continued and people had places to be, no matter that a girl was dead, or the world might be on the verge of a zombie apocalypse, or my entire life was falling apart. "Whether she decides to share that evidence with the minor in her charge is her concern."

The minor in her charge. Gah!! I hated that phrase.

I hated it even more that grown-ups seemed to randomly decide when to treat teenagers like kids and when to treat them like adults. Why was it okay for them to expect me to hold a full-time job and put my life on the line when weird zombies started attacking Carol, but then turn around and deny me information like I was some stupid infant? It made me furious, and for a split second that rabid lust for revenge surged inside of me once more.

How fabulous would it feel to wipe the smug, condescending, condemning looks from all these people's faces? How vindicating to show them what it felt like to be falsely accused? I could find a way to show them. I could—

166

"Come on, let's get out of here. We still have time for donuts before school if we hurry." Monica grabbed my hand and squeezed before reaching for her own bag. "I don't know about you, but I'm feeling the need for some major French cruller therapy."

"I think éclair therapy is more up my alley," I said, sounding as shaky as I felt.

That was the third time in less than twelve hours that I'd had a passing fantasy about using black magic. First with Cliff, then with Mom, and now with the entire SA council of Elders. It was insane, especially considering I knew very little about the black arts.

Where was the urge coming from?

I mean, I was angry, but I wasn't *that* angry. Black magic was soul-destroying, karmic suicide, and body temperatures induced by casting with wicked intent caused permanent brain damage. Jess and her seizures were living proof of that. Were these losers and their suspicions—which I *knew* would be proven false no matter what evidence Mom was withholding—really worth brain damage?

The logical answer was no, but there was still that . . . temptation, which made me determined to get to the bottom of this ASAP.

Which meant I had to refocus my priorities . . .

"Listen, I'm not going to be able to sell tickets for the fund-raiser at lunch today," I said, hunching inside my coat as I followed Monica out into the parking lot and across the street. "I need to talk to Kitty and find out what my parents have been hiding and—"

"And you'll have better luck snooping around while they're at work." She held out her hand. "Give me the tickets. I'll try to sell them for you. Worse comes to worst, we can put you to work organizing everyone else's schedule and fetching cocoa."

"Worse comes to worst, I'm not there at all. Monica, I have to make proving my innocence my first priority. I might not have time to go ice-skating tonight. You know what I'm saying?"

She stopped at the corner and spun to face me after pushing the button for the crosswalk. "You'll make time. No matter what's going on, you've got to make time for normal life."

"But I—"

"No. Matter. What. Even when it seems stupid. Because the second you let the Settler stuff take over, you're not fully alive anymore."

"I won't be fully alive if I'm in jail, either."

She grabbed my sleeve and pulled me across the street, lecturing the entire way. "We're not normal and we never will be, but we have to hold on to our human lives. Otherwise, the dead will take you over. And once that happens, it becomes easier not to care so much about the living." She didn't say it in so many words, but I read the same temptation I'd been feeling in the glance she threw over her shoulder. I wasn't the only one drawn to the more sinister aspect of our gifts.

The relief that dumped into my veins was the most amazing thing Monica had ever given me, and that was saying something after the past few days. I owed her, big-time, and if she thought ice-skating would keep me from the dark side of the force, I would be there.

"Okay. I'll make time."

"No matter what."

I nodded, and followed her into the dingy donut shop next to the 7-Eleven. It had rank coffee, but the fried dough was to die for. "As long as I still have legs by seven o'clock."

"Eh, you don't need legs to sell cocoa. We can just prop you up behind the table or something." She tossed her hair over her shoulder and I saw the CHS version of Monica Parsons come alive.

There were a lot of other people from our school around and she was getting into character. It was weird that I'd never noticed that about her before. Still, she wasn't treating me like the annoying underclassman with poor fashion sense just yet. Maybe we'd finally crossed some bridge and begun a friendship in the real world . . . or maybe it was the fact that I was wearing her clothes.

"What do you want? I'm buying," she said, as we shuffled closer to the counter.

I didn't know whether to laugh or cry. She was just being so great. "Two chocolate éclairs, please. And thanks. So much. For everything. I really—"

"God, don't. Please." Monica's nose wrinkled like I'd just farted on her leg. "Between the love-fest this morning and your puppy-dog eyes, I'm really going to be sick."

"I like puppy-dog eyes." I turned to see Aaron in line directly behind us with Dana and the twins. "Especially Megan's."

"Cut it out, Aaron," Dana snapped, glaring at me. "This isn't the time to be flirting with the enemy. Have some respect for Tabitha. She's going to be in the hospital for like, ever."

Kimberly and Kate joined in the glare-fest, their eyes puffy, as though they'd been crying all night. Probably mourning the loss of their team's flyer. Their stunts just wouldn't be the same without the little turd on top. But at least Tabitha was still alive. We couldn't say the same for poor Bobbie Jane. Still, thinking about Tabitha being rolled out of the swamp on a stretcher made me want to offer some sort of sympathy. Luckily, Monica opened her mouth first.

"Right, Dana, like the respect you showed last night." Monica turned around and nailed Dana with her best "what kind of oozing sore did you leak out of?" look.

"I don't know what you're talking about."

"You were on the phone looking for fresh cheer meat before the ambulance had even pulled out of Pizza Pie," Monica sneered. "I heard you got that new girl, Nina Alexander, to agree to take Tabitha's spot on the team. Don't even try to deny it."

"We had to! Tabitha was a flyer! We had to find someone else small enough to—"

Dana stopped Kate with a hand on her arm. "Forget about it. We don't have to explain ourselves to the Slut Squad. They don't care about Tabitha anyway—all they care about is winning the right to roll around on the gym floor like cats in heat at halftime this Saturday."

"Dana, that's not true," I said. "Last night was horrible, and I think we should just—"

"Whatever," Kate said.

"No one cares what you think, Berry," her twin snapped.

"I do." Aaron smiled, a sweet grin that was out of place in the sea of scowls.

"Oh, shut up, Aaron." Dana rolled her eyes. "Come on, girls, I've suddenly lost my appetite. Let's leave the calorie binge to those with more experience."

"Later, sweetie," Monica said, her tone oozing saccharine. When she turned back to me, however, her whisper was ripe with venom. "You'd better make sure you're at practice this afternoon. We need to be ready to show the boosters something amazing on Saturday and put an end to the question of who owns halftime once and for all."

"I'll be there," I said, the ghost of my old competitive spirit rearing its head.

No matter what else was happening, or how my mom had tried to make me feel stupid for caring so much about pom squad, I did still care about dancing the rest of the games. Of all the things in my life, dancing was one of the things I treasured the most. At no other time did I feel so happy and normal, and there was no way I was giving that up without a fight.

"You look pissed," Aaron piped up from behind me. "I hope not at me."

"No, not at you. It's just a bunch of stuff." I turned around in time to see Josh Pickle—a senior I'd had a very brief not-quite-thing with last fall before Ethan and I discovered our true and undying love—and his friend Andy getting in line behind Aaron. They were eyeing him with thinly disguised suspicion and ignoring me. Which was more than fine. Josh had greatly exaggerated how far our physical contact went the night of our *one* date and had been on my dead-to-me list for quite some time.

He'd gotten the message and chosen a new lab partner, but that didn't stop him from being way too interested in who was flirting with me. Of course, it could be that he was simply shocked to see Aaron trying to get his game on. Most people assumed Aaron was gay just because he was on the cheerleading squad. I, on the other hand, assumed a guy who would endure severe social stigma in the name of getting his hands under a bunch of girls' skirts when he lifted them into the air was probably pervier than your average bear.

And he seemed to have a thing for me. Could I not catch a break this week?

"Thanks." I smiled, trying to force myself into normal mode.

"Hey, I'm so sorry about last night." His smile faded and one large hand came to rest familiarly on my shoulder. "Really, no matter what Dana says, all of us are totally freaked out that Tabitha is hurt and that other girl died. It's just awful."

"Yeah, it was one of the worst nights of my life."

"I'm just glad you're okay. I heard you were hurt trying to fight the gang or something?"

"Not really." My eyes slid over to Monica, seeking support, but she was busy ordering donuts. "It was more like Monica and I got in the way. We were in the back room when they came out of the kitchen."

"But you didn't get bitten or anything? I heard they were biting people?"

"No, no bites," I said, praying for a subject change.

"Scary," he said. "I wish I'd been there."

"Probably better you weren't." I grabbed the bag Monica shoved in my hands, and moved away from the counter. Aaron came too, not even pretending he was in line for any other reason than to talk to me.

"It's *absolutely* better he wasn't. What were you going to do, Aaron? Beat the cracked-out cult members to death with a spirit stick?" Monica rolled her eyes and stalked across the room toward the door, boots clicking on the faded flower tiles. The bitch was back, as Elton John would say. "I'd better see your ass this afternoon at practice *and* tonight, Megan."

"You will," I called after her, my cheeks growing hot when Josh and Andy snickered over the Monicster's parting remark.

"And you hang out with that girl of your own free will?" Aaron asked, his flat delivery actually making me laugh.

"Um . . . not totally. She's the captain. Her word is law and all that." I shrugged and grabbed some napkins from one of the tables. "Dana's the same way, right?"

"No, she's pretty cool." He nodded, clearly finished with the subject. "But let's not talk about squad stuff. I want to cheer you up. What do you say we go for a ride? Maybe get some real breakfast?"

"Thanks, but I can't. I've got to get to school."

"Aw, come on, you need more than donuts for breakfast," he said as I stared out the window into the bright morning light. Across the street, the sun reflected cheerily off the hood of an annoyingly familiar beige sedan.

Argh! My stupid Settler tail. I'd planned on heading back home eventually, but I needed to lose the shadow first. Making an unexpected detour might do the trick, and I did have an errand that would be more easily accomplished with transportation.

Hmmm . . . did I dare? I mean, Aaron *did* have a car. It would certainly save me a lot of time if I got him to drive me back to the Pleasant Mountain clinic, and the less school I missed, the better. I could always ask Ethan, but he was already busy investigating one hospital this morning and probably wouldn't have time to chauffeur me around until later.

"Where's your car parked?" I asked.

"Around back."

I decided to take that as a sign. "I'm not sure I have time for breakfast, but what about a little drive?" Aaron smiled like he'd won the lottery.

"Sure, where do you need to go?" He held the back door for me as we stepped out into the cold. His restored antique Corvette sat only a few feet away, silently beckoning.

"Pleasant Mountain Family Clinic. It's in west Little Rock, right off—"

"Yeah, I know where it is." Aaron shot me a surprised look. "That's where I go. They're really nice there. I know the nurses pretty well."

"Well enough to sweet talk them out of some medical records?" The words were out of my mouth before I had time to consider their wisdom. Exhaustion was clearly eroding my brain-to-mouth filtering system.

"Medical records?"

"Yeah, my parents have been acting really funny lately and my dad's been going to the doctor way more than normal. It's made me worry, but they won't tell me anything," I said, digging into my donut bag as I spoke. I couldn't look at Aaron and tell this particular fib.

How awful was I, to be pretending my dad might be sick? Pretty awful . . . but that didn't stop me from moving forward with my hastily formed plan. "If I could get my hands on their medical records, I know I'd feel so much better."

"The nurses aren't going to just turn them over to you or me." Aaron paused to lean against the hood of his car. "There are laws against that kind of thing. They could get in big trouble."

"Yeah, you're right." I bit into my éclair, but not even the burst of chocolate could lift my spirits.

"So you can't just go in there and ask for them," he continued. "You're probably going to have to steal them."

"Steal them?" I asked, sounding shocked, as if that hadn't been my plan all along. I *was* fairly shocked, however, that Aaron had come around to the idea so easily all on his own.

"He's your dad." He shrugged and stole the last bite of éclair from between my sticky fingers. "You're worried. I think you deserve to know the truth, even if you have to get a little creative to get it. I'd be happy to take you."

I watched him chew and swallow. "Awesome. Thanks so much, I'm sure you can get back before the last bell rings—"

"Screw the bell, I've got study hall first period. Coach Fisk won't even notice I'm gone. I'd feel bad leaving you down there to find your own way back." He practically jogged around the car to open the door for me. "Besides, you'll need someone to create a diversion while you sneak behind the front desk."

"Really, you'd do that?" I asked, gratitude making me ignore the way his hand lingered on my back as he urged me into the passenger's seat.

"Sure. It'll be easy. The nurses over there love me." Aaron grinned, the look in his eyes making it clear he knew the effect he had on most girls, and women for that matter.

Still, no matter how grateful I was, the boy did nothing for me. Maybe that was why I attracted his attention. People always seem to want what they can't have, just because they can't have it. Like me and the whole normal-life thing. Would I want to be average so badly if I was really just the girl next door?

I didn't know, but at the moment, average still sounded pretty darned wonderful.

CHAPTER 15

There was something wrong with me. Obviously. Something girly within me was broken, or I shouldn't have been able to resist the charms of Aaron Christian Peterson. Female heads turned to stare at him as we drove down the street, and the nurse behind the desk at the clinic had a lust-induced seizure of some kind when he stepped in the door.

She was scurrying around fetching coffee minutes later, as though nothing gave her more pleasure than catering to the blond god's every whim.

Her willingness to abandon her post in the name of caffeinating the hottie didn't give me much time to plan, but the less time I had to think, the better. If I stood around dwelling on what I was about to do, I knew I would chicken out. Therefore, the second Aaron followed the nurse into the break room, I checked to make sure the mom with the sick toddler behind me was distracted; then I vaulted over the desk and dashed toward the rows of files at the back of the room.

We were early enough that there weren't any other nurses or doctors milling about, but that wouldn't be the case for long. I knew that they started scheduling appointments at eight fifteen. I had maybe ten minutes before doctors and patients started pouring in and Frisky the desk nurse returned to her post.

Luckily, Pleasant Mountain had a nice and organized filing system. Despite the confusing explosions of numbers on the side of each chart, the patient records were in good ol' alphabetical order. I found the Berrys easily, and Mom and Dad's folders soon after.

I had the main compartment of my backpack open and the files halfway inside when footsteps sounded to my right.

"What are you doing?"

Crap! Think fast, Berry!

"Excuse me? Did you hear me?" The voice was female, but I didn't turn around to see if it was Nurse Frisky or someone else.

Instead, I moaned as if in pain, hunching over my backpack as I shoved the files in and tugged the zipper closed. "Oh . . . oh, no."

"Are you okay?" she asked, the anger fading from her tone. "How did you get back here?"

"I was looking for the bathroom," I groaned, amazed at how quickly the lie came into my weary brain. Maybe I'd have to go without sleep more often. It made me think faster on my feet. "I think I'm going to be sick."

More groaning ensued and the nurse—not Frisky as it turned out, but a shorter, rounder woman wearing that perfume older ladies like that really did make my head explode and my stomach cramp—took my arm and guided me through a little door at the side of the room and back toward the bathroom in the lobby.

"Here you go. Come check in with me at the desk . . . when you're done." She slammed the door, not any more interested in watching a stranger vomit than the average person. You'd expect more from a nurse, but I wasn't going to complain.

Sagging with relief, I kept up my moaning for a second or two before turning on the water. Hopefully that would cover the sound of my *not* retching. Now I just had to kill a few minutes, find Aaron, and sneak out the front door. The hard part was over, but I was still pretty freaked. I had *stolen* something. It was a first if you didn't count the time I filled my pockets with cookies from a salad bar when I was seven.

My hands were shaking as I dampened a paper towel and pressed it to the back of my neck. Some thief I was. My heart raced and I'd broken out in a cold sweat. I faced down rabid Undead with less angst. But then, Settling was in my blood—criminal activity clearly was not.

Which was further evidenced when a soft knock at the door made me scream. "Megan? Are you okay?"

Thank God. It was only Aaron. "Um, yeah. I'm good, I'll be out in a second."

"Yeah, a second would be good. Or maybe less?"

Taking the not-so-subtle hint, I shut off the water, grabbed my backpack, and stuck my head out of the door. "We're good to go? No one's watching the front door?"

"The nurse who caught you just went into the break room."

"How did you know she caught me?"

"The entire office knows. You sounded like you were dying of Ebola or something." He grinned before casting a quick look over his shoulder at the empty hall. "You got the files?"

"Yeah, just barely."

"You had a chance to look at them?"

"No, not yet, I just put them in my backpack for—"

"Good, let's go." He grabbed my hand, pulling me toward the exit. The mom with the sickly little boy was still the only one in the waiting room, and she didn't spare us a second glance as we scurried to the door.

Aaron waited until we were nearly to his car before beginning to laugh. "God, I thought you were toast."

"Me too." I joined him in a slightly hysterical giggle.

"Quick thinking on the barf attack," he said, opening the car door for me. I started to sit down, but Aaron leveraged his body in front of mine, stepping so close I scrambled back until my butt hit the door behind me. Nice guy or not, the dude really needed to work on the concept of personal space.

"Thanks, I—"

One hand gripped the door next to my shoulder, blocking any escape from the square foot of space he'd trapped me into. "But I hope your stomach recovers fast. I'd still like to take you to breakfast."

I struggled to maintain eye contact as his face moved uncomfortably closer. He'd been really helpful. I didn't want to let him know he borderline creeped me out. "We should probably get back to school."

"We've got time. Come on, I'm starving." His other hand landed possessively on my hip, touching me in a way no one but Ethan had ever done, sending shivers of apprehension up my spine that knotted at the base of my neck. This wasn't feeling friendly or casual anymore, but what could I really do?

I couldn't just shove him away after he'd gone out of his way to help me.

"But what if someone sees us skipping class?"

"No one will see us." Closer and closer, until his strange not-Ethan smell invaded my nose. He smelled like too much cologne and some sort of spicy soap. I didn't like his smell. Not the least little bit. "I know this little place downtown by the river. Tiny diner. Only businesspeople go there. We won't see anyone we know."

I sucked in a breath and fought the urge to engage in self-defense moves. "Please, Aaron. I just need to get back to school."

He sighed. "Okay, fine, I'll take you back to school. Just get in the car."

"Um . . ." God, now I didn't want to get in the car. Crazy or not, I suddenly didn't believe that he intended to take me back to Carol. "Maybe I should just catch the bus and you can go grab yourself some breakfast."

"That's ridiculous. I wouldn't think of it." He smiled and stepped even closer.

Now every inch of us was in far-too-close-for-my-comfort contact. Some feminine instinct within me screamed at me to knee the bastard between the legs, but I fought to keep my cool.

"Come on, let's go," he said, grabbing my backpack and pulling it away, even when I made it clear I didn't want to hand it over.

"Hey, listen—"

"Hurry, or we're going to be late." He yanked the backpack away from me and threw it into the backseat before grabbing me by the arm.

I was getting ready to tell him to get his paws off of me—screw worrying about over-reacting—when a hand clamped down on Aaron's shoulder and tugged. "Hey, what the—"

"Get away from her." It was the first time I'd seen Cliff in the glaring light of early morning, but he didn't look any more dead than he had before.

In fact, he looked more alive than ever. His cheeks were flushed with anger and somewhere he'd found a heavy orange and brown sweatshirt and corduroy pants that fit him well enough to show the buff physique beneath his clothes. His greenish-brown eyes practically glowed with purpose behind his glasses, and a muscle jumped in his jaw. He was a man on a mission, and if I'd been Aaron, I would have been freaked to be on the receiving end of a look like that even if Cliff was a full six inches shorter.

"Um, okay . . . and you are?" Aaron laughed uncomfortably, like Cliff was the crazy one and he hadn't been going all high-pressure touchy-feely on me a few seconds ago. But thankfully, he moved away a bit. "I'm Aaron, Megan's friend from school."

"I don't care who you are." Cliff said, and glared at the hand Aaron held toward him, then reached out and took my hand, pulling me over to stand beside him. "Get out of here. Now."

"What the—Megan, do you know this guy?" Aaron asked, casting a concerned look my way. "Do you really want me to leave?"

"Yeah, Cliff is my . . . cousin. He can give me a ride home." I tried to smile, but I was starting to shake all over again. The contrast between how safe I felt with my hand in Cliff's and how anxious I'd been a second ago was messing with my head.

"Okay." He paused, his brow wrinkling as he gave Cliff another subtle once-over. "As long as you're going to be okay?"

"Yeah, I'll be fine. Thanks for all your help," I said, praying he would just leave already.

Aaron completely freaked me out. One second I was sure he was a creep, and the next he had me wondering if I was the one who was insane. Maybe I simply had issues. After all, I'd had these panicky moments with my own boyfriend, someone I loved and was definitely attracted to. Maybe *I* was the freak, and nothing weird had been going on at all.

"All right. Well . . . take care." Aaron smiled before walking around to the driver's side. "And let me know how things go with your dad."

"I will." It was only after his car had disappeared that I realized I was clenching Cliff's hand in a death grip. "Sorry, I didn't realize—"

"Don't worry about it. Are you okay?" He gripped my fingers when I tried to let go and brought his other hand to my face. It was another inappropriate touch from a guy who wasn't my boyfriend, but Cliff's touch didn't make me afraid. It only made me want to touch him more. *Need* to touch him more.

"Not really." Before I consciously decided to close the distance between us, I'd pulled Cliff into a hug. But once his arms were wrapped around me, I stopped thinking about whether holding him was smart. The wave of dizziness came, but underneath was the buzzing, wonderful feeling of being right where I was supposed to be. "Glad you were here."

"I had a feeling you'd come back after last night, so I waited around. Sorry I ran off. I just knew things would go seriously awry if the cops found out I didn't have a pulse."

"It's okay. You were right to run." I'd been angry last night, but Cliff was one hundred percent right. He couldn't let people know what he really was. What I'd learned this morning at the SA meeting made me even more sure of that.

He hugged me tighter. "What were you doing with that guy, B?"

"He was giving me a ride, and he knew some nurses here." I sniffed and buried my nose in Cliff's neck. He smelled so much better than Aaron, smoky like a campfire and other warm, safe things. "He was helping me."

"It sure didn't look like he was 'helping.' That dude's got some seriously disturbing personal energy." Cliff's hands smoothed in comforting circles on my back. "Seeing him touch you made me want to cut his hands off."

I pulled back to look Cliff in the face. "So it *was* creepy?"

"Are you crazy? Of course it was creepy." His hand cupped my face again as he gave me that see-straight-through-you look. "You've got to trust yourself, trust your instincts."

"But maybe he didn't mean to make me uncomfortable. Maybe I wasn't making it clear that I—"

"You were backing away from him like he had the plague." Cliff glared at me and his fingers dug a little into my hair. But this time, the firm touch didn't make me afraid. At least not afraid of Cliff. The fact that I could be thinking more-than-friendly thoughts about him again after vowing never to do so only a few hours ago was another matter entirely. "Why the heck did he think it was okay to keep pushing you? He knows you have a boyfriend, right?"

I didn't say a word, just stared into Cliff's face, now only a few inches away from mine. It didn't take long for him to get the message. He flushed a deeper shade of pink and stepped away, shoving his hands into his pockets. If I needed any confirmation that Cliff's feelings weren't purely platonic, I had it.

Holy crap. How did this happen? How did I manage to get an Unsettled crushing on me? More importantly, how did I let a part of myself start crushing right back on him?

I was an awful girlfriend, an unprofessional Settler, and as soon as I got my life back on track, I had to get Cliff back in his grave. Maybe, once I'd figured out what was in those medical records, I—

"Oh no! The medical records. I left them in my backpack."

"And your backpack is . . . "

"In Aaron's car," I said, kicking at the ground. "He took it and threw it in the backseat."

"Well then, let's go get it." Cliff grabbed my hand, but then thought better of it and let me go. Thankfully the awkward pause only lasted a second. "We can head up to your school and break into his car."

"Or I could just ask him to let me in, Mr. Delinquent."

"Fine," he said, though it was clear he didn't like the idea of me exchanging two words with Aaron. "You can ask him to let you in and I'll hide out somewhere close to make sure he behaves himself. Then we can look over the records on the way downtown."

"Downtown?" I asked, following him toward the bus stop.

"Yeah, we need to take a walk by the river. I've . . . realized a few things, and there's something I want to show you."

I sighed. "Cliff, I have to go to school."

"You're not at school now."

"But I will be, and if I hurry I won't miss more than first period, so maybe the principal won't call my parents. Besides, I've told you, I can't keep Settling you. There are rules about this type of thing, and I have other responsibilities to—"

"What responsibilities? You haven't had another Unsettled since I showed up by your boyfriend's car that night," Cliff said, looking as frustrated as I felt.

He was right, though I hadn't really thought about how weird that was until just now. "How do you know that?"

"I've been keeping an eye on you, Megan. I haven't made any secret of that, so don't look at me like I'm some kind of psycho stalker."

"Oh, right. Wouldn't want to do that." I rolled my eyes, angry, though I couldn't say at exactly who, or what. Cliff was frustrating, yes, but he wasn't a bad guy, and he'd done nothing but help me. Still, I was just sick of my life being so crazy, sick of things I couldn't explain, and Cliff was a big one of those things.

"What's that supposed to mean?"

"Nothing."

"No, it's obviously not nothing." He stopped a few feet away from the awning that covered the bus stop and turned to face me. "Listen, you can try to push me away, but I'm not going anywhere. I'm supposed to be here, and I'm supposed to help you. There's a reason you haven't had any other Unsettled and I'm it."

"You are?"

"There's something I know, something you need to know that—"

"What? What do you know? Just tell me!"

"I will," he shouted back. "Just come with me and I—"

"I don't have time for field trips. I need answers."

"I'm giving you answers! What about those records? You never would have thought to take them without me."

"And I still don't know if whatever is in them will help me or not," I said, gaining momentum. "All I know is that my life was going okay before you and those other weird zombies showed up. And now a girl is dead and I'm in the biggest trouble I've ever been in and nothing is—"

"What? You think I have something to do—"

"Maybe. It's an awful big coincidence, isn't it? I mean, how do I know I can believe anything you say?" The hurt in his eyes made me cringe, but I couldn't seem to stop myself. "So just leave me alone. I don't need—" My new cell buzzed in the pocket of my coat, making me jump. I fished it out and flipped it open. "Hello?"

"Megan, it's Ethan, where are you?"

"I'm in Little Rock, but I'm on my way back to Carol, what's up?" I asked nervously, turning my back on Cliff. I couldn't look at him, not and hope to conceal my guilty conscience from Ethan. Even over the phone he would be able to tell something was up if I wasn't careful.

"I think I've got a lead, and if we hurry we can check it out and get you back at school before lunch. Stay where you are and I'll come pick you up."

I gave him directions to the McDonald's down the street from the Pleasant Mountain clinic and hung up, not bothering to ask what his lead might be. It had to be something good or he wouldn't advocate skipping more class. The Enforcement selection board looked closely at school attendance records and conduct reports when they were interviewing new recruits. They didn't want anyone who couldn't handle real life infiltrating their ranks, and I knew Ethan wanted me in those ranks with him someday.

Speaking of handling real life, was lashing out at one of the few people trying to help me just because he was a freak of Undead nature and filled me with confusing feelings really "handling" anything?

I turned slowly around. "Listen, Cliff, I . . . " My words faded away. Cliff was gone, which made me way sadder than I wanted to admit.

CHAPTER 16

"I'm pretty sure I wasn't supposed to tell you, but—"

"That's seriously messed up," Ethan said as we swung through the drive-through at Micky D's fifteen minutes later. I hated to admit that Aaron was right, but I did need more than donuts for breakfast. "So the Elders have always known what causes SRUs?"

"Guess it's something they've passed down through the ages or something, and why SA stopped working with human governments back in the Dark Ages," I confirmed. "But they don't tell the little Settlers about it unless they screw up like Monica and I did last night."

"Don't they think we should all know the possible consequences of being observed *before* we unleash a zombie epidemic?" Ethan asked, proving we were soul mates. And then, proving it yet again, he leaned out the window and ordered me a sausage, egg, and cheese biscuit with no egg. We'd only eaten breakfast together a few times, but he remembered my hatred of egg and egg products.

"That's what I said. They're crazy, but this proves we're not dealing with SRUs. They would be acting like Rogues, not zombies raised to attack a certain person. So there has to be some other reason these things are so hard to get rid of."

He grunted his agreement; then we both fell silent as he paid for and collected our sandwiches.

"So you really think you were followed?" I asked, keeping my voice to a whisper just in case there were Enforcer operatives lurking behind the plastic Ronald McDonald or the trash can where Ethan paused to throw away the bag that our sandwiches came in.

I was really getting paranoid, but I couldn't seem to help myself. Between our phones being bugged and my mom withholding evidence, I had reason to be suspicious.

"Barker pulled into the parking lot of the hospital just as I was pulling out. I had glasses on, but my car is pretty distinctive."

I started in on my sandwich but found myself unable to swallow the food I'd chewed until Ethan pulled out of the parking lot. "Yeah, you should invest in a windowless white van if we're going to keep with the lurking and sneaking."

"Not a bad idea." He gunned it through the red light ahead and turned east on Highway 11, heading out to less populated areas. "I could think of a few things a windowless van would be good for." He wiggled his eyebrows at me.

"Right." I smiled and tried to laugh, but it came out as more of wheeze. Thankfully, Ethan was too busy finishing his own breakfast and checking all the mirrors to make sure we weren't being followed to notice my minor malfunction.

"So what did you find out?"

"A lot, but . . . there's something else you need to hear first."

"Okay? This is a bad something?" I asked, wadding up the last few uneaten bites of my sandwich in its paper, suddenly losing what was left of my appetite.

"I called Kitty," he said, making a swift right and then a left, presumably to ditch a tail if we'd acquired one. I hadn't seen my SA spies since I'd snuck out the back of the donut shop, but he was probably right to be careful. "About the DNA test for you and your mom."

"Ethan! I should have been the one to do that. I wanted to—"

"I was just trying to help. I knew you probably hadn't had time to call, and I thought the sooner they got started the sooner you'd be able to breathe easy, you know?"

"But I'm not going to be able to breathe easy?" I asked, heart clenching in my chest.

He sighed. "She wouldn't tell me anything except that there wasn't going to be a DNA test because a DNA test was impossible."

"What?" I barely resisted the urge to hit something. "That doesn't make any sense! They're just being pigheaded, stupid—"

"Maybe not. I called Monica after I hung up with Kitty and told her to go back and look through that list of blood types she was researching last night. I don't remember for sure, but I think some of those can cause mutations in DNA."

"Mutations that would make DNA tests impossible?"

"Maybe."

"But I thought Monica said these blood types could only be detected with fresh blood and only with Settler tests," I said, the pieces of the puzzle not adding up in my mind. "If my DNA is gimped up, wouldn't a normal medical test be able to detect—"

"I'm not sure," Ethan said, a little too fast for my liking. If I didn't know better, I'd have thought he was hiding something. "Let's wait and see what Monica finds out. She's going to call me back as soon as she gets a chance to look through her notes."

I looked out the car window and wondered briefly where he was taking me. We'd turned off the old highway and were moving further west than I'd ever been before.

"Okay," I said, feeling the tight rope of hope I'd been walking on snap and send me plummeting into the mouths of the alligators beneath. There wasn't going to be a DNA test, which meant I probably only had a few more hours before Kitty got that blood test back and came to arrest me.

It was looking like I hadn't just been a jerk to tell Cliff to get lost, I'd been an idiot as well. What if he really had information that could help? I had to think of a way to mend the rift between us, and it was past time for me to tell Ethan about my Undead friend.

"Listen, we're going to figure this out. I think I'm getting somewhere with the rest of the investigation. You're not going to believe what I found at the hospital," Ethan said, a note of forced optimism in his voice that I appreciated even if I didn't completely buy it. "I'm not sure *I* believe it, and I saw it all myself."

"I don't know—I'm feeling very open-minded these days. A lot of strange things have been happening." There, I'd given myself a good lead-in to a confession about my recurrent zombie. Now I just had to gather the last of my courage and spill my guts.

"Not this strange. I never even imagined something like this." His jaw clenched as he turned right onto a small country road I'd never been down before.

The way his jaw jumped reminded me of Cliff. I wondered where he'd gone, and what he'd had to tell me. If he took my last words to heart, I'd probably never know. It made me want to punch myself repeatedly in my big, stupid mouth, and not just because what he knew might help clear my name. I would just . . . miss him. Even sitting next to my boyfriend feeling guilty for keeping my "other guy" a secret, I got sniffly when I thought of never seeing Cliff again.

What a hot sloppy angsty mess I was becoming. I really needed to chill out.

"I tracked down a lab coat when I got to the ICU so I could roam around. At first I didn't find much, until I got to where they keep the people who are on life support—coma victims mostly."

"Coma victims?" I asked, not missing the significance he gave the words.

"Yep." Ethan pulled onto a gravel road that led to a barren field that looked like it would be planted with soybeans come spring. He parked the car behind a clutch of leafless trees that formed a barrier between the field and the road, before turning to face me. "I wanted to wait until we were somewhere secure to tell you this." I gazed around the field. Pretty much the middle of nowhere. If anyone were to try and spy on us, we'd see them coming for about a mile. Ethan swept some hair out of his eyes. "I—I think I found the zombies who attacked you last night. They were patients from the ICU, coma patients."

"But zombies are dead, Ethan," I said, his words banishing all thoughts of spilling the Cliff beans. At least for the moment. "That's the whole—"

"I know, it sounds crazy, but the nurses were changing the bandages on their feet when I got there. There were three, maybe four whose feet were cut and bruised." He leaned closer, his excitement clear. "How could that have happened if they weren't out of their beds?"

"Maybe they were out of their beds, but that doesn't mean they were transformed into bloodthirsty freaks," I said, the very idea of living zombies scaring the crap out of me. "The zoo is right next door to the hospital, right? Maybe they just stepped out to take in the new baby elephant. Did you know the zoo has a new baby elephant?"

"Megan."

"It's supposed to be really cute. We should go see it. Once it gets warmer."

"Megan, what's wrong? This is really important," he said, grabbing my shoulder and giving it a little shake. "You need to listen to me. This could be the break we've been waiting for."

"How? Just because some people who were in a coma suddenly woke up and—"

"But that's it, they didn't wake up. At least, they weren't awake this morning. They were all unconscious, every last one." His hand smoothed down my arm, and his fingers interlocked with mine, offering silent support I wished I didn't need. "Which makes it pretty hard to explain how one of the girls ended up with a broken nose and a dude managed to shatter his kneecap."

"Oh God." I closed my eyes, replaying the fight from the night before in my mind and not liking what I saw.

"The theory floating around is that some psycho came in and roughed them up in their beds. Everyone seems to be ignoring the fact that several of the patients have scraped and bruised knuckles. Like they weren't just lying in bed taking abuse—they were dishing out a little of their own."

Crap. What were the chances that this was just a horrible coincidence, and that these people had sustained the same exact injuries I'd inflicted on what I thought were the Undead in some perfectly reasonable way? Or that they'd hurt their hands running into the brick walls outside the hospital or trying to smash the glass keeping them from the precious baby elephant over at the zoo?

Better question, do you really have time for this level of denial?

"So you're saying I beat the crap out of *living* people?" I asked. "Very sick, comatose living people?"

"You didn't know. Besides, they weren't acting like defenseless sick people. You and Monica did what you had to do to keep anyone else from being hurt or killed."

"Still, I—Shit!" I brought my fist down hard on the seat beside me. "I should have realized. The pajamas, the lack of dead smell, it all made sense. I can't believe I—"

"Hey, it's not your fault," Ethan said, grabbing my fist when I made to hit the dashboard. He held my hands captive. "Whoever used those people to attack you is the one to blame. They're sending seriously sick people to do their dirty work."

I swallowed hard, wishing I'd skipped the breakfast sandwich that was now threatening to make a second appearance. "What about the blood? Did they find blood on the patients? Like, on their pajamas or . . . in their mouths?"

I rolled down the window and took a deep breath of cold, crisp winter air.

"Not that I know of. Everything had been pretty well cleaned up. I'm guessing by Enforcement." Ethan cracked his window too, letting in a nice, nausea-killing draft. "There was no trace of blood or mud or anything else on the people's clothes. The clothes they were wearing last night were probably destroyed, but they couldn't get rid of the injuries themselves."

"What about the nurses? Could any of them tell you what happened?"

"No one could remember anything. Smythe did a thorough job." His scowl made it clear what he thought of stealing people's memories. There was a time I would have agreed with him, but if what the Elders had said was true and we risked a zombie apocalypse if anyone found out about our world . . .

Let's just say it put my usually fierce belief in human rights in a slightly different perspective. I mean, what good were rights if we were all afraid to go out of our homes lest we be attacked by the Undead?

But then, wasn't that saying it was okay for Settlers' Affairs or the government or whoever to do whatever they wanted to the people under their control in the name of "protecting" them? There were always things to be afraid of—that didn't mean I wanted Smythe or anyone else to have the power to steal my past, to corrupt my memories, to make me think . . .

Oh no . . . they wouldn't. Would they?

"Ethan." I turned to face him, a horrible suspicion growing in my mind. "What if the Enforcers did something to me? What if they made me forget something I did? So now I can't remember it, but I'm really guilty and that's why they all—"

"That's ridiculous. You would never do something like this," Ethan said, his faith in me as strong as ever. "Why would you? You don't want to hurt anyone, especially yourself. What possible motive could you have?"

"I know, but then why is everyone so sure I summoned these people from their hospital beds? And why is my own mother keeping the truth from me?" I filled him in on the weirdness between Mom and me the night before and the blood-type stuff Monica and I had figured out this morning. "My blood and the blood they found on the coma victims must match and—"

"You've got your answer right there. They only think you did it because the blood matches and you've got a super-rare blood type. That means there has to be somebody else out there with the same weird blood you've got. And believe me, I'm going to do everything possible to find out who it is. I've already put a few things in motion so . . . don't worry."

"A few things?" He was definitely hiding something. "What kind of things?"

"I don't want to worry you if it's nothing. Besides, if you don't know what I'm up to, you can't be held responsible," he said, a hard look in his eyes I'd never seen before.

"Ethan, I don't want you doing anything illegal to—"

"I'm going to do what I think is right, whether that's kosher with SA or not."

"Now you sound like a criminal. You're supposed to be with Protocol," I said, scared by the change in my rule-loving boyfriend.

"I'm not a criminal, I just—" He broke off, choosing his words carefully. "Everything that's happened lately . . . It's made me think more Settlers should start considering what's best for the people we're trying to help instead of just trusting that SA has everything under control."

"Because I'm a freak of nature?" I turned to look at the silent field with its barren rows of unplanted earth. God, I wished it wasn't winter and everything didn't feel so . . . dead.

"It's not just you, and it's not just Carol." His fingers brushed my

195

chin, urging my eyes back to his. "There's been an increase in Rogue and Reanimated Corpse activity across the entire country. The world is changing and we've got to change with it. The people working black magic certainly are."

"What does that mean?"

"I've just noticed some things, that's all. Things that don't make sense."

"What sort of—"

"I promise, once I have something concrete, you'll be the first to know." He put his arm around me and pulled me closer to his side of the car. "But that's totally weird about your mom. I wouldn't have thought she'd do something like that."

"Yeah, I know," I said, allowing the change of subject. I was sick of people hiding things from me, but I was also sick of fighting. Besides, I knew Ethan well enough by now to know he wasn't going to budge. If he'd decided he wasn't ready to spill whatever beans he was holding, no amount of pleading, whining, or threat of violence on my part was going to make a difference.

"I mean, she's always seemed so cool."

"I guess." I wrapped my arms around Ethan and buried my face in his chest. I didn't want to think about Mom or her weirdness right now. I didn't want to think about anything except Ethan and how good it felt to be close to him.

I guess he was feeling the same way, because when I lifted my face his lips were waiting right there in the perfect position. Just like it had that day in the hospital parking lot, our kiss went from sweet to steamy in under six seconds. My skin was immediately alive with the amazingness of his lips, his touch, his smell—everything that meant

Ethan when he was this close. Perfectly close.

We angled our heads, our kiss growing even hotter. Before I really thought about what was happening, he was pushing my coat off my shoulders and I was doing the same. Then we were back together, smushed as close as two people could get.

Or maybe not *quite* as close as two people could get—there were ways to get closer.

Ethan's fingers were a little cold as they slid beneath my sweater, but that wasn't what pulled me out of the happy kiss haze. For some reason, the feel of his bare hands on my bare skin made me think of Aaron, of how awful it had felt to have him touch me. Then I started thinking about how annoyed Ethan had been when I'd pulled away that day at the hospital and how I couldn't pull away now or he'd get annoyed again.

He was my boyfriend, for God's sake, and we'd been going out for practically forever in nineteen-year-old-boy time. How much longer would he wait for me if I kept freaking out every time he tried to take the natural next step in our relationship?

But then, should I really do something just because I didn't want Ethan to freak? Shouldn't he be patient and understanding about having a younger girlfriend? Even if she was technically not *that* young and more than old enough to be rounding the bases?

I mean, how many girls my age did I know who were already on the Pill? A lot. And I didn't judge them. I wasn't super conservative, and I didn't have any morally compelling reason not to pounce Ethan. I didn't plan on waiting until marriage. I loved Ethan, and I knew he loved and respected me too. So what the *heck* was my problem?

"You feel so good," he mumbled against my lips.

"You too." It wasn't quite a lie, but it wasn't quite the truth either. He *did* feel good, but *I* didn't. I was approaching seriously crazy head space at a rate not healthy for a teenage girl. But what could I do? How could I gracefully put an end to something that was quickly growing way more intense than any make-out session we'd ever had?

As I inwardly stressed, we continued to kiss like the world was coming to an end and Ethan's hand inched higher. And higher. And then even higher, until, for the first time in my entire life, a boy was touching me there. The old pink training bra I'd borrowed from Monica this morning because her real bras were too big for my wee chest was still on and all that, but still! Touching. *There*. Sort of cupping and brushing and obviously thinking about sliding under the lightly padded lace and taking this to a whole other level.

It was supposed to be great, if my mom's romance novels were to believed, so I tried to let the greatness happen. But after a second or two I couldn't deny that I just wasn't feeling the mind-numbing passion, or whatever it was, I was supposed to be feeling. It was definitely interesting, tingly, wonderful in its way, but there was something wrong. I was too distracted, too knotted up in my head to relax into what was going on with my body.

And maybe I would always be that way. Maybe I would always be the weird girl who freaked out when her boyfriends tried to get to second base, and I would die alone and childless—because it's a known fact that baby making involves much touching and running of bases—but I couldn't worry about that right now. Just like I couldn't make myself go somewhere I wasn't ready to go just because I thought I should.

"Stop," I said, gently pushing at Ethan's arm.

"Megan, I—"

"Please, stop." I pushed a little harder, but he still didn't move his hand, which made my heart beat even faster and a sour taste rise in my mouth. He wasn't Aaron. I shouldn't be feeling so anxious, but I couldn't help it. I wanted my space, and I wanted it now.

"I have stopped," he said, hand still firmly in place. "I just want—"

"Get your hands off of me!" I yelled, losing my cool. I shoved Ethan's now–eagerly departing hand away and backed against the car door—my heart racing, feeling angry with Ethan and myself and Aaron for getting me started down this spaz-attack path.

"Fine," he said, his expression a crushing mix of shock and hurt and irritation. "Just say something next time, will you?"

"I *did* say something."

Ethan sighed. "Yeah, you did, but not until—"

"Not until what?"

"Never mind." He started the car with sharp, abrupt movements that left no doubt he was angry. "Where am I taking you? Back to school?"

"Home. I need to find the paperwork my mom is hiding, and she should be leaving for work right about now."

"Home it is," he said, pulling back onto the road and turning the car toward my house. "Though you know your parents are going to get a call from the office if you skip this much school."

You didn't seem too worried about that a second ago, I thought. Aloud I said, "Hopefully it won't take me too long and I can be back to school by lunch hour. But now that we're pretty sure whoever is sicking these zombies on me is using the living, I can't waste anymore time. I don't want to risk hurting innocent people while I'm trying to keep them from hurting innocent people."

"You're right. I'll follow up on a few other things while you're busy at your house," he said, his words perfectly nice but his tone telling me there had been serious damage done.

"Okay. Thanks."

"No problem. Anything to help." We both spent the rest of the ride in silence. I was trying not to cry, and I guess Ethan was just mad. He kind of looked mad. Or maybe he was trying not to cry too. I shouldn't be sexist and assume he was too tough to cry just because he was a boy.

After all, if a wretched girlfriend like me couldn't bring a guy to tears, what could?

CHAPTER 17

The good thing about leading a double life is that there are times when you're just too busy to stress out.

By the time I ransacked our house thankfully finding the file without too much trouble, raced back to school just in time to join the seniors returning from lunch, finished class, changed into my dance clothes and practiced for an hour and a half, and showered and changed into the ice-skating clothes I'd snagged from the house during my ransacking earlier, I had managed to *not* think about my dire situation for six whole hours.

Or at least not think about it that much. The coma zombies, my weird blood, the psycho who was trying to kill or frame me, and the chance I could go to jail forever for a crime I didn't commit were never too far from my mind.

The unread paperwork from my house was like a lead weight in my purse dragging me down to the bottom of an ocean of psychosis. I was jittery and paranoid all day long, torn between the urge to wait for a semi-private moment to read the file and just ripping the darn thing open in the girls' bathroom in between classes and putting an end to the horrible suspense.

In the end, I decided I would have to break down and read the thing in public as soon as I got the chance. I didn't have any more time to waste. On my way out of practice, I noticed that my normal beige SA tail had been replaced by a sleek black SUV with tinted windows exactly like the one Kitty drove. It followed me at a discreet distance as I jogged the five blocks over to where we were holding the sweetheart skate. The SUV turned off a few streets before the gravel road leading to the pond, but I wasn't fooled.

I expected to be snatched off the street and taken into SA custody any second. In fact, when that skin-prickling "watched" feeling started up again seconds after I'd grabbed a spot on the bleachers and begun to tug on my skates, my first thought was that it was Kitty and that I should get ready to run if I wasn't prepared to rot in a jail cell.

I peeked through the hair falling around my face, scanning the edge of the pond, but there wasn't a sign of Kitty or anyone from Settlers' Affairs. Finally, I spotted the source of the prickles—a zombie lurking in the woods on the other side.

It was Cliff. Even concealed by the winter wonderland of twinkling lights strung in the trees, I could tell it was him, but I didn't make any move to acknowledge his presence, no matter how thrilled I was to see him. I couldn't risk him being spotted by my Settler tail. Just the fact that he was here, still lurking, watching out for me, was a great sign.

Besides, I had a feeling he would be losing it big-time if he were forced to sit next to me while I laced my skates and Aaron tried his best to look up my skirt.

"Those are really cool skates," Aaron said, eyes still glued to my hemline. The boy had deliberately chosen the seat two below mine and wasn't overly subtle in his attempts to get a peek under my red and white kilt.

"Thanks. They're vintage from the eighties." I couldn't freak on him. I still needed my backpack with my parents' medical records inside and should have known better than to wear a skirt to ice-skate in anyway.

But I'd been trying to follow Monica's advice and at least pretend I still cared about normal things. And in my normal life I wouldn't have been able to resist the lure of my kilt with the matching red sweater. With a white turtleneck and heavy knee-high socks, the outfit was warm enough to wear without a coat and looked great with my mom's red ice skates. I looked fairly cute for a girl on the verge of a breakdown, and I was certain I'd snag a few couples' skates before the night was through.

Heck, I already had one buyer, whether I liked it or not.

"You're going to save me at least one song, right?" Aaron finally lifted his eyes as I finished with my laces and pressed my knees tightly together.

"Won't Dana kill you?" I smiled, doing my best to be friendly, though I really wanted to tell him to give me my backpack and scram. "I mean, you're the only boy for sale. I'm sure you'll be in demand."

And I was sure he would be. Girls were already roaming around, shooting Aaron "yummy, I want" looks even though it would be at least thirty minutes until the DJ arrived to start spinning the tracks for our little soiree. Hopefully Aaron would find one or two who enjoyed his inappropriate touchy-feelyness and they would all live happily ever after, making certain he never touched *me* again.

But for now, I gritted my teeth and tried to smile when his hand landed on my knee. "I don't care what she says. It's just one skate."

"Okay, sure. Sounds good." I vaulted to a standing position before his fingers could creep any closer to the hem of my skirt. "But until then I'd love to look at those records. You said you brought my bag?"

"Yeah, I looked all over school for you this afternoon but couldn't find you anywhere. Guess you were hiding from me, huh?" he asked, with a weird giggle.

"Nope, just busy." I smiled, determined not to give Aaron the "you are a creepy stalker leave me alone" talk until after I retrieved my backpack. "But you have it now?"

"I've got it in my car. You want to take a walk with me to the parking lot?"

Did I want to take a walk? Hello? Skates? I gave my feet a pointed look. "Um, walking might be difficult."

"Oh, right," he said. "I could give you a piggyback ride."

"Don't think that would be a good idea in a skirt."

"Well, you could just put your shoes back on." He sounded weirdly frustrated, which made me shuffle a few extra inches away, closer to where I'd left my purse.

"Or you could just go get the backpack," I said, plucking my purse from the bench.

Aaron smiled, but I didn't miss the vein bulging at the side of his forehead. "Right. I guess I'll do that."

"Okay." I stared at him for a few awkward seconds, waiting for him to go, before pulling out the paperwork I'd snatched from my mom's lingerie drawer. The medical files weren't the only reading material on my list, and it was past time for me to get educated about my own case. "Um . . . all right . . . I'm just going to take a little practice skate and work on some reading for the classes I missed this morning."

"Reading and skating at the same time?"

"What can I say? I'm a multitasker," I called out over my shoulder as I eased out onto the frozen pond, grateful to leave Aaron behind me. His crushy weirdness was the last thing I needed right now.

The ice was still a little rough, but the machine London's dad had brought to condition the surface really made a difference. It was almost like skating at the indoor rink in Little Rock, but ten times as beautiful. There was a dusting of snow falling, and delicate white lights hung in the trees surrounding the skating area. Over to the right, the place where we used to build snowmen when we were kids had been transformed into a mini carnival. There were three tents selling yummy-smelling food and two fire-pit things for roasting marshmallows. Everything had come together perfectly, including the attendance.

Thirty minutes to go time, and there were already a few people on the ice and more trickling in from the parking lot. The advance couple skate sales predicted a large influx of boy-type people in the next two hours. By the end of the night, we were going to make the booster club some serious cash. *And* we'd know who won the fund-raising competition.

Unfortunately, I sensed I wasn't going to give a crap about any of that once I finished my required reading. It wasn't just a lack of time and privacy that made me put off reading the paperwork. A part of me didn't *want* to know what my parents had been keeping from me. I had a horrible feeling that what was inside this bland-looking beige folder was going to change my life. Forever. And not in a good way.

So it was no surprise when I felt like I was going to throw up or pass out or both as I flipped open the folder and started to read.

The first page of the report was a brief and relatively unsurprising summary of what I'd been charged with. But the second page—instead of diving straight into the evidence and blood samples and all that as I'd expected—contained a three-paragraph report detailing the findings of a paternity inquest.

"Idiopathic infertility, causation unidentified," I said aloud, focusing on transforming the clinical words under my dad's name into something my addled brain could digest.

Infertility, duh, I knew what that meant—can't make babies. I wasn't so clear on the definition of "idiopathic," but it probably didn't matter. The message here was clear. My dad couldn't have kids, he had "never fathered a child."

Never fathered a child.

My throat closed up and my entire body went numb, and I knew I had to get off the ice before I wiped out. Thankfully, my spot on the bleachers was free with Aaron nowhere to be seen. As soon as I caught an opening in the crowd, I darted over.

Struggling to take a deep breath, I snapped the folder shut, squeezing it closed until my fingers turned white, as if I could trap the horrible things I'd read inside. But it was already too late. The truth was squirming around in my brain, like some horrible worm set on devouring my happy past.

Dad wasn't *my* dad. I didn't get my athletic ability from him, I couldn't really have his thumb, and I wasn't one-fourth Italian. Or if I was, it wasn't from his genes.

Somewhere out there was another man, a complete stranger, who was the other half of me. But how could that have happened? Mom and Dad were married for years before I was born. Had mom gone to a sperm bank or something when they learned Dad couldn't have kids?

"Yeah, right," I mumbled.

I had messed-up supernatural blood. What were the chances I was the product of a sperm bank? Not good. The most likely story was that my mom had *cheated* on my dad. She'd gone and banged another guy and gotten knocked up while they were still living in California. Knowing my mom—how much she loved my dad and how important honesty had always been to her—it seemed psychotic to even think of her as a cheater, but it would explain so much, especially if . . .

I forced myself to open the folder again and turn past the report proving my father wasn't my father. On the very next page, things got interesting. The Enforcers had ordered a blood analysis, comparing the blood they had on file for me at SA headquarters with blood found on the hospital beds of patients at University Medical Center's intensive care unit. The blood type—AB negative—was identical, as I'd suspected. But it also said that both samples had tested positive for the same rare virus, ensuring a nearly one hundred percent probability that they had come from the same person. From there it hadn't taken SA long to decide who was to blame. After all, they already knew a Settler with AB negative blood who had the virus. Me.

The third page in the file contained the results of an amnio done on my mom while she was pregnant, an amnio that gave all the details about the virus the unborn baby was infected with and recommended termination of the fetus. Termination of *me*. Guess I knew what Mom's big "mistake" was now. *I* was the mistake.

I sucked in a deep breath as everything I'd just read swam around in my brain. It wasn't a rare blood *type* that I had at all, it was a virus. A freaking *disease*!

"WB retrovirus. Type two." I mumbled the words aloud as I scrolled through the description contained in the amnio results.

The Type II part was apparently significant because it was present only in women, not men, where Type I could be carried by either a male or female. So my mom's argument—quoted in the last page, right there in black and white—that my bio father, who also had the virus, might be responsible for the attacks was discounted.

My *bio* father. I had a bio father, and he was apparently enough of an evil bastard that my mom would suspect him of attacking me with living zombies. And, according to the file, he'd given me a virus just by being my stupid bio father. A virus that had altered my DNA, making me some kind of super-powerful freak. It had also released potentially harmful metallic elements into my blood, making me "predisposed to violent psychotic breaks involving the use of forbidden magics."

My cheeks flamed even as the rest of me grew cold. Kitty and the Elders and God only knew who else knew about this. They knew that the man I'd always loved like a father wasn't my dad, and that I was really the spawn of some evil maniac *and* had a crazy-making virus.

Of course, just reading about psychotic breaks was enough to make me *certain* I was having one. Because I was just *that* crazy. Here I'd thought I was just a little high-strung, but now I knew I was a breakdown waiting to happen. I was a freak, a virus-ridden freak whose parents had lied to her her entire life. It made me feel like I was suffocating. Dad couldn't *not* be my dad. I loved him so much, and I'd assumed he loved me.

But what if he didn't? What if he secretly hated me for being someone else's kid? A psychopath's kid? A diseased psychopath's unholy offspring—

"Megan, I couldn't find the backpack. I think I left it in my locker at school like an idiot. You want to come with me to grab it?" God! Not Aaron again. Couldn't he take a freaking hint? "Hey . . . are you okay?"

I shoved the file back in my purse as fast as I could, keeping my face down. "Fine, I'm fine." I didn't want anyone to see me crying, especially not Aaron. His idea of comfort would no doubt involve his hands in places I didn't want, and I just couldn't deal with that right now. I'd probably punch him in the nose because that was what people on the verge of a psychotic break did.

"You don't sound fine. Are you crying?"

"No, I just . . . I think it's something I ate." I swiped at my cheeks and slung my purse over my shoulder. I had to get away from Aaron. Now. "Or maybe something I didn't eat. I didn't have time to grab anything after practice. I think I should go hit the tents before we get started."

"I'll come with you," he said, following me onto the ice in his street shoes.

"I'd really rather be alone right now, but thanks."

"Come on, let me buy you a funnel cake. We can eat it in my car."

"No thanks, I—"

"I bet you'll feel better if you sit in a warm car for a few minutes." He reached for my arm, but I managed to slip away before he could catch my elbow.

"No," I snapped, skating faster toward the tents, not sure where I was going to go when I reached the edge of the ice, just knowing I had to get away from Aaron. What was *with* this guy?

"What about some hot chocolate?" He caught me this time, his infuriating paws closing around my waist.

"Aaron, leave me— Ah!" My one hundred and eighty–degree turn to face Aaron turned into a three hundred and sixty–degree spin into a major fall. I hit the ice chin-first with a very unladylike "oomph." Though I doubted anyone noticed my grunt, considering my skirt was suddenly up around my armpits.

I scrambled to right myself, but between the slippery ice and Aaron's efforts to "help" me up, I couldn't seem to get my kilt back down where it was supposed to be.

"Omg! Granny panties, much?" The high-pitched voice was met by giggles. I looked up to see Nina, the new flyer for the cheerleaders, doing her best to earn her gold scrunchie of evil. Kimberly, Kate, Lee, and a couple other cheer-witches stood next to her, laughing, quickly drawing attention to our side of the pond.

By the time I got to my feet and pulled my skirt down, half the student body of CHS had seen my "granny panties." And they *were* grannyish. I hadn't had time to do laundry in nearly two weeks and was down to my comfy briefs, which were big on fabric and extremely low on sex appeal.

Like it would have been any better wearing a black thong? The voice of reason was so dead-on. There was no "right" underwear to be wearing in a situation like this. Just like there was no "right" response to the laughter floating toward me from what felt like *every* direction.

Still, I was pretty sure running from the ice in tears wasn't the coolest choice I could have made, especially since I tripped again at the edge of the lake and nearly bit the dust a second time. I was halfway to busting my face in the frozen dirt when two hands grabbed me and set me back on my feet.

"Come on, this way."

I clung to the hand Cliff slipped into mine and followed him through the woods, away from the sound of Aaron's voice calling my name, not even caring that I shouldn't. No matter how strange it was to feel more comforted by the hand of a dead boy than by that of an alive one, there was no denying I'd rather be here in the woods hiding with Cliff than with Aaron. I was just lucky he still wanted to be around me.

"I'm sorry," I whispered, sniffing as we found an isolated place under the trees, far from the crashing sound of Aaron pursuing me through the fallen leaves in the opposite direction. "I'm really sorry I said those mean things earlier."

"Don't worry about it. I'm sorry too . . . about your dad. I should have told you this morning," he said, finding a sheltered place behind one of the larger trees. "Last night, after I left the clinic, I had a vision, the biggest vision yet, really. I knew what you were going to read in that file—I even saw you fall down on the ice. I should have told you instead of letting you find out while you were alone."

"No, it's okay." I sniffed again and swiped the last of the tears from my face. "I don't think there is a good way to find out my dad isn't my dad." Oh crap, shouldn't have gone there. I was going to start crying again, and after I'd just gotten myself relatively cleaned up.

Cliff pulled me in for one of those hard, loving hugs like my grandmother always gave. My maternal grandmother, who was still my *real* grandmother. God, I hadn't even thought about all my dad's family not being my real family anymore. This just kept getting worse and worse.

"Of course he's still your dad—genes don't change that," Cliff said, hugging me even tighter. "That other dude is just a sperm donor."

"But I have a virus," I said, my voice cracking.

Cliff laughed. "You make it sound like a death sentence. From what I've seen, that virus only makes you stronger than other Settlers. Which is not necessarily a bad thing."

"It's also supposed to make me break psychotically."

"Nothing could make you break psychotically. You're too tough." Cliff pulled back to look me in the eyes.

He was short enough that the action put our noses a few inches apart and our lips only a little further away than that. I knew I shouldn't have been thinking about his lips, but I couldn't seem to help myself. As powerfully as Aaron skeeved me out, and as much as what I felt for Ethan scared me with its intensity, Cliff put me at ease just as powerfully. He made me feel safe and weirdly relaxed, a little dizzy, and more than a little . . . curious.

"Did you hear me, Megan Berry?" he asked, his words a warm whisper that caressed my parted lips. "You're strong and smart and you can handle anything that comes your way. You've got to handle it, because—"

I shut him up by pressing my lips to his. I hadn't consciously decided to kiss him, but I just couldn't deal with hearing about what I *had* to handle. I didn't feel like I could handle anything right now— not my family, or my boyfriend, or Settling, or even getting up the courage to go back out on the ice and face the people who had seen my underwear.

And I certainly couldn't handle learning that Cliff was a way better kisser than I'd imagined.

He didn't hesitate for a second, simply cupped my face in his warm hands and pulled me closer, like he'd known exactly how he wanted to kiss me for a long time. His lips were confident, but at the same time unbelievably gentle. Cliff didn't make me feel pressured—he made me feel alive and warm and wonderful.

Dizziness spun through my head, and that giddy, low-blood-sugar feeling descended with a vengeance, but I didn't care. I didn't care about anything but—

"Megan?"

Oh God, no. It couldn't be. But there wasn't much chance I was mistaken. We'd only been going out for few months, but I would have known that voice anywhere.

CHAPTER 18

I read in a book one time that a woman's voice was "dripping with pain." I remember thinking it was a weird way to describe a sound. But now I understood. When Ethan said my name, I could feel his pain dripping all over me, like some sort of horrible acid that burned my skin and made my heart feel like it was going to explode.

I jumped away from Cliff, but it was too late. The shock and hurt on Ethan's face left no doubt he'd seen what I'd been up to.

"Ethan, I—"

"Don't. Just don't," he said, swallowing so hard I could see his Adam's apple bob up and down.

"Please, don't go," I called after him. "I'm sorry, I never meant—"

"I don't care what you meant." He stopped and spun around, glaring at me with what looked like tears in his eyes. "This isn't going to work. I won't let you treat me like some sort of rapist while you mess around with another guy behind my back."

"I wasn't messing around, I swear," I hiccupped, tears streaming down my face. This couldn't be happening! I couldn't have ruined everything with the boy I loved with one stupid kiss. What had I done? "It was just one time."

"One time is enough," he whispered. "I'm done."

"Ethan, I—"

"I don't want to see you anymore."

"Ethan!" I tried to follow him as he stormed away, but I was so dizzy that I would have tripped over my skates and fallen if Cliff hadn't caught me a second time.

This time, however, his touch didn't make me feel better. It just reminded me what a horrible person I was. It suddenly hit me that I was just like my mom—a cheater. A lying, filthy cheater too stupid to think about how many lives I could screw up with just one kiss.

"I'm sorry, I just . . . ." I pulled away and buried my face in my hands. I couldn't stand to look at him right now. It wasn't his fault, but that didn't make it any easier. "I'm awful. I can't believe I—"

"You just got some horrible news. You weren't yourself," he said. "Once you talk to Ethan and let him know about your dad, he'll understand this was an accident. A reaction to stress or a moment of insanity or—"

"But it wasn't," I whispered, using my sleeve to clean up my face. Gross, but better messy sleeve than messy nose. "I wanted to kiss you."

Cliff was silent for a second. "No, you didn't. Not really."

"No . . . I think I—"

"No. You didn't." Cliff's voice was way firmer than anything I'd ever heard from him before. "This is my fault. I should have told you."

"Should have told me what?"

He sighed and shoved his glasses back up his nose. "I haven't been coming to see you because I need Settling or even because I want to help. I mean, I *do* want to help, but that's not . . . It's just . . . Man, this is harder than I thought."

"What's harder than you thought?" I asked, knowing I wasn't

going to like what Cliff had to say. God, I was *sick* of everyone hiding things from me! "Tell me!"

"I— I've been feeding on you. I *have* to feed on you or I'll—"

"*Feeding* on me?"

"On your energy. Sort of like a battery?" He blushed bright red, clearly as embarrassed as I was skeeved. "Your power is what's keeping me out of my grave, what's making me strong so I can help you. It's *connecting* us, which might make you feel . . . I mean, it's certainly made me feel . . . Though I think I would have felt that anyway because I just think you're—"

"You've been lying to me." I felt something deep inside me freeze over. "This whole time."

"No! Not at first. I didn't know at first, but then I had that vision last night. More like a visitation really. It was like nothing I've ever—"

"Great. Congratulations." I spun on my skate and headed back toward the ice, needing to be far away from Cliff and the dizziness and guilt and anger he inspired.

"Megan, come back. We have to get down to the river. In my vision, I saw—"

"I don't care," I tossed over my shoulder. "You're a liar!"

Leaves crunched under Cliff's feet as he ran after me. "Not about this. I swear! And I swear I'll tell you everything, I just—" I heard Cliff cry out and turned in time to see his eyelids fluttering and his eyes roll back in his head.

"Cliff?" He groaned as he fell to his knees, clutching at his head. "Are you okay?"

"Run, Megan. Get to the river. You have to get to the river.

They're coming. Tonight. They're—"

"Who's coming?"

"They're not like the others. But if they rise . . . You have to go. Don't let them stop you, don't—" He cried out and fell the rest of the way to the ground, toppling into the fresh snow.

"Cliff?" I squatted down and pressed a hand to his cheek. He was burning up, and when I touched him flinched like he was in pain.

"*Habeo are transit.*"

"What?"

"*Habeo are transit.* It's a spell you have to remember. Hopefully we won't need it but—"

"What the heck? Now you're some sort of magical expert?"

"No, but I've been hearing those words in my head since that day we went for a walk outside your house, and now I know what they mean," he said, the intensity in his eyes scaring me a little. "It's a spell, and it's the way you'll be able to get the one heart you need if—"

"One heart?" The words made me shiver.

"If these zombies rise tonight, you're going to need a heart to put them back in the ground. I'm not sure how you're going to—"

"A heart? Great." I rolled my eyes and backed away. "God, Cliff, that's basically black magic. Messing around with blood and internal organs and stuff? You've got to get a special permit to get anything like that and then drive up to this SA-approved slaughterhouse in Missouri to—"

"Not an animal heart, a human heart."

"Shit." I shook my head, feeling sick just thinking about what he was saying. Human sacrifice. That was black magic—midnight black—even if you got the heart from someone who was already dead. "No freaking way."

"I'm sorry. I should have told you sooner and let you get used to the idea," he said.

"I'm never going to get used to the idea because—" I broke off, something on the wind demanding my attention.

"You've got to—"

"Wait a second." I turned, already praying I wasn't smelling what I thought I was smelling. But it was there, the scent of grave dirt and rotted corpse, mingling with the smell of funnel cakes frying in the food tents.

Zombies. Real zombies—not the coma kind this time—and they were hella close, if the faint groans were any indication.

"I have to go."

"No! You can't fight them!"

"Well, I'm not going to feed them a human heart."

"They're not the zombies you have to worry about!" Cliff yelled after me, but I ignored him, hurrying toward the ice as fast as my clumsy feet would carry me. "You have to get down to the river, by the bridge! There's no time to waste."

I stumbled over a fallen tree and hit the ground, but was up again a second later. Cliff was right, there was no time to waste. Screams suddenly sounded from the ice—raw, terrified screams.

"No, Megan. Don't fight them," Cliff called after me.

Sorry, Cliff, but I couldn't leave over a dozen people vulnerable to zombie attack.

I burst onto the ice so fast I nearly fell down again, but managed to regain my balance in time to glide to the left, getting out of the path of a couple of CHS kids who were running screaming from the ice. Behind them, I caught a glimpse of the unholy heck that had broken loose in the past few minutes.

The ice that was once clean and unmarked except for the tracks made by a few eager skaters was already spattered with blood. Two patches of crimson stained the pond, horrific roses blooming larger and larger as the zombies ripped into their victims. They were real zombies this time, dozens of them. Their eyes glowed red, pus dripped from the edges of their mouths, and the stench of rotted flesh filled the air, mingling with the scent of hot dogs, making gorge rise in my throat.

But there was no time for yacking or people were going to die. Again.

Thankfully, my Settlers' Affairs tail was already out of her car and on the job, *pax frater corpus*-ing one of the two zombies who had managed to get its mouth into living flesh. Kitty's tiny hands flashed as she struck the feral corpse with her silver knife and chanted the words that would put it down and keep it down until a Protocol team could come remove the body.

"Megan! Get the other one, while I call for backup!" she screamed as she pulled her cell from her back pocket. I nodded and turned toward the other RC, a part of me elated to see that Kitty still had some faith in me.

Refusing to think about the unique challenges of taking down the Undead on ice, or my epic klutziness, I raced toward the other RC. It was a she, judging by the remnants of her dress, but she'd long ago lost most of her flesh. The face that snapped up to growl at me as I interrupted her feast was skeletal, with only a few leathery flaps of skin clinging to cheek and jaw bones.

"Help me! Help!" The man beneath her screamed and clutched at his right thigh, which already sported a huge hole.

"*Pax frater corpus, potestatum spirituum!*" The momentum from my punch carried me over the RC I'd just whacked in the face and sent me spinning out of control a few feet away—Kristi Yamaguchi I obviously was not, but it got the job done.

By the time I steadied myself, the zombie was sacked out, looking as dead as she truly was. Across the ice, Kitty was off the phone and headed toward another patch of zombies. Hopefully that meant backup wasn't too far away, and Protocol officers would be here soon to snatch both the corpses we'd put down and take them away. I couldn't take the time to dispose of the bodies myself. There wasn't even time to help the man my RC had nearly made a snack of, other than to urge him to apply direct pressure to his wound while he waited for the paramedics before racing away.

There were too many of the Undead for Kitty to handle alone. Dozens already covered the ice, and dozens more poured from the woods, shuffling relentlessly toward the few completely freaked-out living still trying to flee toward the parking lot. The only bright spot was that most of the skaters had escaped, and the cheerleaders and pom squad had also vacated the premises, so there were very few human eyes to observe as I commenced kicking zombie tail.

"*Inmundorum ut eicerent eos et curarent,*" I chanted, continuing the *pax frater* spell as I cut a quick diagonal across the pond, whacking a zombie on my left and a couple on my right as I went.

No matter how disturbing its origins, at the moment I was thankful for my super-Settling power. Any other Settler would have had to speak the entire spell to disable one zombie *and* pierce the

Undead's flesh with something metallic while they were at it, making the process both tedious and dangerous. But all I needed was a snippet of the spell, tightly focused energy, and a moment of forceful physical connection—aka a mean right hook or a well-placed kick—to take out my target.

"*Omnem languorem et omnem infirmitatem!*" I was finishing with a couple of male zombies when I caught a glimpse of Ethan and Monica.

Ethan! He was still here, and in danger. I had to get over and help him, to make sure we had the chance to make up before either one of us died. Not something normal couples had to worry about, but we were far from normal—the past few days had proved that to me in a way even the mess in September hadn't.

He and Monica were standing back-to-back *pax frater*-ing a crowd of Undead who had cornered them on the far end of the ice. There were two or three zombie asses to kick on the way over to their side of the pond, but the largest concentration of RCs seemed to be coming from the woods behind them. Rolling Meadows Cemetery was less than a half a mile on the other side. That had to be where our black artist had raised these corpses.

"Megan! The skate rental! There were kids in there." Monica caught my eye as I moved toward them. She pointed frantically toward the skate-rental tent before turning back to the zombies.

Executing a one-eighty that would have made the Ice Capades proud, I skated back in the direction I'd come. I hated to leave Ethan and Monica, but Kitty was headed their way and there were more SA officials running in from the parking area. They could definitely hold their own, and my unique talents were probably better for fighting in close quarters. I might have the best chance of getting the kids out unharmed.

Just imagining zombies feasting on people too little to even think of defending themselves had my heart racing triple-time as I ran off the ice and awkwardly trotted the few feet to the entrance of the tent.

"Oh shit." The cuss word escaped before I realized I was in the presence of children and should probably watch my language. But then again, these boys and girls were being exposed to something a whole lot worse than my potty mouth.

Three zombies had commanded control of the tent, cornering five kids and Penny—who had volunteered for skate-rental duty to avoid the nerve-racking experience of selling couples' skate tickets. Penny was fending them off with a pair of skates turned around blade-first, but she was well on her way to being overwhelmed. The two older boys were trying to join the fight, but they couldn't have been more than ten or eleven and were no match for the supernatural strength of fully grown zombies.

The only thing that had saved them—or the three little kids cowering beneath the benches where they had been trying on skates before the Undead descended—was that Penny was the one bleeding. RCs were usually raised with a specific target in mind but were easily distracted by the energy emitted by blood, and Penny was providing plenty of that. Crimson streamed down her pale, freckled face from a gouge in her scalp. It didn't look like a zombie bite, so she must have been injured some other way.

Not that it mattered—the zombies would still finish her off if I couldn't get them away from her. Fast.

"Penny, this way! Run to me!" We needed to get the zombies away from the kids, and I needed the zombies out of that crowded corner if I was going to make sure I took care of all three of them before they took care of me.

"Megan!" Penny's wide, frantic eyes darted to mine, relief and terror mingling on her face. "Oh God, please, go get help!"

"Help us," the boy next to her yelled, his words turning into a horrified scream as he barely deflected a lunging zombie with the skate in his hand.

"Mama! Mama!" The little girl under the bench wasn't the only one wailing for her mother, but she was definitely the loudest. She was making so much noise I had to scream to be heard.

"Come on, Penny, run to me!"

"I can't," she moaned, screaming again as the zombie directly in front of her got one hand around her arm and leaned toward her face.

She whacked him with the skate in her other hand, slamming it into his face again and again with a strength I hadn't known she possessed, but it wasn't going to be enough. The others were closing in, and running was no longer an option.

I ran toward them, scrolling through my options as I went. I couldn't work the *exuro* spell and risk burning everyone alive. I wasn't even sure it was safe to invoke the *reverto* command—assuming it might work with so many zombies raised at once—in such close quarters. Penny or one of the kids would definitely get in the path of the spell, and I didn't know what that would do to human flesh.

Allegedly, Settler magic doesn't have much effect upon humans aside from a slight stinging sensation, but my powers weren't of the average Settler variety. I had a freaky virus and had to be careful. I couldn't risk electrocuting the people I was trying to save. The *pax frater* required direct contact with the RC, so I supposed it was my best choice. I'd just have to be sure not to touch anything but the zombies.

Unfortunately, I couldn't really control who touched *me*.

I hadn't made it close enough for the punch I was throwing to connect with the nearest zombie when the little girl wailing for her mother darted from beneath the bench, launching herself at my legs.

"*Pax frater cor—*" I swallowed the spell as fast as I could, sucking my power back inside myself, but it was too late.

One second, pudgy little three- or four-year-old hands were latched onto my thigh; the next, the little girl was screaming. I saw smoke rising from her tiny red palms and reached for her, some part of me instinctively wanting to offer comfort. But she skittered away, crawling across the floor, the look in her wide brown eyes making it clear I was as much a monster as the slobbery rotten things behind me.

The look would have been sufficiently crushing on its own, but a second later it got a whole lot of help from the SA officer at the entrance to the tent.

"You're coming with me, Berry," Smythe said, the anger twisting his features making it clear he thought I'd hurt the little girl on purpose. "I'll be back for you in two minutes."

"Just get the kids out," I yelled, kicking a zombie away from Penny as Smythe gathered the littlest kids from beneath the bench and hustled them out the way he'd come.

"I'll be back," he said, channeling the Terminator in true Smythe fashion.

I turned back to the Undead, determined not to think about this latest injustice, and slammed my fist into the closest zombie. "*Pax frater crrpp*—" This time my words were cut off by a thick hand over my mouth.

If I couldn't speak, I couldn't cast, which meant I was just about as helpless against the freakishly strong Undead as any sixteen-year-old girl. Whether the zombie behind me somehow knew that—doubtful, since it was your average drooly flesh-eater—or it was just dumb luck that its hand had connected with my mouth, I couldn't say.

All I could do was scream and struggle as teeth tore into my shoulder. It was the same shoulder where I already sported a zombie bite scar from when I was ten. Now it just remained to be seen whether I'd live to add another scar to my collection or bleed out right here in the skate tent, taken out by three measly RCs. I'd kicked the tail of at least four times this many at once in the past, but I guess that old saying is true—it only takes one.

White-hot pain, sharp and fierce, cut through my body, shooting through my nerve endings until I was on agony overload. Tears leaked from my eyes and my knees buckled as I fell to the ground, my struggles growing weaker as the zombie's teeth tore deeper into my skin, getting closer to the bone.

Crap, it hurt so bad. Where was Smythe? Hadn't he gotten the three little ones somewhere safe by now? Wasn't he coming back for me? Or was he just going to let me and Penny and the two older boys die, therefore avoiding relocation and taking care of the "Wicked Megan" problem in one fell swoop?

I screamed around the hand over my mouth as the zombie shook its head back and forth like a dog with a hunk of steak. Suddenly

I couldn't think, I couldn't plan—all I could do was feel and pray wordlessly not to feel anymore. The pain had to stop—it just had to. I would do anything to make it stop, anything to—

"Megan, lie down!" It was a male voice. It must have been Smythe, even though it didn't sound like him. "Lie down now or you're going to die! Do it! Lie down!"

I did as I was told, falling flat, bringing the zombie on my shoulder along for the ride. Seconds later the air filled with a whirring sound and bits of flying flesh and bone. I squeezed my eyes closed and held as still as I could, realizing my life was in Smythe's hands. If he didn't pull away in time, whatever they were using to chop the zombie off my shoulder would chop my head off as well.

CHAPTER 19

Strong hands appeared. The zombie on top of me was gone. The whirring sound ground to a halt and some sort of sanding machine fell to the ground beside me.

"Skate sharpener," I groaned, assessing the damage to my shoulder and deciding I would live. "Good call."

"God, Megan, are you okay?" Penny dropped to her knees and clutched at my hand. Tears still stained her face, but the only sniffling was coming from behind me. One of the two boys still in the tent was crying a little, but no one was screaming anymore. Smythe must have taken care of the other two zombies as well.

"Come on, get up, we have to get out of here," the male voice said, but it wasn't Smythe whose face appeared or Smythe's hands that slid under my armpits, hauling me to my feet. It was Aaron, his face splattered with red from where he'd used the skate sharpener to take out the three zombies.

I cried out as pain shot through my shoulder again, but did my best to help him. He was right—we had to get out of here. Or at least *they* had to get out of here. I had to stay and make sure the rest of the RCs were contained.

"You okay? Can you walk?" Aaron asked.

"Yeah, I have to go. I have to find Monica and—"

"No, you have to come with me. The parking lot is full of all these random people and I heard two big guys saying they were coming for you."

Crap. The rest of Settlers' Affairs must have arrived and Smythe must have already told them I was a toddler burner! Now they'd arrest me and I'd never make it down to the river to check out the Super Very Bad Thing Cliff had warned me about.

I peeked out of the entrance to the tent to see Smythe and several Protocol officers battling a clutch of RCs, but it wasn't going well. They seemed . . . weaker than I'd ever seen them before. Their spells weren't packing the same punch and neither were their attacks. Being observed by even the few dozen people who had seen Settlers in action tonight must have taken its toll. It was a chilling thought that brought home just how much there was to lose if I didn't figure out who was really responsible for all these attacks.

"Aaron, we need to get to your car," I said, not relishing the idea of enlisting Aaron's help, but at the moment he was my only available ally. At least, the only one with transportation. "Unobserved by all those people out there if we can make it happen."

"I've got something even better. The cheer van is parked in a clearing on the other side of the pond, and I've got the keys." He grabbed my hand and turned back to Penny. "Here Pen, take the keys to my car. You and the kids get inside and lock the doors."

"But I don't have a license. I don't even have a learner's permit," she said, her pale face growing even paler.

"You don't have to drive—just get the kids in the car and lock the doors."

"But I—"

"Don't worry. The police should be here soon," Aaron said, before she could stress any further. "I heard sirens just a few seconds before I came in here. Go ahead, go." He pushed the keys into her hand and herded her and the kids to the entrance to the tent, where he peeked out to make sure the coast was clear. "Okay, go, run!"

"But what about you guys?"

"Go, Penny, we'll be fine," I said, making shooing motions with my hands.

"Just be careful, Megan. You too, Aaron," she said, then turned and ran for it, the two kids trailing after her as she made a beeline for the parking lot. Thankfully, there were plenty of Settlers controlling the Undead in the direction they were headed.

The entire parking lot was swarming with SA and Protocol officers, and I was betting the siren Aaron had heard was our SA plant on the Carol police force. With something this big, every Settler in Carol would be doing their damnedest not to let real cops on the scene until they had the situation under control. The safety of the world depended on it, and too many people had already seen these OOGPs. We needed to contain the situation and get super busy with a decent cover-up strategy.

Hopefully the Elders would be up to the challenge, though their behavior lately certainly hadn't encouraged a lot of confidence on my part. That was why I had to make sure I got down to the river to handle whatever it was Cliff had seen. I no longer trusted SA as far as I could throw Elder Thomas with a bum shoulder.

"Come on, let's go." I headed out and around the tent before Aaron could reply, making it clear he was along for the ride not the other way around. I wasn't about to tell him about my zombie-slaying qualifications, but it would be best if he got the message I was in charge.

I toddled toward the ice, my skates making land walking far less speedy than I would have liked. Kitty, Monica, and Ethan were still halfway across the pond in the heat of battle, but I couldn't stop to help them. I had to get out of here before Smythe or anyone else could take me into custody.

"God, those freaks are scary," Aaron said as we hurried toward the clearing where he'd said the van was parked. For some reason, though, he didn't sound that scared. Maybe he was just too pigheaded to understand the real threat. He was probably still buying the "cult members on drugs" story the Settler on the police force had spread the previous night. I mean, if he weren't denser than solid rock, he surely would have gotten the hint that I wasn't into him by now, but no such luck. He still insisted on clinging to my hand as we ran.

I followed him down a narrow path and out into the clearing where the big gold and black cheer van was sitting a few feet away from the generators. The thing was enormous and certainly capable of fitting the dozen members of the cheerleading squad plus one dance team guest. So it made me wonder . . . why weren't any of the cheerleaders *in* the van?

"God, Aaron, where were you?" Dana fisted her hands on her hips.

"Yeah, we've been waiting for like, forever," Kate said.

"I got a little tied up in the skate tent, but we're cool. Let's get inside," Aaron said, as sirens sounded in the distance.

"Aaron's right, I think we should get out of here," I said, trying to think of a good excuse to convince the cheerleaders to drive me into Little Rock. "Probably somewhere far away, across the river. Just in case those . . . um . . . cult members come back."

"You mean the zombies?" Lee Chin rolled her eyes before hurrying toward the driver's-side door of the van.

Oh. Crap. They knew the RCs were zombies?

"Stupid zombies," a girl whose name I didn't remember piped up. She was covered in bite marks and sporting a very un-perky expression. "This was a lame idea."

"This is going to make sure we have the time we need." Aaron's hand tightened around my wrist. "Besides, I told you we might get bitten if we worked that one spell. No one said this would be easy."

"No one said you had to raise so many, either, Aaron. You *so* overdid it."

"*You* did this? You— Ah!" My question turned into a scream as Aaron spun me into him and locked his arms around my torso. An explosion of agony ripped through my wounded shoulder as he lifted me and climbed into the back of the van.

"I didn't overdo it," he said. "There are just enough to cause the distraction we need."

"This isn't a distraction," Kimberly whined. "This is a—"

"Just get in the van," Dana said.

Aaron plopped onto one of the padded benches on the right side, forcing me to sit on his lap, while the rest of the squad claimed seats on the bench facing us or in the two rows of front-facing seats at the head of the van. The doors slammed shut and Lee Chin gunned the vehicle to life.

I was about ten seconds away from being kidnapped by a bunch of zombie-raising cheerleaders. God! And to think Ethan and I had *laughed* at the very possibility a few days ago. Even staring them in their perky yet evil faces, it was still hard to swallow.

It was so surreal, in fact, that we were pulling out of the clearing and onto the road before my lips remembered how to form words.

"You've got to let me out," I said, fear settling in as the reality of what was happening struck full force. "I work with those people fighting the zombies. They're going to come looking for me, and you're not going to like what happens to you when they learn what you've done."

Kimberly and Kate, seated directly across from us, snickered.

"I'm serious. You have no idea what you're—"

"We're not scared of Settlers' Affairs. We've got more powerful people on our side," Dana said in this calm, easy voice that made it clear she believed what she was saying. I, for one, was too shocked to form a quick rebuttal.

How did she know about Settlers' Affairs? We were a top-secret organization, for God's sake! We'd operated under the radar for hundreds of years, since the beginning of human civilization. World leaders were still clueless as to our existence, so how in the heck had a bunch of bleached-blond Stepford wannabes gotten the memo? This *so* proved that SA was totally sucking at their job. If they were half as with-it as they thought they were, this never would have happened.

"Listen," I said in my most reasonable tone as Lee Chin pulled down the ramp leading to the highway heading toward Little Rock. A second ago her choice of direction would have thrilled me, but that was before getting *away* from the evil cheerleaders became my new first priority. "I don't know who you've got on your side, but I—"

"Yeah, you do, Megan." Aaron gave me a little squeeze that might have been called affectionate if I weren't his captive and it hadn't disturbed the ravaged skin near my shoulder. "You and Jess used to be BFFs. Or have you forgotten?"

"She certainly hasn't forgotten you," Dana added with a smug grin.

"Jess?" I asked, unable to believe what I was hearing. This couldn't be happening. The Jess nightmare was over, had been for months. "But she's in prison."

"Not for long." I heard the smile in Aaron's voice and was tempted to slam my head back into his nose, but forced myself to hold still. I was only going to have one chance to put up a fight. I had to make sure my timing was right. "We're getting her out tonight."

"If Aaron hasn't screwed everything up," the girl with all the bite marks said.

"Shut up, Felicity." Aaron's arms tightened around me, making me wince. "This was a team effort last time I checked."

"You shut up." Felicity's eyes narrowed in Aaron's direction. "You're the only one who could raise the living ones, and you screwed it up. Twice. Then you had all day to kidnap her, but couldn't get it done, even though you had her in your freaking car this morning."

"We were being followed. I couldn't just—"

"So if we fail, it's going to be all your fault."

"We won't fail," Aaron whispered, his tone cold enough to make me shiver. "We've got Megan and everything is going to be fine."

"But one of the living ones was supposed to bite her, not one of the dead ones. And no one said anything about kidnapping," Felicity argued, while I forced myself to stay quiet and absorb as much of the insanity as I could.

"It's cool," Kimberly said. "She's not going to be around to tell anyone about it."

Well, there went any doubt about whether or not they planned to kill me. This just kept getting better and better.

"But we weren't supposed to have to do this. One of the zombies was supposed to—"

"It's not too late," Aaron said. "Everything will be fine."

"Oh yeah? We're supposed to raise the army at ten and it's already eight. How are—"

"I'll take care of it," Aaron snapped. "I've made plans."

"How? You're not going to be able to make it to a hospital and—"

"Shut up!" Aaron screamed so loud half the girls in the car jumped. "I told you. I've. Made. Plans."

"Aaron will take care of it, Felicity," Dana said, her words seeming to calm the entire van. She was a natural leader, that one. Too bad she had to use her talent for evil.

I still wasn't sure what these freaks were up to, but there was no doubt it was bad news. That part about the "army" rising at ten o'clock sounded especially nasty. Jess had a history of big, violent gestures when it came to wielding her black magic, and it sounded like her time in prison hadn't mellowed her out a bit.

Geez, how had this happened? How had she managed to organize a coven of evil cheerleaders while she was supposed to be rotting behind bars? Settlers' Affairs had some *major* explaining to do.

"He'd better take care of it," Felicity said.

"If I were you, I'd start watching my mouth." Aaron squeezed me so tight I couldn't help but whimper. "Unless you want your ass left on shore tonight."

"You wouldn't dare, you—"

"Stop it," Dana said, raising her voice to be heard. "Lee, take the next exit."

Lee Chin nodded and turned off just after we crossed the bridge. Now we were driving right along the river, which was entirely too much of a coincidence. Whatever the cheerleaders were up to, this must have been what Cliff was trying to warn me about.

"This is not the time to turn on each other," Dana continued. "We're a team, and if we keep acting like one, everything is going to work out just like we planned."

"But it's so hard," Kate whispered. "It wasn't supposed to be this hard."

"Isn't being young and beautiful forever worth a little effort?" Dana asked, barely concealing her frustration. "I mean, we didn't win state last year sitting on our bottoms. We practiced every day and made sacrifices."

The van was quiet for a moment before Lee Chin piped up from the driver's seat. "But no one had to die for us to win state."

Dana's head snapped around to the front. "Fine, Lee, if you want out, pull over."

"I don't want out," Lee said hastily. "It's just that no one said we were going to kill her."

"And you don't have to," I said, seeing what might be my only chance to inject some sanity into this situation. "I know black magic can really mess with your head. Believe me, I understand. But you guys don't have to go through with this. We can stop it all right now.

Let me call SA and we can talk to them, explain what Jess was trying to make you do and—"

"She isn't *making* us do anything. We went looking for her and said we were willing to do whatever it took to work the spell."

"Aaron's right," Dana said. "This was what we all wanted. The vote was unanimous."

"Besides, we knew people were going to die," Aaron said, not bothering to conceal his contempt for the naysayers in the vehicle. "What does it matter if one of the dead people happens to be someone we know? It's not like any of you are friends with Megan."

There was much nodding of heads as this was generally agreed to by everyone in the van. Gah! What assholes they were.

"But what about Tabitha?" I asked. "I'm sure she wasn't supposed to—"

"Tabitha screwed up," Dana said. "She should have vacated the woods as soon as she dropped the zombies. I mean, there are snakes and stuff in the swamp. And those big rats they say aren't rats but totally are. What are those called?"

"Nutria," Nina, the new girl, said. So far she'd been sitting pretty quietly in the corner near the back, and I'd been hoping she might prove to be a bit more sane than the others. No such luck. "They are so gross."

"Totally!" Dana smiled. "Which just proves Nina is a way better choice to be young and beautiful forever. I mean, at least she's smart."

More mutters of agreement and nodding of heads ensued. Nina beamed.

"This is crazy—you all realize that, don't you?" I asked, struggling to keep the hysteria from my tone. "Whatever Jess has told you she can do, it's a lie. She can't make you young and beautiful forever. She's just using you to get to me. She's crazy! You know that, right? She's been after me ever since we were ten years old and—"

"Shut her up, Aaron," Dana said.

"Gladly." Aaron's hand slammed down over my mouth. "Slow down, Lee. I'm getting out in two blocks."

"What?" Felicity asked. "But we're already set up—"

"I told you I've made plans. I've got a special date waiting for Megan and me at the old hospital. I figured if bringing the living Undead to her wasn't working, I'd bring her to the living Undead."

"Awesome!" Dana beamed at Aaron as Lee Chin pulled over to the side of the road. "So you're going to—"

"Take care of Megan's part in this, get the blood of the living Undead after he's bitten her, and then meet you all at the site."

"Are you sure?" Lee asked. "We can wait for you here."

"Yeah, Aaron. You don't want to be late," Dana said. "We can't work the summoning or the youth and beauty incantation without that blood."

"Don't worry." Aaron pulled me to my feet and dragged me toward the back of the van. "It's only a couple of blocks. I'll be there in plenty of time. This is something I think I should do alone. If I get caught, I wouldn't want any of you to go down for murder."

As we dropped to the pavement, I caught looks of complete freaked-outed-ness on the faces of a few of the girls. Crazy or not, there were definitely those who thought this was wrong.

It would have made me hopeful . . . if any of them had stayed behind. Instead, Nina and Felicity slammed the doors shut and the van pulled away, disappearing down the deserted street.

Now it was only Aaron and I, headed toward a very creepy abandoned building that was crumbling into the river a few feet away.

The river. Just like Cliff said. If I'd listened to him, maybe he and I would be nipping this army-of-the-dead thing in the bud, and I wouldn't be locked in a psycho cheerleader's arms on my way to die in a fashion I was sure wasn't going to be fun.

CHAPTER 20

"This used to be a children's hospital. For kids with tuberculosis. They closed it in the fifties," Aaron said, his hand still clamped over my mouth. Guess he didn't want me to interrupt his amateur tour guide routine. "You're not going to believe the view from the roof. It's gorgeous."

He kissed my head, close enough to my ear to make me stumble on the stupid skates I was still wearing. If he tried to take this kissy-kissy crap any further, I was going to puke.

"Come on, let's get a closer look." Aaron dragged me toward the entrance, a great mass of gray stone with sharp angles and vertical lines.

It also made me think of teeth—big, scary teeth pocked with cavities protecting a black hole of a mouth that hadn't been fed in a long time. The building was hungry, and no measly chain-link fence across the doorway was going to keep it from sucking me inside and picking my bones clean. Call me crazy, but it seemed like a good time to fight for my life, *before* Aaron managed to get us inside to meet up with my living Undead "mystery date."

I moaned, then let my entire body go limp, faking a girlish swoon.

"Hey now, we're not there yet." When Aaron bent to adjust his grip, I struck.

Kicking with my feet, I hurled myself at his legs, knocking us both to the ground. My shoulder exploded with pain, but I ignored it and the little black and white spots pricking at the edges of my vision. I rolled over, slamming my good fist into Aaron's stomach as I went.

"Bitch!" He grunted and reached for me, but I kicked him upside the head with my skate, sending him back to the ground with a groan.

My hands shook as I tore at my laces, loosening them just enough to slip the skates off my feet, knowing my trusty weapons would have to go if I was going to have any chance of outdistancing Aaron.

"Megan! Get back here!" Aaron surged back into a seated position—blood dripping down his face—but I was already on my feet and running for it.

If I hadn't been injured, I might have stayed to fight even though Aaron was six inches taller and outweighed me by fifty pounds. Barker and Smythe had taught me ways to take down bigger opponents, but not when I had a throbbing, gaping wound and only limited use of one arm.

So I ran, sprinting down the dark street in my sock feet toward the lights of a liquor store a few blocks away. This area of downtown was all but deserted except for gangs, crack addicts, and bums, and was hardly the place for a sixteen-year-old girl to be walking the streets, but I would have been relieved to see anyone at all. Even getting robbed to support someone's coke habit sounded great compared to death by insane male cheerleader.

"Megan! Come back here!" Aaron roared, obviously not concerned about being overheard. "Come! Back! Here!"

My heart raced even faster and a frightened sound escaped my lips. The boy behind me was crazy. Totally out of his mind. If he caught me, he was going to feed me to a zombie. And it was going to be unthinkably awful, far worse than anything the Undead could ever have done on their own.

Zombies—real zombies or these poor coma victims Aaron had been raising—were only vessels, after all, and couldn't hold a candle to the pure evil of the people who raised them to do their dirty work. A zombie would munch on your flesh, but it wouldn't derive pleasure from watching you suffer.

But Aaron would. I knew that, and it scared me more than any OOGP.

"Help! Help me!" I screamed as I got close to the liquor store. I was quick, but Aaron had longer legs and the speed of the crazy. He was catching up fast. I had to run harder, had to get to the freaking door before—

"No!" I half sobbed, half screamed the word as I finally reached the door and jerked on the handle, only to find it locked and the lit store deserted. It was a Friday night, for God's sake! Why was a liquor store closed at eight o'clock?

Oh God. The locked door from Cliff's vision. I had to get away from this place. Fast.

But I didn't even have time to release the handle, let alone try to run, before Aaron was on me, slamming my body against the glass door.

"Do not run from me! Do you hear me?" he screamed directly into my face, holding me captive with hands fisted in my hair. I winced and gritted my teeth as fresh agony bloomed in my shoulder and now in my scalp. "There isn't time."

"Okay, okay," I whispered, silent tears rolling down my face as I struggled to breathe. I felt like I was going to pass out. If only I'd slept more than a few hours last night, maybe I wouldn't feel so weak—maybe I could have run faster or fought harder and wouldn't feel so trapped and helpless.

"No, it's not okay." Aaron's eyes grew even flatter as he wrapped his hands around my throat, apparently deciding that me having trouble breathing was working for him. It looked like Cliff's vision was coming true, every horrible detail. "But it's going to be okay. We're going to make it okay." Then, he smiled like we were BFFs again.

God, he was crazy. So crazy. I wanted my mom and dad, I wanted Ethan, someone who could take all this bad, scary stuff away.

Why had Ethan and I fought? Why had I kissed another guy when I loved Ethan more than anything? And why did I have to get close to dying to realize it wasn't the physical stuff that had me freaked, but realizing I would fall even harder if Ethan and I took things to the next level? That was what scared me, to think I could need him any more than I already did.

And that was why Cliff was safe. I didn't love Cliff, and by pure virtue of the fact that he was a dead guy bound for the grave, I knew I never would. I wouldn't get the chance, and so Cliff would never get the chance to hurt me.

It all made sense now. If only I could have told Ethan, maybe he would have understood.

"Please." My voice wasn't much more than a whisper, a beaten thing drifting in the bruised cotton of my oxygen-starved mind.

"Just go to sleep," Aaron said.

I tried to resume struggling, but couldn't manage more than a twitch or two, even though my inner voice was screaming that I couldn't let this happen. I couldn't black out. There was a serious chance I wouldn't wake up again. I had to fight . . . had to . . .

"When you wake up everything will be better. I promise."

Aaron bent his head, as if he would kiss me on the lips this time, but everything went dark before I could know for certain. As I lost consciousness, I tried to be thankful for the little things.

• • •

When I woke up, I kept my eyes shut while I did a quick mental check in on my situation to see if it was still Extremely Dire or I'd been downgraded to threat-level Majorly Awful. Unfortunately, Extremely Dire still seemed the rule of the day.

My head hurt like nobody's business, my hands were bound behind my back, and I was very thirsty and very cold. Wherever Aaron had taken me, I was still outside. The cold wind whipping across my chapped lips and the soft prick of snow as it hit my cheeks and melted confirmed that much. My face was numb and stiff and probably in danger of frostbite, but I was alive.

Alive was good. Staying that way, however, would be even better. So I didn't open my eyes right away. Better to try to figure out where Aaron was and what he was up to before I—

"I know you're awake. I saw your eyelids move."

God! I hated this guy. Hated him with the white-hot intensity of a billion Boy Scout campfires. "I bet you were a Boy Scout, weren't you, Aaron? You look like you were a Boy Scout," I croaked as I slowly opened my eyes. It sounded like I'd taken up a pack-a-day smoking habit . . . or nearly been strangled to death. Take your pick.

"Yep, for five years. My dad was scout leader." We were indeed outside—on the roof of the old hospital, if I had to guess—and Aaron was sitting a few feet away, black and red candles burning in a semicircle around him and what looked like a dead body wrapped in a sleeping bag. The living Undead he'd mentioned, I supposed? Some poor coma victim he'd appropriated for his own evil purposes? "One of the perks of being an only child. My parents had a lot of time to devote. If you'd taken the time to do your research, you'd know that."

Okay. He was even crazier than I'd thought. Which was pretty freaking crazy. "My research? Why should I have been *researching* you, Aaron? I thought you were a friend."

"You thought I was a creep," he said, proving he wasn't as oblivious as I'd thought. Nuttier than your average granola bar, yes, but not oblivious. "You'd get this little curl in your lip every time I touched you."

"You had no business touching me."

"You have no business being alive," he snapped. "Not anymore."

"Aaron, please," I said, sensing reasoning with him was futile, but knowing I had to try. Lying on my side with my arms tied behind my back didn't leave me many other options. At least not until I could get my hands free. Slowly I wiggled my fingers, willing the rope to stretch. "You don't want to do this. That person needs to be in the hospital."

"The entire Veterans' Hospital smells like piss. He'll be better off dead." Aaron waved away my concern with a little smile. "And maybe losing a patient will teach the staff a lesson. Getting him out was way too easy. I just walked in, stuck him in a wheelchair, and walked out.

Their security blows. Shows how much we care about the brave men and women who served our country."

Okay, so much for pleading for mystery dude's life. I was going to have to change tactics. "Fine, but you're wasting his life and mine. I swear Jess can't do what she's told you she can do. She can't make you and the rest of the cheerleaders young and beautiful forever. There's no spell capable of—"

"I know she can't. That's just what we told the others to get them to cooperate." Aaron pulled a small bag from behind him and began to unpack bunches of herbs. "Jess needed a coven of thirteen to raise the army. I knew I'd never get Dana or the others to agree to do that just to help Jess, so I thought of something else they'd want and offered them that instead."

"And they just believed you? Didn't they—"

"After they saw how powerful Jess and I are together, they were ready to believe just about anything. Plus, we worked a little spell to show them what they'd look like in twenty-five years." He laughed. "Most of them were so fat it was easy to convince them to sell a little piece of their soul to keep away those pesky middle-aged pounds."

"But Jess has been in prison, *maximum-security* prison. How did you—"

"I can channel her spirit. She can inhabit my body and give me the power I need," he said, this dreamy look on his face that revealed how pleasurable he found this alleged experience, though I'd never known anyone who successfully "channeled" another person, at least not a living person. That was pure legend as far as I knew. "That's how I raised the zombies tonight and the patients from the hospital."

"Aaron, I don't know what you think—"

"That's because you're not asking the right questions," he snapped impatiently. "After seeing you escape the living Undead without a bite on you, I expected more. But I guess you're all brawn and no brain."

"So what should I be asking?"

"What's in it for me?"

"Fine." I sighed, shifting on the cold ground. "What's in it for me?"

"Not you, you idiot. *Me*."

"Oh." Okay, so I was a little slow on the uptake, but I *had* just regained consciousness. "What's—"

"Life. I get to live," Aaron explained as he pounded away at the herbs he'd placed in a small clay bowl. "You've got very special blood, you know. Witch blood, the most powerful blood on earth."

Witch blood. Could that be what the "WB" in "WB virus" stood for? If so, how the heck had Aaron found out I had it when I didn't even know myself?

"I drink the blood of a living Undead who has tasted witch blood and I get to live," he went on. "I'm terminal. Brain tumor. Inoperable."

"Sorry."

"No, you're not."

"No, you're right. I'm not," I said, straining at my bonds until I could barely feel my fingers. I had no idea whether what Aaron said was true, but he believed it, and that was all that mattered.

"That's cool. I'm planning to kill you. So I guess we're even. The spell doesn't actually require your death, just your blood, but I—"

"How did you even learn about this spell? I've never heard of—"

"You've never heard of a lot of things. Didn't even know you were a witch, did you?"

"How can you be sure Jess isn't lying to you too?" I asked, refusing to focus on my cluelessness. "Telling you what you want to hear so you'll help her raise her stupid army or whatever? She lied to me for years. *Years*. And I was supposed to be her best friend."

"Possible." He shrugged. "But I'm kind of out of options. Besides, I doubt she's lying. She didn't need living Undead for her plans. She's been helping me raise them just to heal me, and it's been taking it out of her big-time, the poor thing. She's been in the hospital three times."

Aha! So Jess's seizures weren't from what she'd done last fall, but from much more recent dabbling in the black arts. I should have guessed she was up to something. She was never the type to give up after one measly defeat.

"For a little while we thought she'd be able to donate the witch blood, since she was at the hospital anyway, but the living Undead have to take the blood straight from the source, and there was no one in a coma at the Settler clinic. Besides, her guards never left her alone. The best she could do was slip some of her blood out the window to me when no one was looking."

So *that* was where the blood on the hospital beds had come from. Jess had witch blood. Her mom had been deep into dark magic, and I'd always wondered how Jess had become so powerful in only six years of practicing the black arts. Probably wasn't so hard if you'd inherited the WB virus from your mother. And since Jess was a chick, it would explain why the virus type was the one only present in females.

Finally, real proof that I wasn't the bad guy! Now . . . if I could only live to tell the Enforcers about it. They could get a blood sample from Jess, run the special test, and, bam, they'd have their zombie raiser! I couldn't even fault them for not realizing the truth sooner. After all, why would they run special blood tests on Jess? She was in prison, not considered a threat to anyone, and Monica had said magical blood types were only present in the tiniest portion of the population.

But now they'd know to test that witch, and I could finally put the insanity of the past week behind me. I just had to stall until I figured a way out of here or someone from SA found me. Surely, no matter how incompetent they'd been lately, they would realize I'd fled Carol and come looking. Kitty had told us about tracking spells Enforcers can work if they have the blood or hair of the person they're looking for, and she certainly had plenty of mine on hand.

"So how did you find out about Jess, anyway?" I asked, continuing to struggle with my bonds, encouraged by a slight loosening in the rope around my right wrist. "No one at school knew she worked black magic."

"I was in a support group for terminally ill patients. Jess contacted Elsa, one of the other girls in my group, but things between them . . . didn't work out." Aaron pulled back the sleeping bag to reveal the slack and lifeless-looking face of an older man.

"Contacted?" The news was enough to shock me into stillness for a few precious seconds. "How did she *contact* anyone?"

"I don't know. Elsa didn't tell me how they met, but they kept in touch with notes."

"Notes?" I had become a parrot. A shocked, horrified parrot capable only of repeating the ridiculous things coming out of Aaron's mouth.

"Yeah, little notes like back in elementary school. That's how Jess and I did it too. We'd stick our notes to each other in a hole in an old headstone at Rolling Meadows Cemetery." He smiled. "I saved all of them. I think I'm going to make a scrapbook."

A scrapbook. He was going to make a scrapbook. I doubted they made stickers for a notes-from-a-freak-who-helped-me-bring-about-a-zombie-plague page, but there was no need to dash Aaron's crafty dreams. I had more important things to focus on, like the fact that Settlers' Affairs had *massively* screwed up.

If I made it off this roof alive, I was going to insist on an investigation into the Carol and Little Rock branches of SA by the National High Council. They'd allowed Jess to *sneak notes* out of a *maximum-security prison*. That level of incompetence was ridiculous at best and criminal at worst.

I was no longer certain all the "oversights" lately were simply the product of bumbling, narrow-minded Elders. There might very well be a traitor in our midst. A traitor who had facilitated Jess's evil plans, and who wanted me dead and Arkansas plunged into a state of zombie emergency.

"Jess needed someone with a terminal disease. Only someone close to death is capable of channeling another person's spirit, and that was the only way for Jess to work her magic in the outside world." He smiled. "She was hoping Elsa could help her out. But Elsa died too soon. When you think about it, it *is* pretty amazing that we found each other. There were kids in my support group from all over the state, but Jess and I both grew up in Carol. It made it so much easier to develop a deep, magical connection. We knew all the same people, had a lot of the same friends, same values, even went to the same church before she left town."

"She didn't leave town—she was arrested for crimes against humanity!" I shouted, unable to keep my freak-out under control as Aaron began tracing the runes of reanimation on the unconscious man's face. He was going to raise him like he'd raised the other coma victims and turn him into a bloodthirsty monster with me as the intended meal. I had to keep him talking, had to figure out some way to get out of here. "She's a monster, she's not—"

"Shh! She's inside me now . . . her power, her spirit . . . She can hear you." His eyes got this faraway look that made him even creepier. "No, I know, you're not a monster, you're an angel," he said, allegedly talking . . . to Jess? Who was inside his head somewhere? Maybe chatting it up with all the other voices in that crazy melon of his?

"She's a psychotic freak," I said, half hoping the nutcase was right and Jess *could* hear everything I was saying. "And I'm going to make sure she pays for everything she's done."

Aaron scowled as his eyes refocused on me. "That psychotic freak is going to be my wife if everything tonight works out the way we planned, so I'd appreciate it if—"

"What?! Jess is gay. You know that, right? She prefers *girls*, a girl named Beth, to be specific. So I don't get—"

"People change, and we're in love."

"In love? You're *crazy*, and even if you weren't, you're too young to get married." They were like an episode of *Engaged & Underage: Psycho-Killer Black-Magic Edition*.

Aaron laughed. "Well, you're entitled to your opinion. We weren't planning to invite you to the wedding anyway." He finished with the herbs and stood up. "Listen, I've really enjoyed you, Megan, but we're out of time. I hope you know how much I appreciate this.

And honestly, you should die proud. If you hadn't been so good at your job, one of the other living Undead would have bitten you and we wouldn't be here right now."

The man on the ground stirred and twitched, and a low groan escaped his parted lips.

"Aaron, don't do this. You don't want to murder me, I know you don't."

"I don't have a choice."

"Yes, you do! This isn't—"

"One with witch blood must give blood to the living Undead, and I must drink of the living Undead until death if I'm going to live." Aaron backed away when the man groaned even louder. "That means I'm going to kill this guy after he bites you. If you were free, you wouldn't let me get away with that, would you?"

"Please, please," I begged, scooting backwards until I ran into a wall of brick. The edge of the roof. There was nowhere else to run. Or scoot.

"Sorry, but Jess is pretty excited about you dying a criminal." He paused and tilted his head to the side, as if listening to a voice only he could hear. "She also thinks it would be cool to use your blood on the altar tonight. I told her you're still a virgin, so there's no need to use one of the cheerleaders' blood."

"How would you know what I have or haven't—"

"It's totally obvious, even if I hadn't been spying on you and your boyfriend. You won't even let the poor guy get to second base—there's no way you've headed in for a home run."

Great. Once again, my lack of experience of the nookie variety was biting me in the ass. You'd think I would have learned my lesson the first time I was targeted for my virgin blood and just done it already!

"She really hates you, you know," Aaron continued. "Even after she found out her mom wasn't really dead—"

"What?" Jess's mom wasn't dead? What the freaking heck?

"Don't worry. You don't need to worry about that. Or your dad. That's why I kept those medical records from you. I didn't want you to have to learn what a creep your dad was right before you died. Didn't seem fair." He shook his head sadly. "But you found out anyway, right? At the pond? I didn't figure anything else could make you so upset. Sorry about that."

"Right. I can tell it's really breaking you up inside." Something moved at the edge of my vision, and a spark of hope leapt inside me, but I did my best not to follow the shape with my eyes.

No matter who—or what—it was, there was no way my situation could get any worse. I had to hold on to what little hope I had left and pray someone had come to help me. Maybe one of the cheerleaders had a change of heart. Or maybe Ethan and Monica figured out where I was.

It was a long shot, since no one saw me leave, but man, did I want to see another Settler face right now. If only I'd told one of them about Cliff and his warnings when I had the chance! Then they would have known to look for me somewhere near the river.

Another flash of movement behind Aaron, but this time it was easy not to look. I had eyes only for the living Undead man who was reanimating in earnest, rolling over and pushing to his feet among much groaning and moaning. "I really do feel bad," Aaron said. "I'm probably not going to be able to watch the actual biting part, you know."

What a prince.

The coma victim was up now, lumbering to his feet, shaking his head like a dog getting out of the water. The movement knocked the sock cap off his head, and two long braids fell down around his face, making him look like a deranged Willie Nelson.

Frantically, I pushed myself into a seated position against the bricks behind me. It didn't put me in a much better position for combat, but it did give me a peek at who had joined us on the roof.

It was Cliff! Sweet, wonderful Cliff who was even now creeping up behind my kidnapper. Unfortunately, I wasn't sure he'd made it in time.

Undead Willie lunged for my throat and I screamed a raw yelp that couldn't compete with the feral groans issuing from the man's foaming mouth.

CHAPTER 21

While Cliff tackled Aaron to the ground, the coma dude's cold hand latched onto my shoulder and his mouth strained toward the exposed skin of my neck.

"Get off!" I bent my knees to my chest and then kicked directly into the man's groin. The fact that I was only wearing socks took the edge off the blow, but he still groaned and fell to his knees, giving me a few seconds to reposition myself for the next attack.

Which was coming fast. The longer Willie was reanimated, the faster he moved. Pretty soon, there would be no way for me to hold him off.

"Cliff, help!" I yelled, even though a part of me was as terrified of Cliff as the coma zombie.

The sounds coming from across the rooftop weren't pretty. At All. Aaron was screaming like his fingers were being chomped off one by one—which they very well might have been; the man on top of me was in the way, so I couldn't see what Cliff was up to—and the smell of hot, sickeningly sweet blood filled the air, reminding me Cliff *was* a zombie, no matter how lifelike.

But I didn't have any time to angst out about how Cliff was taking Aaron down; I just needed him to hurry and get it done before Braid Guy opened my jugular.

"Unh!" Willie dove for my ankles, clearly meaning to disable the part of me that had delivered the groin kick.

Living zombies so sucked ass! I mean, at least the dead Undead didn't learn from their mistakes. They were scary and wicked persistent, but, mercifully, as dumb as the dirt they crawled out of.

"Cliff!" I dodged the man's first grab, but the second time his hand lashed out, he caught me around the calf, his fingers digging into my skin with a force that made me cry out.

"Megan, help!" Aaron wailed, his voice cracking as his words turned into another scream of pure agony. "Help me!"

He *had* to be kidding. He was asking *me* to come save his ass? The girl he'd intended to be zombie chow?

It was so ridiculous I started laughing. Really laughing. Giving myself a stitch in my side, losing it even as I kicked and flailed and did my best to keep Willie from digging into my calf like it was something from a KFC bucket. I was laughing so hard tears were streaming down my face by the time the guy actually latched his teeth into my flesh and chomped.

"Ahhh!!" I screamed, a sound so filled with rage I could feel it vibrating through my every cell. That was it! I'd had enough! The walls holding my power fell with an almost audible popping noise, and I cast. "*Reverto!*"

I hadn't had any success disabling living zombies on my own up until this point, but then, I'd never dared cast this way before. As I sent my power sweeping out toward the man chewing my leg, I held nothing back. I hit Willie with everything in me. I used every ounce of my Settler power as well as that curled, sleeping thread of dark energy I'd never dared use before.

I'd always been afraid to call upon that black force, what I now suspected was a legacy of my witch blood, but at the moment, I didn't care. I didn't care who got hurt; I didn't care what karmic price I paid; I just wanted to destroy the thing that threatened me, to make Aaron and this man on top of me disappear. Forever.

No sooner had I recovered from the recoil of the *reveto* spell when the man's mouth went slack and a shudder ran through his body. The smell of burning skin and hair filled the air, mingling with the odor of fresh blood wafting from Aaron and Cliff's side of the roof. Then, slowly, Willie stood and turned back toward the one who had raised him, the one whose blood he had to taste to return to his rest.

Cliff—who had Aaron pinned to the ground—stood up and backed away, swiping at his bloodstained hands as he went.

"Thank God, I—no. No!" Aaron barely had time to get to his feet before Willie fell on him, his open mouth latching around the tear Cliff had made in Aaron's arm.

Braid Dude's jaw muscles clenched and blood gushed down his chin, but it didn't seem to quiet him in the least. In fact, he only grew more frenzied, his fingers clawing at Aaron, knocking him backwards, the pair of them locked in a deadly embrace that ended a few short feet away when Aaron's knees hit the wall surrounding the roof and they began to fall.

"No!" As soon as I realized what was happening, I shoved my back into the wall, pushed myself into a standing position, and ran, but it was too late. By the time I reached the edge, they'd had already smashed onto the pavement below.

"Oh my God." Cliff joined me, leaning over to peer at the broken bodies. Neither of them was moving, and it didn't look like they ever would again. "It happened so fast."

I didn't say anything, just stared down the seven stories to the ground, trying to come to terms with the fact that I was a murderer.

"This isn't your fault," Cliff said, sounding remarkably calm for a guy who had just ripped another person open right in front of me. But at least he pulled back before anyone was seriously hurt, let alone killed.

"No, it is. When I cast, I—I knew what I was doing." I bit my lip and backed away from the edge. "I wanted to make them both disappear and—"

"You were only defending yourself."

I turned to face Cliff, wondering why the trace of blood on his right cheek didn't trouble me the way it usually would. Maybe I was turning into a monster, finally losing touch with whatever it was that made me a normal, freaked-out-by-bloodshed-and-death girl. "That man was innocent, and Aaron was—I could have figured something out . . . I didn't have to kill them."

"You *didn't* kill them. Don't do this to yourself. Aaron was trying to kill *you*. And that poor man looked like he'd been in a coma for a long time. Death was probably a blessing."

"I don't care! I still didn't want to—"

"I know, I know." Cliff brushed my hair out of my face, then turned me around to work on the knots binding my wrists behind my back, his touch as soft and gentle as always.

He'd just gone rabid zombie on a guy five minutes ago, and now he was back to playing the sweet, supportive friend. It was enough to freak me out. As soon as my hands were free, I wasted no time pulling away from him and spinning around.

"Don't look at me like that," he said.

"Like what? Like you're a killer too?"

"I've never killed anyone and neither have you." He sighed and swiped at his hands, wiping away the last of Aaron's blood with a calm that only made my freak out worse.

"But you told me you've been *feeding* on me. How do I know you haven't been chowing down on human flesh when I'm not around?"

"I've been feeding on your *energy*, your magic. Believe me, you've got plenty to spare."

"I do not. I get dizzy when I'm around you."

"I'm sorry, I'll try not to take so much," he said, his look growing harder. "But I'm not going to stop taking what I need to survive, and I'm not going back to my grave. We're at the beginning of something bad, Megan. Something really bad."

"We are, aren't we?" I didn't know exactly what Cliff was talking about, but I'd felt the same way for weeks. There *was* something bad coming, and my gut told me it was something more than Jess and her plans to kill me or raise a zombie army.

"We are. And you need me. That's why I came back after I died, to help you. There are lots of people like me," he said, then quickly added, "Well, not a lot, but more than you'd think."

"How do you know?" I asked. "I thought you didn't know what—"

"I didn't, at first." He glanced down at his feet, having the grace to look embarrassed for withholding information for once. "You know my vision the other night? A woman like me came to me in—"

"Like you?"

"Dead but . . . not," he said, noticeably refusing to use the word *zombie*. "She explained what I am. She told me that when the balance of the world is threatened, seers don't die. We come back to help the living, especially people like you who have the power to help more people than we ever could alone. I believed her, and I need you to believe me."

"I do." And, weirdly enough, I did. Just like my gut told me trouble was coming, it told me Cliff was an ally I needed on my side. Besides, hadn't I more than learned my lesson about ignoring what this boy had to say? "I don't really understand it all, but—"

"It's okay. You don't have to understand. You just have to trust me."

"I do, and I should have listened." I fought the shivers that threatened to overtake me as the horror of the past hour and a half set in. "Thank you for coming. If you hadn't—"

"You saved yourself—all I did was provide a distraction. Besides, if I hadn't messed up, you wouldn't have been here in the first place. It's my fault," he said, pulling me in for a hug I appreciated, even if I *had* experienced a breakthrough about my true feelings for him and Ethan. Just friends or not, Cliff gave good hug. "I should have made you come to the river with me today."

"You're too nice, that's your problem." I pulled away and smiled.

"Probably my fatal flaw." He returned my smile, but his grin only lasted a second. "Maybe everyone's fatal flaw if we don't get down to the water. I saw the place in my vision—it's not far from the bridge, right next to downtown, and there are a *lot* of dead bodies resting there. It's some sort of mass grave from the Civil War."

"Aaron said he and Jess tricked the cheerleaders into forming a coven so they could raise an *army* of zombies. Guess they meant it literally," I said. "I'm guessing they're going to attack downtown, make the Settlers expose what they really are and—"

"Start a zombie apocalypse. I know, I saw it," he said, heading toward the stairs. I followed, being careful not to step in the circle of blood Aaron had drawn. "I also saw that you're the only one who can stop it. You're going to have to use your power. All your power. Like you did up here."

Great. Well, at least he wasn't talking about the heart thing anymore.

"And be ready to use the spell if we absolutely have to. The *habeo are transit* spell will help you get the . . . thing you'll need."

Scratch that, spoke too soon. Or thought too soon, anyway.

I didn't say anything, but there was no way in heck I planned to work spells I didn't know, especially ones involving human organs. I didn't even want to dip my baby toe back into the dark place inside me. Not if there was any other way. That shadowy place was dangerous, to me and everyone else.

The sharp, pungent smell of rot and rodent droppings assaulted my nose as Cliff and I started down the stairs. It was crazy dark in the stairwell—the only light coming from a skylight—but I could still see well enough to pick my way around the debris. Thank God. The last thing I needed was to step on a used needle in my sock feet and contract some sort of human cooties. I had enough to handle with my supernatural virus.

Speaking of my supernatural virus . . .

"Aaron knew about my virus, and my dad," I said as we circled around the fifth-floor landing and kept moving toward the ground. "But I didn't get a name or anything."

"Why do you need a name?" Cliff asked in this overly casual voice. "You don't want to get to know the guy, do you?"

I sighed, not even wanting to ask what Cliff wasn't telling me. "Maybe."

"Really?"

"I don't know." Did I want to get to know my bio dad? I mean, if he was as rotten as my mom had made him out to be, it would probably only make me feel really bad to realize I was related to such a piece of scat. Make me wonder if I had inherited his evil along with his witch blood. But then, there was a part of me that said it was something I *had* to do. "I sort of feel like I should, even if I don't want to."

"Sounds pretty hard."

"Yeah," I agreed. "Maybe we'll all die tonight and I won't have to worry about it."

"Very funny."

"I try." We pushed the door open at the bottom of the stairs and picked our way across the lobby, which was littered with signs of recent human habitation. Guess if you're a homeless person, you don't care about mouse droppings or seriously creepy atmosphere.

We stopped at the chain-link fence and Cliff pulled aside a broken section so I could duck through, while I briefly filled him in on the whole Aaron and Jess connection. "Aaron said he and Jess needed a coven of thirteen. With Aaron . . . gone, they're not going to have enough people."

"I don't know." Cliff slipped through the fence after me, and we shuffled slowly through the pitch-blackness near the entrance to the building. "I'm thinking we should still—"

A shadow detached itself from the side of the building and tackled Cliff before I could move a muscle to help him. Cliff cried out in surprise as he fell to the ground, but he rallied with a swiftness that was scary, going from zero to zombie in less than a second.

With a feral growl he bucked the black-clad figure off his back and flipped her over, pinning the flailing girl beneath him to the ground without any more effort than it took to pin a bug to a board

The girl screamed into Cliff's face—which seemed to have no effect except to annoy the heck out of him, which wasn't a good idea when he was in zombie mode—and let forth a stream of obscenities before finally stringing words together in sentence form. "What the *hell are* you?"

"Wait!" I grabbed Cliff's arm and tugged, recognizing the "you are unworthy of licking my shoe" tone immediately. "It's Monica. She's a Settler, and a friend."

Cliff made a surprised sound in the back of his throat. He still didn't move, but at least he quit with the growling.

"Berry, call this thing off. Now!"

"Let her up, Cliff."

Cliff slowly released Monica's wrists and stood up. "Hey, you attacked *me*. I was just defending myself."

"It talks. Like, really talks." Monica scrambled to her feet and moved out of the shadows, darting freaked looks between me and Cliff. "What have you done, Megan? Did you raise—"

"I didn't raise Cliff. He's a normal Unsettled." Monica's arched eyebrows made it clear what she thought of that explanation. "Okay, so he's not normal. I've tried to Settle him, but he won't—" God, I really didn't want to get into the zombie-psychic-who-is-feeding-off-my-energy-and-bad-things-are-going-to-happen-he-saw-it-in-his-vision stuff, so I chose the simplest explanation. "He's a seer. He saw what was going to happen tonight and he's trying to help me."

"Right." She laughed, a frustrated bark of a sound that revealed the level of her pissed-offedness.

"No, really. He is. He's been helping me all week. We can trust him."

Monica shot a slightly less suspicious look between me and Cliff before sighing in defeat. "Okay, fine. Whatever. We'll talk about how much you suck for keeping secrets later." She still didn't look appeased, but evidently figured we didn't have time to argue. "Where's Aaron? He's the one responsible for—"

"Yeah, I know. He just tried to kill me."

"Shit! Well, where is he? I used a tracking spell to find you, but I didn't—"

"He's . . . gone. He fell off the roof."

"Good," Monica said, though that didn't make me feel any better that I'd accidentally killed people. Even someone crazy and evil with an inoperable brain tumor or someone who'd been in a coma for years. "He was the one who raised all those RCs at the pond. His fingerprints were all over the gravestones."

"SA actually ran fingerprints?"

"No, Ethan did. Luckily, Aaron's were on file from some FBI missing-children-prevention packet or something," Monica said, still inching further away from Cliff, as though he gave her the creeps. "Ethan figured out that Jess had to have an accomplice on the outside and—"

"He knew it was Jess? Why didn't he tell me?" I asked, my voice rising to a pitch that made Cliff wince. "Talk about keeping secrets. I can't—"

"Ethan only figured it out tonight, freak. He noticed that Jess ended up at the SA clinic right after both the weird zombie attacks. He convinced SA to run additional tests on her blood, and they just found out she's AB negative and positive for the same weird blood thing you've got."

"It's a virus, a blood virus."

"So what? Who cares?" She shrugged, somehow making me feel better with her utter lack of compassion. "The good news is that you're cleared. They can't run DNA tests to prove who the blood belonged to, but anyone with a brain will know it was Jess. Ethan is at the hospital and is going to try to get her to confess. She started having seizures again after—"

"Good. Call Ethan and tell him to keep her there. Don't let her out."

"Of course she's not getting out. Even with practically every Settler in the area up in Carol, they didn't leave her unguarded," Monica said. "Which reminds me, we've got to get back up there and help Enforcement get this contained. Tons of people saw us, and everyone's already losing power. It's crazy! We've got to get memories wiped or—"

"No, we've got to get down to the river now," Cliff said, his jaw muscle jumping. "We've got ten, maybe fifteen minutes tops. They're raising them at ten o'clock."

"What the heck is he talking about?" Monica snapped.

"The stuff in Carol was just a diversion," I said, following Cliff as he started across the parking lot. "A distraction while Jess's coven raises an army of zombies to attack downtown. They wanted to make sure Settlers couldn't contain it before tons of people saw the zombies."

"Oh my God," Monica said, her face growing even paler than normal. "So that means—"

"If we don't get moving, there won't be any functioning Settlers left in Arkansas, and we're going to have a plague on our hands." Cliff pointed to the ground as we circled around the building. "They're going to have their thirteen after all."

I turned to look at the spot where Aaron and the other man had fallen to their deaths less than fifteen minutes ago. Only one form was still on the ground. Despite the massive amounts of blood coating the cracked pavement, Aaron was gone.

CHAPTER 22

"When we get there, I'll take care of whatever's on the altar and do my best to disperse the cheerleaders," Monica said, barely panting, even though we were flat-out sprinting down the bike trail beside the river.

We'd left the majorly sketchy side of town behind a few minutes ago and were getting close to the newly revitalized downtown area. The sounds of people drinking and eating and dancing at the nearby bars and River Market restaurants got louder with every second. The zombies certainly wouldn't have any trouble finding fresh meat once they were out of their graves. We had to hurry.

"You and your zombie pet should probably take Aaron if he's really channeling someone else's magic."

"I'm not a pet," Cliff growled. "And he *is* channeling Jess's magic."

"So it's still talking?"

"Monica, please." I wished she wouldn't take her anger at me out on Cliff, but there wasn't time to have a heart-to-heart about it. "I believe Aaron is channeling Jess's spirit. There's no other explanation for how a guy with no history of even dabbling in the black arts worked all this big-time magic. Besides, Ethan said Jess was still unconscious, right?"

Monica had called Ethan to give him the 411 and ask him to bring help ASAP. He'd said he and one of Jess's guards were on their way and they'd call for more backup en route. They'd seen no reason to leave more than two guards with Jess since she was still blacked out, hooked up to a dozen different machines, and on the verge of going into a coma, if the SA doctor's speculation was correct.

Wouldn't *that* be high irony after what she'd tried to do for Aaron?

"That still doesn't prove anything," Monica said. "I've never heard of a living person channeling another living person."

"It's because Aaron was terminally ill. That's why—"

"Whatever. Let's just get there and take care of this mess." Monica cut across a patch of stiff dead grass, making me jealous of her shoes. The whole running-in-socks thing wasn't working for me. Heck, the whole running thing wasn't working for me. I could barely breathe. I had to start training harder. Or maybe sleeping more.

Or maybe figure out another way to feed my pet zombie.

Cliff was taking his share of my energy. I could feel it now, a subtle draw on my reserves that I normally wouldn't even notice, but it made me worry if I'd be strong enough to take on Jess. Or Jess in Aaron, or whatever. I mean, I was a heck of a Settler, and we had the same witch blood, but she'd been training to use hers for years, and I knew next to nothing about real magic. Settler commands didn't really count in my mind, since they were only useful with the dead.

It made me worry I was going to follow in poor Bobbie Jane's footsteps, that I was getting ready to fight the fight I couldn't win.

No, no way. My inner voice rebelled against the concept of failure, but the rest of me couldn't quite get on board the positivity train.

Positivity is difficult to achieve when it feels like your lungs are about to collapse.

"I may have to take care of Aaron alone. I think Megan's going to be busy." Cliff, like Monica, was not at all out of breath. But then, he didn't need to breathe. Lucky. "There's something unnatural about the circle."

"Yeah? What?" Monica asked.

"I don't know yet," Cliff said defensively. "But Megan's going to have to use her power, her full power, and she doesn't have much practice. So I think the rest of us should just stay out of the way."

"Stay out of the way?" Monica laughed. "And just let the zombies take over—"

"Megan's going to stop them. If we just let her handle—"

"Megan already got herself kidnapped and nearly killed. By a *cheerleader*. Call me crazy, but I'm not going to trust her to 'handle' anything."

Ouch. But she was right. I'd definitely had better days. Better weeks, for that matter.

"You're going to have to trust her. You don't have the power to—"

"Cliff, it's okay," I said, taking Cliff's hand, knowing it would calm him the same way touching him calmed me. Unfortunately, Ethan picked that moment to pull up beside us. His Mini Cooper jumped the curb and rolled across the frozen grass with enough speed that for a second, I didn't know if he was going to stop before he plowed right into me and Cliff.

I quickly dropped Cliff's hand, but it was too late. Ethan's über-scowl as he and the man in the passenger's seat jumped out of the car left no doubt that he'd witnessed what he saw as another sign of my betrayal. But he didn't say a word about it. He didn't even look at me as he and the tall black man—who looked vaguely familiar from SA headquarters in Little Rock—crossed the grass.

"This is Cruz. Cruz, Megan and Monica, the other Settlers," Ethan said.

"And I'm Cliff," Cliff said, reaching out to shake Cruz's hand. Cruz nodded and clasped Cliff's hand in his, thankfully not seeming to notice that Cliff was dead.

"Cliff?" Ethan asked, finally turning the full force of his glare in Cliff's direction as he connected the dots. "You're the guy from the other night. The zombie from my grandpa's farm."

"Unsettled. Not real fond of the zombie label," Cliff said, glaring right back at Ethan.

"I don't care what you're fond of." Ethan stepped closer to Cliff, looking ready to smash the shorter guy's face in. "I don't know what you are, or why you're here, but—"

"He's here to help me," I said, stepping in between them. "He's a seer and he's not going back to his grave until we get all this black magic under control."

"He's a zombie, Megan," Ethan repeated, looking me straight in the eye, the expression on his face leaving no doubt as to what he really wanted to say. Fortunately for me, he was too well mannered to call me a disgusting zombie-kissing cheater in front of Monica or Cruz. Still, the look connected like a sucker punch to the gut, taking the last of my breath away.

"Dude's a zombie?" Cruz asked, sounding surprised but not hostile. "What kind of zombie? I've never seen—"

"It's not going to matter what kind of zombie if we don't get down there," Cliff said, pointing toward a bunch of flickering lights about a half mile away. "They're starting the spell—can't you feel it?"

And I could, like a hundred little needles scraping against my skin, promising pain and pleasure all at the same time. I closed my eyes and shuddered, not liking the churning deep in my bones one bit. I could feel the black magic calling to me, calling to the dark part of my power I'd finally set free up on the roof. It wanted to be free again, wanted to join in the—

"Then let's go," Monica said, snapping me out of my daze. God, I had to focus. And keep a tight rein on my power. No matter what Cliff said, I knew letting the "other" part of me out to play would be a very bad idea. "Where's the rest of our backup?"

"Cruz is it." Ethan stepped away from Cliff, but the angry buzz of energy between the two remained. "With the crisis in Carol, SA refused to send anyone until a disturbance down here is confirmed. Barker and Smythe are waiting for a call from Cruz."

"I've got my cell," Cruz said, his friendly face offering reassurance I wished I could cling to. "As soon as I see a circle or an Out-of-Grave Phenomenon, I'll be on the horn. You've got my word."

"By then it will be too late," I said, despair blooming in my chest.

"What about Kitty?" Monica asked, the anxiety clear in her voice as well. "Surely she'd be able to see that—"

"I couldn't get Kitty on the phone. We're it," Ethan said with a note of finality that put an end to any further discussion.

"Okay then," Monica said, getting her all-business face on. "Then let's get moving." She headed off the trail and down the snow-dusted hill, taking a straight shot toward a circle of candles burning beneath the bridge. "Megan and her zombie can come in from the south and the three of us take the north?"

"Sounds good," Ethan said. "Wait for a signal, Megan. With only four of us, we'll be better off if we surprise them and attack all at once."

"Okay, be careful."

"Yeah, you too," Ethan said before he, Cruz, and Monica veered north and Cliff and I veered south. His chilly tone made it pretty clear he hated my guts and didn't care if I was careful.

Still, I turned to look over my shoulder as Cliff and I hurried toward the riverbank, unable to keep from trying to catch Ethan's eye one last time. My heart did a celebratory touchdown dance when he turned around at the exact same moment, a worried look on his face.

He cared! He still cared!

Ethan turned back around fast, but I'd already learned what I needed to know. We still had a chance. If we could make it through tonight, maybe I could make him understand, and he'd forgive me and we'd—

"Get down!" Cliff tackled me to the ground, pressing his hand over my mouth as we rolled. Thank God my shoulder was feeling the tiniest bit better, or there was no way I would have been able to keep from screaming and we would have been spotted for sure.

Or maybe not. The girls huddled in the darkness a few feet away sounded pretty freaked out. They might not have noticed if we'd walked right into the middle of their circle and set up a picnic.

"Are you sure you're okay, Aaron?" Lee Chin's voice was shaking, but at least she wasn't crying, not like several of the others. Poor cheerleaders. Apparently evil witchery just wasn't as much fun as they'd thought it would be.

"Just shut up and light the altar. Hurry." Aaron sounded . . . *so* not right, kind of like a cross between a tracheotomy patient and a gargling donkey.

"Aaron, I think you should go to the doctor. There's so much blood and your head looks—" Dana's words ended in a strangled sound as Aaron's hand reached out and latched around her throat.

"Don't think. Light. The altar. Now."

"I'm out of here," Felicity said, backing away from the clutch of shadows. "This isn't what—"

"Leave and you die," Aaron said, the chilling note in his voice enough to freeze Felicity in her tracks. "Get in position and light the altar. There are Settlers on the way. They'll escape the binding spell under the bridge sooner or later. We have to be ready."

Crap! The candles under the bridge were a trap. Anyone who got close to them would be stuck there. I started to get up, to try to warn Ethan and Monica and Cruz before it was too late, but Cliff grabbed my hand and shook his head, pointing back toward the coven. Reluctantly, I relaxed back onto the ground. He was right. Shutting down this spell was my first priority.

"So what's the plan?" Cliff whispered, so close to my ear it felt like he was speaking directly into my mind.

The plan. Okay, we needed a plan. Too bad it was so hard to think with the smell wafting from the altar. It wasn't even lit yet, but already I could feel the dark power of the herbs sliding across my skin, calling to me, making me want to join the circle and dance until the dead beneath us rose from their mass grave.

I shook my head, forcing away the seductive voice in my head, praying Cliff wouldn't feel my weakness. "Wait until the altar's lit and they step back, then rush the center and grab the ingredients and scatter them in the river. I'll take care of Aaron," I whispered.

"You're going to have to use your power on him again, your full power, I'm not sure how, but I know it's the only way to avoid using that spell I—"

"Right," I said, still unwilling to even *think* about that just yet, but knowing better than to argue with Cliff. He'd been right too many times for me to doubt him. If he said I needed to use my full power, I would, but only as a very last resort. "But we'll both have to be fast. We can't let them start chanting or we'll be trapped outside the circle."

"Everyone take your blade and cut your right hand." Aaron took a long, liquid breath as Felicity flicked her lighter open and touched it to the altar, sending the herbs flaring to life. "Now repeat after me."

Crap! They were starting the chant. We had to move. "Come on, hurry."

"No, wait," Cliff said. "Something's not right, something's—"

"There's no time." I was on my feet and running toward the circle before Cliff could mutter another word of protest.

"Drop the knives," I yelled as I breached the edge of the circle, knocking Dana to the ground as I rushed toward Aaron, only stopping when I saw the size of the huge knife in his hands. Yikes. Severely wrecked by his fall from the roof or not, he could still do some damage with a weapon like that.

"Oh. My. God. This is so precious." Blood bubbled from a hole in the side of Aaron's neck as he made a sound that vaguely resembled laughter.

Unfortunately, that wasn't the grossest thing about the dude. Now that the fire was lit, I could see that the back of his head was smashed flat, and shiny gray stuff was dripping down his neck into the collar of his shirt. His eyes, once a gorgeous shade of blue, were now cloudy and shot through with red, and his mouth was filled with blood that leaked down the sides of his lips every time he spoke. He was, in short, one of the scariest freaking things I'd ever seen, especially when he smiled.

"You're here to save the day." His grin faded a watt or two. "I can't believe you figured out where we were so quickly. I'd be impressed if I didn't hate you."

"The feeling's mutual." I gave him my full attention when it became clear the rest of the girls weren't making any move toward me or the altar.

The altar that Cliff was supposed to be dismantling even as I spoke. Gah! Where was he? It was like he'd just disappeared, which did not give me a warm, fuzzy feeling inside or lend me much confidence about telling Aaron to surrender. Still, I tried to make my voice as scary as possible when I issued my ultimatum. "You've got one chance to stop this. Put the knife down and turn yourself in to SA custody."

"Or what?" Aaron took a menacing step forward, but I didn't flinch.

"Or you're going to die for real this time," I said.

"Because you're going to kill me? You, Megan Berry, Miss 'I can't kill these bugs for science class, will you please do it for me'?" He laughed again, but this time the giggle sounded way too familiar, sending a chill down my spine. "I'm impressed. You've become so *dark*. Guess that witch blood is working for you. If you'd discovered it sooner, maybe we could have been friends for real."

It was crazy, but the look in Aaron's eyes, the sound of his laugh, the way his voice floated up at the end of his sentences—he just didn't seem like Aaron anymore. He seemed like—I mean, I'd rationally known he could be channeling Jess's spirit and her magic, but I hadn't expected . . . I hadn't really thought . . .

"Jess?" I asked, my freaked-outed-ness clear in my high, thin voice.

"Jess? Oh no! Jess, is that you in Aaron's body?" Aaron's hands flew to his ravaged face and his eyes grew wide with fake shock before narrowing in hatred. "Yes, it is. I got stuck here when you *killed* him, you bitch. He was channeling my spirit to raise the living Undead. When you pushed him off the roof, I was trapped inside his body! A freaking *dead* body! And, unlike you, I don't get off on dead guys."

"But I—"

"You pushed Aaron off the roof?" Lee Chin asked, horror clear in her voice.

"You *killed* Aaron?" Kate and Kimberly breathed at the exact same time.

The tide was turning, and not in my favor. I had to talk fast.

"No, I didn't. Aaron was trying to kill me. I was only defending myself. He's the one responsible for his own death." I turned back to Jess/Aaron. "Just like your mother would have been responsible for her death, *if* she had even died," I said, gambling that what Aaron had said about Jess's mother not being dead was the truth.

"Shut up. Don't you dare say a word about my mother."

"How does that feel, Jess? To know you dedicated your life to avenging some woman who couldn't even be bothered to let you know she wasn't dead?"

"Shut up! My mother loves me. She would be here if she could." Jess in Aaron's body took another step forward and gripped her machete even more tightly. "I know she'll wish she was here to watch the person who sent her daughter to prison finally get what she deserves."

"That's what I don't get," I said, praying Cliff was working on that whole getting-into-the-circle-to-clear-the-altar thing. "Why do you still want to kill me when you *know* I didn't kill your mother?"

"You ruined my life, and now you killed my fiancé!"

"I did not ruin your life, and I thought you were gay!"

"You killed him and trapped me in his *dead* body," Jess yelled, ignoring my very logical arguments. "Have you noticed that, Megan? That my head is leaking brains?" Jess/Aaron swiped a hand across the back of Aaron's head and hurled a bit of the sticky mess in my direction, getting close enough to make me flinch.

"Okay, fine!" I yelled, matching her volume. "Then what the heck is with the army of the dead and the zombie epidemic and—"

"The Settlers were never going to let me out of prison, so I figured I'd get rid of the Settlers." Jess grinned as she traced a few runes in the air. I tried to back away, but it was like moving through molasses. It was suddenly impossible to force my muscles to function. Jess had evidently learned a few new tricks while she was supposed to be rotting in prison. "As soon as the borders close, I've got it on very good authority that no one is ever going to mess with me again.

I'll walk free and be princess of the very scary land of quarantined Arkansas."

"Megan, don't look at her hands!" Cliff yelled from somewhere behind me.

"Grab him, girls!" Jess ordered, not stopping her mesmerizing little finger dance for a second. No matter how hard I tried, I couldn't seem to look away. "You remember how we wanted to be princesses when we were little, Megs? How we'd dress up in all my old Halloween costumes and steal Clara's jewelry from the safe in Dad's room? Now I'm really going to be one. Isn't that awesome?"

She was nuts. Completely nuts. I mean, she'd obviously never been all there, but now black magic had truly rotted what was left of her brain. There would be no reasoning with her. Which meant I was probably going to have to kill Aaron a second time.

The realization simultaneously turned my stomach and made the darkness within me do the happy dance. Which made me even sicker.

"What do we do with him?" Lee Chin asked from behind me, where I could hear her and several of the other girls grunting as they fought to hold on to a struggling Cliff.

"Throw him on the fire. Dead virgin blood will probably work as good as the living stuff. Did you know your little lover zombie was a virgin, Megan? That he died without—"

"Fight her, Megan!" Cliff cried, very real fear in his voice for the first time.

"No!" I screamed, fighting to move as my heart raced with fear. "Lee, Jessica can't make you young and beautiful forever. She's been lying to you just to—"

"They'll never believe you, Megs," Jess/Aaron said. "They've seen what I can do. They're too afraid to doubt me. You should be afraid too."

"Put him in the ground!" Cliff yelled. "Hurry, before—"

The machete flew at me before I could think to move. It was simply clenched in Aaron/Jess's hands one second and hurtling toward me the next. If Cliff hadn't twisted free from the cheerleaders and thrown himself between me and the knife at that exact second, I would have taken the blade right in the chest.

"Cliff!" I fell down beside him, the sight of the knife buried to the hilt in his neck finally breaking the hold Jess had on me.

"Don't! Just watch yourself," he said, his eyes pleading with me from his pale face. He was so badly hurt he could barely move his lips, but his first thought was still for my safety. He was just so good. Too good. "Put him in the ground, Megan. Put them both in the ground."

I surged to my feet, facing Jess/Aaron across what was left of Cliff, my rage so thick I could feel it crawling across my skin.

She'd destroyed him. Even a dead guy couldn't survive the kind of wound Cliff had sustained. The blade had almost completely severed his head from his body, and decapitation was one of the only ways to take down a zombie without magic.

That meant a wonderful person wasn't going to be around anymore because of this evil freak. This wicked waste of flesh who was already responsible for the deaths of an innocent Settler, and a poor man whose only mistake had been being in a coma at a hospital with lousy security.

Jessica Thompson was a disease, a pestilence that deserved to be wiped off the face of the earth. And it looked like I was the one who was going to do the wiping.

"Drag the dead guy onto the altar, girls. We've got some zombies to raise," Jess said.

"Move a muscle and I'll make you bleed," I said, freezing Lee Chin and Felicity where they stood.

"Get back in position or I'll make sure that the river barge leaves without you. Then you can stay here with the dead people instead of being young and beautiful forever," Jess countered, sending the girls scurrying to do her bidding. The smug look on her/Aaron's face as she turned back to me sent my anger spiraling impossibly higher. "Looks like I win. Again."

"You've never won shit, Jessica. And you're not going to win now."

"Oooo, cussing. Aren't you a bad, bad girl?"

"You have no idea," I said, and then I was running straight for her, dropping every wall I'd ever used to control my Settler power, hurling every ounce of rage in my body straight at the witch in front of me.

CHAPTER 23

I didn't know any witch-type spells—I dealt with magic for the dead, not the living—and I didn't want to call upon the darker power within me unless there was no other option. Settler power was what I knew, what I was best at. So I did the only thing I could think of in the ten seconds it took me to reach Aaron/Jess. I invoked the "return to earth" command, determined to put them in the ground just like Cliff had told me to.

"*Reverto terra!*" I hit Aaron's chest with both fists, shoving with all my physical strength and every ounce of my power.

Still, I never expected him to fly ten feet into the air, or for the earth beneath him to open like some toothless mouth and suck him beneath the soil. It all happened so fast, I barely had time to recover my balance before Aaron/Jess had disappeared.

"Oh my God. She killed Aaron again." Kimberly brilliantly stated the obvious while Dana ran to the place where Aaron had vanished.

"Good, let's get out of here while we still can," Felicity said. "I don't care if I'm going to be fat anymore!"

"No," Dana shouted. "Get back in position."

"But we—"

"Now!" Dana screamed, turning to run back to her place between

Kimberly and Kate as the earth beneath us began to rumble.

Looked like Aaron/Jess wasn't quite ready to lie down and die. Fine with me—I had plenty more kick-ass in my arsenal. I wasn't feeling the least bit drained. In fact, I was practically itching to invoke the *exuro* command and give Jess a taste of what it was like to be burned alive.

"Megan, you've got to—" Cliff's words ended in a groan of agony as the ground beneath him buckled and a very angry living-inhabited corpse burst from the earth.

"*Tergum!*" Before Aaron/Jess had even finished speaking the word, I was flying backwards on a collision course with the stone altar.

I cried out as my lower back connected with the rock, making what I guessed was my right kidney explode in a supernova of pain. The sensation was so intense, I was practically blinded by it for a few seconds. By the time I pulled myself together enough to even think about standing up, the circle had closed and Aaron/Jess was halfway through the spell to raise the dead. The cheerleaders didn't seem to be helping much—most of them were bawling their eyes out, in fact—but it didn't seem to matter.

"Thanks for the power, Megan," Aaron/Jess said, yelling to be heard over the rumbling of the earth. "I appreciate the gift."

Oh God, what had I done? Settler magic made a corpse channeling a living soul stronger. We'd only studied that particular phenomenon for about ten seconds in Enforcer training, but I should have remembered.

That was what was weird about this circle—*that* was what Cliff had felt from the start. There was a living person inside a dead body, which meant the only way to take down Aaron/Jess was with a mixture of magic for the living and the dead. A Settler with witch blood was Arkansas's only hope. *I* was Arkansas's only hope, and I'd gone and screwed it up and given Jess exactly what she needed.

Now all they needed was blood—the blood of an innocent, to be precise.

"*Haustum*," Aaron/Jess gurgled, a smile stretching across Aaron's ravaged lips as Jess watched realization dawn in my eyes.

The zombie bite on my shoulder suddenly broke open and blood gushed, hot and wet, across the altar behind me. I screamed, doing my best to pull away, but it was as if I'd been glued to the stone. The pain ripped through me with enough force to make my bones ache, and I could feel my power draining away even as the blood drained from my body.

Never had I wished so desperately that I was issue-free when it came to sex. If Ethan and I had just gone ahead and done it already, Jess wouldn't have been able to use my blood to raise her army of the dead. Now it was too late. I could feel the dead coming, squirming through the ground below, yearning toward the surface and the blood they craved. I'd failed. Jess had won, and there was nothing to do but lie here and wait for—

No! My inner voice had never been so loud. It was so adamant, in fact, that it actually made me flinch. *You've got the same power she does, and every word she says is a weapon.*

The inner voice was right. I might not have spent years studying black magic, but I had ears and a mouth, and so far both were working just fine. I also had a great memory, at least good enough to recall the word she'd used to make me bleed, and I was suddenly having a lot fewer issues with dabbling in the dark arts.

"*Haustum*," I yelled, summoning both my Settler power and the darker power lurking beneath it. I aimed my palms in Aaron/Jess's direction just as skeletal hands thrust up from the ground all around me.

The obvious wounds on Aaron's neck and head and what I was guessing were internal injuries began to gush blood. At first, Aaron/Jess didn't even seem to notice, since the dead can't feel pain, but then Aaron's knees buckled and his bloodshot eyes widened in alarm.

"No. No freaking . . . way . . . " Jess's words faded away, and, within a few seconds, the body that had been Aaron crumpled to the ground, finally as lifeless as it should have been an hour ago.

"Oh crap," Dana said. "I don't think that's supposed to happen."

"What do you mean you don't think—Ah!" Felicity's words ended in a scream as a rotted face burst from the ground and a zombie mouth latched around her ankle. "They're going to eat us! Jess and Aaron were wrong!"

"Run, everyone! Get to the barge!" Dana and the other girls turned and ran for it while Felicity kicked at the zombie that had her in its jaws, making her escape in time to catch up with the others as they fled toward the river.

I jumped to my feet, wavering unsteadily. I'd lost a lot of blood and used up a lot of power. There was no way I'd be able to take down all the zombies bursting from the ground by myself. I needed help.

I turned toward the burning candles under the bridge, determined to find a way to free Ethan, Cruz, and Monica, when I tripped over Cliff and went down hard.

"Behind you," he said, the open wound at his neck gurgling sickly. He'd managed to pull out the machete and was clutching it between his hands, but lacked the strength to put it to use—as evidenced by the fact that all he could do was lie there as the now-bloodless Aaron hurled himself on top of me.

"You suck! So hard!" he screamed, Jess's voice coming through clearer than ever, hands clawing into my calves when I tried to scramble away.

I sucked? Really, *that* was what she came up with? After she'd killed and lied and pretty much doomed our state to zombie plague unless we stopped the RCs crawling out of the ground? *I* sucked?

"Let go!" I kicked Aaron's body in the face, but Jess clung tight, holding me still as two zombies with glowing red eyes emerged from the earth right in front of me. "*Pax frater corpus postestatum.*" I smacked each of them in the head and they froze, which was a relief after the week of zombies who wouldn't say die. These were just normal RCs, after all, just—

"Ahh!" I screamed as the two dudes I'd just *pax frater*-ed surged back to life and started snapping at my yummy flesh.

"They were raised partly with your power, you idiot. You can't stop them!"

"Then you stop them, or I'll—*Absisto!*" I froze the Munch Brothers in place, but knew the freezing command wouldn't hold for long.

"I wouldn't even if I could. No one here has the power to make them go back to their graves." Aaron/Jess gouged cold, corpselike fingers even deeper into my leg. "You're finally going to pay for everything you've done."

I surged into a seated position away from zombie mouths, grabbed what was left of Aaron's hair, and tugged—hard, distracting him/her just long enough to twist my leg free.

"Megan! Put out the fire!" Kitty screamed. I looked up to see Ethan, Monica, Cruz, and Kitty at the edge of the circle, which unfortunately looked like it *hadn't* been broken when the cheerleaders made a mad dash for the river. Ethan, Cruz, and Monica were kicking the tails of the zombies who made it out of the circle, but when they tried to get too close to the altar, they were repelled by the invisible walls of the spell. "Put out the fire so we can help you."

I scrambled to my feet and lunged for the altar, willing to throw my body on there to smother the flames if that was what I had to do, but Aaron/Jess tripped me, flipping me onto my back. She leapt on top of me a second later, pinning me to the ground and sliding her large, Aaron hands around my neck for the second time that night.

Argh! No way was I blacking out again.

"Get off!" I tried to buck Jess off, but Aaron's body was too heavy and his hands too strong. Spots danced in front of my eyes while zombies continued to pour from the earth.

Two dozen or more were out of the ground now, shuffling toward me and Aaron/Jess with eyes glowing red in the leathery remains of their faces. Scraps of weathered blue and gray uniforms hung on their bleached bones, blowing like miniature flags in the cold wind sweeping in from the river.

"They won't stay down!" I heard someone scream from outside the circle.

"Stop them before they cross the street. Contain the area!" Kitty yelled.

God, no. Jess wasn't lying. Nothing could stop these things. We were fighting a losing battle, shoveling shit against the tide, as my grandmother would say. Cliff's horrible vision was going to come to pass, despite all his efforts to stop it.

My eyes drifted to what remained of Cliff, and I was shocked to see his eyes were still open. Open and latched onto me.

"*Habeo are transit*," he whispered, his voice so soft I could barely hear it over the groans of the Undead and the shouts of the Settlers.

"*Habeo are transit*," I repeated, recognizing the spell he'd warned me we might need. I had no idea what speaking the words would do, but after all the times he'd tried to guide me to the right path and I'd stubbornly insisted on doing what I damned well pleased, I owed him a little bit of faith.

Heck, I owed him a lot of faith.

So I repeated it again, and again, chanting with him even though Aaron/Jess intensified her efforts at my throat and I could barely force the words out. I chanted until the zombies falling to their knees beside me faded from my awareness, until I couldn't feel the cold of the hard, snowy ground or the heat from the nearby fire or the pain from being strangled or my dozen other wounds, until I was so at peace I couldn't feel my body at all.

In fact, I felt like I was outside myself looking in, like I was watching the zombies begin to pile on top of me and Aaron/Jess from a few feet away, watching from inside . . . Cliff.

Hurry, Megan! Now we can put them back.

"Cliff?" I asked, but the words came out all gurgly sounding, because I was actually using Cliff's lips to talk instead of my own.

I wasn't losing it—I really *was* inside Cliff's body, hearing Cliff's voice in the head we now shared. I could feel Cliff's . . . Cliffness, for lack of a better word, snuggled close beside my me-ness, and it felt right. It felt like I'd known his soul for ages, longer than I'd been alive, like he was a part of me I'd misplaced and finally gotten back.

If there had been time, I'm sure I would have spent a good hour or two freaking out about how unbelievably weird all of that was, but unless I wanted to watch myself be eaten alive, I had to do something. Fast.

Put them under!

I can't! I replied, finding it easier to communicate with my thoughts than through Cliff's poor ravaged throat. *They'll just come right back up again. The freezing command won't do much either. And I can't work the* reverto *spell because my blood raised them and my body really doesn't need a few hundred more bite marks.*

Oh. God. A few hundred. There really were a few *hundred* zombies burbling from the ground, clawing their way free from the cold earth inside the circle. Those who didn't linger for a taste of Megan were spilling out onto the snow-covered grass like ants on a Hostess snowball snack cake, intent on reaching downtown and the warm, beating hearts of a thousand or more Little Rock citizens.

Warm, beating hearts. There are so many . . . but they only need one. Cliff echoed my thought in that faraway voice he got when he was getting all "seer" on me. One heart. One human heart could stop all this, and now I knew exactly where we were going to get it.

We had shoved ourselves to our feet and started toward the pile of zombies swarming around Aaron/Jess and my spiritless body before I could consciously agree to the plan I saw forming in his mind, but that was okay.

There was a reason Cliff didn't go back to his grave, and it wasn't just to guide me to where I needed to be tonight, or to face whatever Very Bad Thing was coming next. If I hadn't realized it before, I certainly did now. Cliff gave me strength in the same way that I gave him the vital energy he needed to stay out of his grave. I certainly never would have been able to shove my hand into someone's chest and pull out their still-beating heart on my own. Even to save the *world*, let alone Arkansas.

You have no idea what you're capable of. I didn't know if it was my thought or Cliff's, a condemnation or a compliment, and pretty soon I didn't care.

"No!" Aaron/Jess screamed as Cliff's/my hand disappeared into Aaron's body, parting through flesh and bone like a knife through butter, our fingers closing around the surprisingly hard muscle at the center of his chest. We didn't pause for dramatic effect, we didn't meet Aaron/Jess's eyes for one last moment of grim recognition, we just pulled the sticky organ free and hurled it across the grass.

Even though there was hardly any blood left in the heart after the spell I'd cast earlier, the zombies still swarmed, abandoning my body, returning from where they had prowled outside the magic circle to pounce on the heart of the one who'd raised them, the one who had put this entire nightmarish sequence of events in motion. Any heart would have served the same purpose, but Cliff and I found it rather fitting that it was Jess/Aaron's.

You've got to go, Megan, Cliff urged as more and more Reanimated Corpses surged into the circle to feed on the vital energy of the heart and return to their graves. *Go back to your body.*

But I don't know how. And what about you?

I'm not sure I'm going to make it, and you don't want to be trapped here.

No! What do you need? What can I—

Goodbye, Megan. I'll miss you. The next thing I knew, Cliff had somehow drop-kicked me out of his body. At least that's what it felt like.

One second I was inside him not feeling much of anything, the next I was landing in my body with a groan, barely opening my eyes in time to see Ethan bending down over me.

"Megan? Are you okay?" he asked. His feelings were clear in his eyes.

Ethan still loved me, even after everything he'd seen tonight—corpse-kissing, hand-holding, heart-ripping, and all. For some reason, that was the straw that broke the camel's hump. Or back. Or whatever.

I reached for him and he hugged me and I cried. And cried. And cried.

CHAPTER 24

"You want some more popcorn? Or maybe an extremely large box of Swedish fish?" Dad asked from his seat beside me. "I know the lady working the register—bet I can get us a deal."

I followed his gaze across the basketball court to the booster club snack table, where Mom was working the first shift at the cash box. As if sensing she was being observed, she looked up and smiled. I tried to smile back, but it wasn't easy. So I waved instead, mostly to make Dad happy.

We'd had a long family talk over Saturday morning pancakes, but it was going to take time for my and Mom's relationship to recover. Though after hearing her side of the story, I could *sort of* understand why she hadn't told me the truth, at least at first.

My bio dad was a creep who had wooed Mom while Dad was deployed to Korea for a year. He'd known she was a Settler and had thought she could help him learn more black magic if he seduced it out of her. When he'd figured out she didn't know the kind of spells he was looking for, he'd drained her blood and left her to die alone in our house. If Dad hadn't come home a day later, she never would have made it.

After that, she'd confessed everything to SA and *that* was why she and Dad had been relocated—not the "discovered Settling a corpse" story she'd always told me. She'd found out she was pregnant a few weeks after the move. Dad had already forgiven her for cheating—he felt he hadn't been a very good deployed husband and had probably contributed to the whole tempted-by-a-hot-but-evil-witch thing—but they decided to go in for tests to see if the baby was his anyway.

Turns out "it"—me—*wasn't* his child, *and* an amnio revealed "it" had the WB virus, just like "its" dad.

Mom, who had wanted me even though I had an evil daddy, had been scared to death that SA would make her have an abortion since the WB virus had been proven to cause psychotic evilness in Settlers before. But Elder Thomas had agreed to keep the results of the test secret. She'd buried the report and promised she wouldn't say anything to anyone as long as the baby seemed okay.

So I guessed I owed Thomas big-time. Owed her my life, really, but that didn't make me like her any more than I did before. And I didn't feel the slightest smidgen of guilt that she and the entire Carol and Little Rock SA councils were under investigation by the National High Council, especially since I hadn't been the one to blow the whistle, after all.

Kitty was responsible for that. Apparently, she'd been investigating the Carol Settlers' Affairs office since all the crap went down last September, and had become convinced there was a mole somewhere in the Arkansas organization. A very high-ranking mole who was behind the entire "Arkansas taken over by zombies" plot!

Crazy to believe, but Kitty had all the evidence to prove that Jess's efforts had been facilitated by someone *inside* SA and that Aaron hadn't even been the first terminal patient she'd hooked up with.

Several others had died while Jess was figuring out how to work the channeling spell without killing the body she was inhabiting.

Of course, *why* someone in SA would want Arkansas zombie-apocalypsed and, more important, *who* was guilty were things Kitty hadn't been able to figure out. Whoever it was had covered their tracks and had enough power to wipe the memories of the few people who might have witnessed something sketchy.

So we were all in wait-and-be-highly-suspicious-of-each-other-while-we-see-what-the-High-Council-investigation-comes-up-with mode. Which was fine with me. I liked wait-and-see mode. It was highly preferable to everyone-trying-to-put-Megan-in-jail mode, and the High Council people seemed to *really* know what they were doing. They made Kitty look like a disorganized spaz in comparison, and she was clearly my hero at the moment.

She'd used the fresh blood sample she took from me to prove that the virus in my blood was active, but not mutating the way it would be if I were manifesting large amounts of black magic, confirming I was as innocent as she'd thought. She hadn't been able to tell me or anyone else she'd been working with to clear my name because of the high-ranking mole, but I still totally wanted to be like her when I grew up.

Ethan was also my hero, of course. He'd figured out the Jess/Aaron connection, which had stumped even Kitty. She'd known she was looking for a terminal patient, but hadn't suspected Aaron was her guy thanks to his studly cheerleader front. Needless to say, she was impressed with Ethan, and word was that he was going to be offered an Enforcement job in the next few months.

I was sure he was thrilled. Not that we'd talked . . .

"So what do you say? Nasty gummy fish or more popcorn?" Dad asked.

"I'm already stuffed." I turned back to him with a smile, trying not to think about Ethan or the fact that he hadn't called to see how I was feeling today.

Using my latent power had increased my ability to heal, but Ethan wouldn't know that. All the specifics of what I was were being kept tightly under wraps. Settlers' Affairs didn't want it to get out that they had a Settler with WB virus on active duty. They were afraid it would attract the wrong kind of attention from people like Jess and Aaron, and whoever this mystery mole was, who would want to use my power and blood for their own evil purposes.

They were so afraid that, even though the Enforcers had mind-wiped everyone who'd seen the pond zombies, instilling the injured with memories of rabid dogs loose on the ice and erasing the memories of their coven days from the cheerleading squads' bleached-blond heads, I'd been worried they were going to lock me up just to keep anyone else from getting their hands on me.

But they hadn't. Yet. The SA council and the Enforcers were actually being very cool. They'd even apologized for judging me unfairly after Elder Thomas spilled the beans about the WB virus thing a few days ago.

So mostly, it was good news all around. Or as good as could be expected.

The not-so-good news, however, was that no one could find Aaron. Or Jess. Or whoever he/she was at that moment when I reached into Aaron's body and pulled out that heart. By the time our reinforcements arrived, Aaron had vanished and none of us could remember seeing him move. In all the craziness of the zombies swarming back under the ground, he'd disappeared.

And so had another corpse, one I was considerably more attached to.

Cliff was also missing by the time the big beige SA cars and ambulances arrived, and I hadn't felt the slightest tug on my energy since. It made me worry, though I was certain, deep down, that I'd *know* if he'd gone back to his grave.

I mean, we *had* shared a body and reached into a person and pulled out a heart together. We were undeniably connected, a fact Kitty had confirmed with some much-needed sharing about former prophets who had come to the aid of powerful Settlers in times of earthly crisis. She said it was a sign that I was working for the right side that someone like Cliff had found me, and that our instinct about taking Aaron's heart had been dead-on. The *habeo are transit* spell might have some consequences down the line as far as mutating our power was concerned, but there had been no other way to stop the zombies Aaron/Jess had summoned.

Kitty had recommended we just chill and wait and see what happened with my mojo before freaking out, however. Having had more than enough freaking, I agreed, especially when a second test of my blood revealed all was still quiet on the getting-messed-up-by-black-magic front.

Which made me feel better . . . but not that much better.

I'd lost more than two pints of blood and a few chunks of skin last night—I'd lost a piece of myself I could never get back. I was a darker person and the world a darker place, and I knew I would never see either the same way again.

"It's probably good you're not dancing tonight. Our whole family could use a little R and R," Dad said, snapping me back to the present just as the buzzer sounded, signaling the beginning of halftime.

"Yeah, I'm not too broken up about it." The cheerleaders were claiming the first halftime of the basketball season and participation in whatever "super-special" opening game event the boosters had planned.

The fund-raiser had ended up a draw, so we would now be *sharing* halftime with our cheerleader enemies, alternating every other game. Of course, only Monica and I knew just how vile the cheerleaders really were, but that didn't stop Alana and a few other pom squadders from booing as Dana strode to mid-court with a microphone in her hand.

I, however, didn't utter a sound. Monica and I had been warned not to attract cheerleader attention for the next few days. Erasing memories as traumatic as what Enforcement had removed from the cheerleader's brains was tricky business. Seeing too much of the people involved in those memories too soon after the procedure could cause Dana and Lee and the others to start remembering things no Settler wanted them to remember. We'd come scary close to having our world exposed and our power destroyed, and no one wanted to risk another Class Three containment crisis.

Monica and I wouldn't have been allowed to go to the game at all, in fact, if Kitty hadn't argued that our absence was as likely to incite curiosity as our attendance. So we were here, but lurking in the upper bleachers, both of us sacked out next to our parents. Monica still wasn't talking to me after last night, but I could tell she wasn't going to hold a grudge for too long. She had at least texted to make sure I was recovering . . . unlike Ethan.

God, Ethan. Where was he? I had been sure he would be here tonight, but so far there had been no sign of him.

Dana cleared her throat as the last of the boos faded. "I'd like to dedicate this special performance to Aaron Peterson, who's been missing since the rabid-dog attack last night. Aaron, we miss you and hope to see you soon."

Um, no they didn't, not looking the way he did when I last saw him, but at least it seemed that the Enforcer mind wipe was holding strong. Dana even had a little tremble in her voice as she introduced the head of the booster club and then ran to join the rest of the squad behind a giant breakthrough poster on the other side of the court.

"Thank you, Dana," Mr. Cotter said. "The Carol High boosters are so glad to see all of you here to celebrate our new gym. It was my pleasure to cut the opening-game ribbon earlier tonight, and now it is my privilege to make the following special announcement. In honor of our new gym, and a new era of CHS athletics, we'd like to introduce the *new* Carol High mascot—the Carol Cavemen!"

Then, I kid you not, that horrible "Walk the Dinosaur" song from the 1980s boomed out of our new state-of-the-art sound system, and all twelve cheerleaders burst through the breakthrough sign dressed in . . . caveman costumes. We're talking cheetah halter tops, big mallets, and furry pelt diapers. Yes. *Diapers*. Made of *fur*.

Their ponytails were as blond and perky as always and their makeup tastefully applied, but nothing could make up for the fact that they were dancing around to one of the worst songs of all time in diapers. (Have I mentioned the diapers? The *fur* diapers?)

It took the laughter a few minutes to really get started—probably because we were all fighting off symptoms of clinical shock after learning that our fabulous, fierce Cougars had been replaced by *Cavemen*—but once it did, it was loud enough to drown out the music completely. One by one, the cheerleaders lost the beat and their place in the routine and started bumping into each other, turning their pitiable performance into a true travesty.

"This is painful to watch," I mumbled to Dad.

"Yeah. I think I'll go hit the men's room until it's over," Dad said. "You could visit your mom at the snack table, or I think I saw Ethan head outside a second ago."

"What?!" He'd seen Ethan a *second* ago and had waited until *now* to tell me?

"He isn't a smoker, is he? I don't want you dating a smo—"

I was on my feet before he could finish his sentence. "He's not a smoker—he was probably leaving!" I bit my lip as I realized how crazy I must sound. I'd gone from zero to mournful in two point two seconds. If I didn't watch it, Dad was going to realize something was up. "I'm going to go try to catch him. Be back in a few."

"Okay, but call my cell if he's giving you a ride home."

I acknowledged his order with a wave and made a relatively dignified dash to the front doors and out into the cool night air, even though my heart was racing a thousand miles a minute.

No matter what I'd felt for Cliff, no matter how strong the paranormal connection between us, Ethan was the one for me. He was my home base, my best friend, and the only person who I trusted with my life but who terrified me at the same time.

But the terrified part was okay. Because that was part of what love was about: feeling something so powerful it was scary, but staying and feeling it anyway. That's what my dad and mom had done. They'd stayed and fought for each other, forgiven each other, and—

"And you're sure you're ready?" Kitty asked. She and Ethan were standing by Kitty's enormous truck, looking decidedly chummy. "You'll have to leave Arkansas. The closest certification program is in Nashville."

"My bags are already packed. I'm just waiting for the word," Ethan said, sending my heart crashing into my stomach where the wreckage burst into flames. He was leaving? To go to Nashville? And his bags were *already packed*?

"It probably won't be for a month or two. We've got to get your paperwork and background check through the system. But I don't anticipate any problems," Kitty said, grinning up at her latest protégé. "You've done some great work. Everyone's really excited to see you join the team."

"It's what I've wanted to do for awhile." Ethan was practically glowing as he shook Kitty's tiny hand. "Thanks for the recommendation."

"No thanks necessary. You earned it." Kitty hopped up into the driver's seat. "Come by the training office on Monday and we'll get everything started."

Ethan said goodbye and Kitty drove away, and I knew I should scram. But instead I lingered in the shadows near the door, watching as Ethan walked toward his car, sniffling in confusion as he walked right past it and made a beeline to where I was hiding a dozen feet from the gym exit. I obviously needed to work on my super-secret-eavesdropping skills. As he closed the last few feet between us, I debated making a run for the safety of the girls' room but decided against it. I needed to talk to him, and this might be my last chance.

I had to let him know how sorry I was, and that I'd always care about him no matter what. I had to be strong and rational and not turn this into some sort of Megan blubber-fest.

"So you're leaving and you weren't even going to tell me?" I blubbered, opening my mouth and inserting my decidedly weak and irrational foot.

"You've done a lot of things lately without telling me. So I guess we're even, huh?" he asked, in that deep, sexy voice he always had when he was angry or upset. I wondered which it was right now? Probably angry, if the scowl on his perfect, kissable lips was any indication.

I flinched but didn't look away. This was it. Time to take my medicine. "Yeah. I guess. I'm still sorry, you know. Really, really sorry. This past week has been . . . really hard. I'm not saying that's a valid excuse, but I . . . "

His scowl softened for a second. "I know. Kitty told me everything last night. I can't believe your mom never told you about your real dad."

"I was keeping secrets from myself too," I said, refusing to give into the temptation to bask in the warm glow of Ethan's sympathy. It was time to get real, with him and myself. "Everything that has happened since September had me really mixed up. My powers returning and the zombie attacks and Jess. Even the good stuff, like Enforcer training and us—it was just a lot to handle in a really short amount of time."

He stepped closer and I felt the invisible wall between us start to crumble. "Then why didn't you just say something? I could have understood if you needed time or—"

"I didn't understand it myself until last night." I looked up into his eyes, willing him to see how much I cared about him. "I was sure I was going to die, and all I could think about was you. That I was stupid to have been so scared."

Ethan's hand touched mine, just the barest brush of his fingers, but it was enough to make my entire self ache. "It wasn't stupid. I know you've never been in a serious relationship before."

"No, it's not just that. It's not even sex, so much," I said, blushing until my cheeks burned. Maybe I wasn't so jaded and dark after all. I could still get embarrassed saying the *s* word. "It's just . . . you mean so much to me. I've never felt this way about anyone else. I've never loved someone—"

"Then why the thing with the zombie, Megan?" Ethan asked, the hurt clear in his eyes, though he didn't step away. "If you love me so much, why were you making out with another guy?"

"I don't know," I said, fighting tears for the zillionth time in the past few days. "I think it was because I was so confused about us and he was safe."

"Safe?" He was mad again. "And what am I? A serial killer?"

"I don't love him," I said, scrambling to explain myself. "Cliff is a super-nice guy, but he isn't even alive, so there's no way he could hurt me the way you could."

"I'd never hurt you. Don't you realize that by—"

"Maybe not on purpose, but what if you just fell out of love with me one day?" I asked, ignoring the stares we were getting from people headed back into the game. "Or got tired of me being younger? Or met someone you liked more?"

"What if I got hit by a bus, or you got killed during one of these freakish Undead outbreaks you seem to attract like it's going out of style?" he asked, squeezing my hand in his. "Don't you think that scares me? Thinking about all the people who are going to want a piece of you if they find out what you are? Something bad could always happen, but if you're too afraid of the bad, you can't ever enjoy the good."

"I know!" God, Ethan totally got it. Of course he did. He was way smarter than I was when it came to stuff like this. "I finally figured that out. It just took me a while. I'm sorry. But I . . ." Okay, here it was, this was the BIG moment. I might have thought Ethan and I had been here before, but we hadn't, not like this.

"But you what?"

"But I love you. I really love you." My heart raced and I suddenly felt like I was going to throw up, but I didn't let myself stop or look away from Ethan's eyes. "If you can't forgive me, I understand, but I really wish you would because I . . . I think things would be a lot better."

"You think?" The hand not holding mine snuck up to play at the back of my neck, making me shiver for reasons that had nothing to do with the cold night air.

"I *know*." I leaned closer, wanting to be in Ethan's arms more than I have ever wanted anything. I wanted to feel his lips on mine, to kiss him and kiss him and let those kisses take us wherever they would. I didn't want to hold back anymore, didn't want to worry about anything, just wanted to be as close to him as I could get. I was finally ready. Completely ready. Too bad it had taken another near-death experience to make me realize that truth.

He stared down at me and I could tell that he was thinking the same thing. But in the end, when he leaned down, his lips landed on my forehead, not my lips. "I love you, and it's okay."

"You forgive me?"

"I do."

"You do?" I asked.

"I do, but I don't think we should jump right back into anything. You're right—you've been through a lot, and it's not over yet. You and your parents have a lot to deal with, the Enforcers are going to be isolating you for special training, and I heard Kitty talking about full-time bodyguards for at least a few months, until they see who knows about you having witch blood. So . . . I think we should take our time."

I sighed, a part of me wanting to burst into full-blown sobs at the idea of "taking time," but another part of me a little relieved. I wanted to be with Ethan more than anything, but I was also really, really tired. No matter how much I wanted my life back on track *right now*, it was going to take some adjustment to get used to the new lay of the land.

"So what do you think? Friends for now?" he asked, still playing with my hair in a way that wasn't really strictly friendly—not that I was going to complain.

"Friends who hug." I threw my arms around his waist and hugged him tight.

"I can do hugs." He wrapped his arms around me in a mostly platonic way, but I felt his lips brush the top of my head and heard the telltale sniff as he inhaled the scent of my shampoo. He'd told me a dozen times how just smelling that shampoo made him want to drag me into a dark corner and never let me go. "And maybe a kiss or two. If you'll put your Frisbee hat back on."

"It's called a beret, which sounds a lot cooler than 'Frisbee hat.'"

"Right, whatever," he said, dropping another kiss on my forehead.

I smiled, and a sense of calm settled in my usually angst-ridden guts. Ethan and I were going to be fine. We'd take our time, but in the end, when I was ready and he was ready, we'd be us again. I was sure of it.

"So, you want to go get some ice cream? I heard you're supposed to be pounding back the calories to help you heal," he asked, pulling away from our hug.

"I thought all details relating to my condition were supposed to be top secret?"

"Yeah, they are, but Kitty gave Monica and me the scoop. I guess she figured we'd earned insider information for being the only two people smart enough to know you were innocent from the start." He grinned, pleased with himself. "And I'm really craving a hot fudge sundae."

"How can you crave ice cream when it's this cold?" I asked, holding on to the hand he placed in mine and following him to his car.

"Not just ice cream, a *hot fudge sundae*. The fudge is hot, countering the coldness of the ice cream and making it the perfect all-weather snack food."

"Oh, I see." I laughed and dug around in my coat pocket for my cell to call my parents, letting Ethan open the door for me. "I guess I can't argue with—Oh, Ethan, what did you do?"

"What?" he asked, acting like he didn't know what I was talking about.

"This." I grabbed the elegantly wrapped black box with the silver ribbon from the passenger's seat, marveling at the fact that Ethan had gone to the trouble to spell out my name on the gift tag with glitter. "It's not anywhere close to my birthday."

"Megan, I didn't—"

But I was already tearing into the paper, revealing the carved wooden box inside. Impatiently, I fumbled with the ornate latch. I'm not one of those take-your-time-and-savor-it kind of unwrappers. I want to know what's inside, and I want to know *now*.

Of course, that might change. After this particular gift, I didn't know if I'd ever look at wrapping paper the same way again.

"Ohmygod!" I dropped the box as fast as I'd picked it up, which was my second mistake, because dropping it made the severed hand inside come rolling *out*.

"What the heck?" Ethan crouched down to get a better look at the thing, wisely not touching it. He was in Protocol mode now. He wouldn't touch evidence and risk losing fingerprints or any magical remnants that might be stuck to the skin. "There's a note."

Ethan pulled a tissue from his pocket and used it to carefully pry open the edge of the crisply folded paper that had been resting beneath the hand.

Dearest Megan,

I heard from a little bird you'd taken your first heart. Don't you know a good witch always starts with a hand? Here's one to hold you over until your training can truly begin.

All the best, love,

Your father

Ethan stood up fast and scanned the parking lot even as he grabbed his phone and dialed for backup, but I stayed where I was. If I stood up, if I spoke, then this would be real, and I didn't want it to be real. Not yet. Not ever.

Just when I'd thought it was over, it was really only beginning. My biological father had found me and scared me more than anyone ever had. All that, and I didn't even know his name.

I do. His name is Addison Strain. He's not here yet, but he will be. Soon. I joined Ethan, spinning in a wild circle, searching for any sign of the boy who owned that voice. It was Cliff, speaking in my mind, just like he had when we'd shared a body for those brief moments last night.

Where are you? Did you see who—

I didn't see who put it there, but I'll keep my eyes open. And I'll be here when you need me. Be careful, Megan. Out of the corner of my eye I caught a flash of a dark green sweater and shoulder-length brown hair at the edge of the parking lot. It was Cliff, but a very pale Cliff, with a huge bandage wrapped around his neck.

My stomach turned as I remembered the way his throat had been ripped open, then turned again as Cliff vanished and my gaze dropped to the hand. "I think I'm going to be sick."

"Right, we'll see you in five." Ethan snapped his phone shut and wrapped his arms around me. "Just take deep breaths. Kitty's on her way back, and Monica is going to grab your parents and be right out. We'll find out who did this and make sure you're safe. Don't worry."

I buried my face in Ethan's chest and took a deep breath, pulling the comforting smell of him into my soul, searching for the calm I'd felt only a few minutes ago. Surprisingly, I found it was still there, buried beneath the fear and anxiety, waiting for me to call it to the surface.

"Okay. I'm going to be okay." I pulled away from Ethan and

stood up a little straighter. What had just happened was crazy and horrible, but that seemed like it was the story of my life. This time, however, I was determined to be the one writing the next chapter.

Ethan smiled, that special smile he only showed me. "Of course you are. I never doubted it." He took my hand in his and squeezed as we turned to watch the gym doors, ready for whatever happened next.

ACKNOWLEDGMENTS

Thanks again to all the people at Razorbill who put their talent to work on "Undead Much", with special thanks to Lexa Hillyer, my amazing editor. You made this book a joy, Lexa!

More special thanks to my agent, Caren Johnson. I could never juggle everything without you, thanks for all you do.

And then some more special thanks to the Diamond State Romance Authors, Jamie Fender, and Stacia Kane for friendship and girl talk.

And then yet even more special thanks to my family—my mom and dad, my adorable husband who I love more every day, and my preshush children and stepchildren who keep me on my toes and have taught me as much as I'll ever teach them.

And then still more special, heartfelt thanks to my readers. Every email I've gotten about Megan and Ethan and the Settler world has completely blown me away. Thank you for reading and for loving my characters as much as I do.

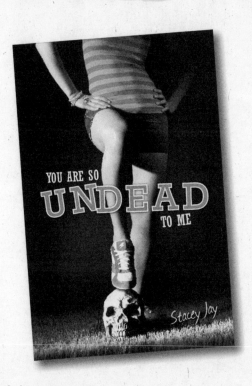